Deeds of Darkness

The chronicles of Hugh de Singleton, surgeon

Deeds of Darkness

**The tenth chronicle of
Hugh de Singleton, surgeon**

MEL STARR

LION FICTION

Published by Lion Fiction
an imprint of
Lion Hudson IP Ltd
Wilkinson House, Jordan Hill Road
Oxford OX2 8DR, England
www.lionhudson.com/fiction

ISBN 978 1 78264 245 9
e-ISBN 978 1 78264 246 6

First edition 2017

A catalogue record for this book is available from the British Library

Printed and bound in the USA, September 2017, LH37

For Charis, Meleah, and Elijah

"Have no fellowship with the unfruitful deeds of Darkness,
but expose them."

Ephesians 5:11

Acknowledgments

Several years ago, when Dan Runyon, Professor of English at Spring Arbor University, learned that I had written an as yet unpublished medieval mystery, he invited me to speak to his fiction-writing class about the trials of a rookie writer seeking a publisher. He sent sample chapters of Master Hugh's first chronicle, *The Unquiet Bones*, to his friend Tony Collins. Thanks, Dan.

Thanks to Tony Collins and all those at Lion Hudson who saw Master Hugh's potential.

Dr. John Blair, of Queen's College, Oxford, has written several papers about Bampton history. These have been invaluable in creating an accurate time and place for Master Hugh. Tony and Lis Page have also been a great source of information about Bampton. I owe them much. Sadly, Tony died of cancer in March 2015. He is greatly missed.

Ms. Malgorzata Deron, of Poznan, Poland, offered to update and maintain my website. She has done an excellent job, managing to find time in addition to her duties as Professor of Linguistics. To see her work, visit www.melstarr.net.

Glossary

Ague: term used in the medieval period for any illness marked by sweating, fever, and recurring chills.

Ambler: an easy-riding horse, because it moved both right legs together, then both left legs.

Bailiff: a lord's chief manorial representative. He oversaw all operations, collected rents and fines, and enforced labor service. Not a popular fellow.

Balloc broth: a spiced broth, used most often in preparation of pike or eels.

Blancmange: literally, "white food." A mixture of rice, almonds, lard, salt, and perhaps sugar and ginger, cooked to softness and ground to a smooth paste.

Braes: medieval underpants.

Bruit: a sauce of white wine, breadcrumbs, onions, and spices.

Burgher: a merchant of a town – a burgh.

Candlemas: February 2. Marked the purification of Mary. Women traditionally paraded to the village church carrying lighted candles. Tillage of fields resumed this day.

Capon: a castrated male chicken.

Chamberlain: the keeper of a lord's chamber, wardrobe, and personal items.

Chauces: tight-fitting trousers, often particolored, having different colors for each leg.

Chrisom: a white cloth placed on an infant at baptism as a symbol of innocence.

Churching: four to six weeks after childbirth a mother processed to the church with other women, carrying a lighted candle. She met the priest at the church door, was sprinkled

9

with holy water, then was led into the church for mass. Thus a ritual purification after childbirth.

Compline: the seventh and last of the monastic canonical hours, observed at sunset.

Copperas: iron sulfate.

Cordwainer: a dealer in leather and leather goods imported from Cordova, Spain.

Corn: a kernel of any grain. Maize – American corn – was unknown in Europe at the time.

Cotehardie: the primary medieval outer garment. Women's were floor-length, men's ranged from the thigh- to ankle-length.

Cotter: a poor villager, usually holding five acres or less. He had to labor for wealthier villagers to make ends meet.

Cresset: a bowl of oil with a floating wick used for lighting.

Daub: a clay and plaster mix, reinforced with straw and horsehair, used to plaster the exterior of a house.

Demesne: land directly exploited by a lord, and worked by his villeins, as opposed to land a lord might rent to tenants.

Dexter: the right hand or right direction.

Dibble stick: a stick used to penetrate soil in planting peas and beans.

Dredge: mixed grains planted together in a field – often barley and oats.

Easter Sepulcher: a niche in the wall of a church or chapel where the host and a cross were placed on Good Friday and removed on Easter Sunday morning. Often closed with a velvet curtain.

Egg leach: a thickened custard, enriched with almonds, spices, and flour.

Farthing: a small coin worth one-fourth of a penny.

Fast day: Wednesday, Friday, and Saturday. Not the fasting of modern usage, when no food is consumed, but days upon which no meat, eggs, or animal products were consumed. Fish was on the menu for those who could afford it.

Fee (knight's): a death duty, or inheritance tax. Magna Carta specified 100 shillings for a knight to possess a deceased father's lands. Also referred to the number of men at arms a knight was to provide in time of war.

Gathering: eight leaves of parchment, made by folding a prepared hide three times.

Gentleman: a nobleman. The term had nothing to do with character or behavior.

God's sib: a woman who attended another woman while she was in labor, from which comes the word "gossip."

Goliard: a student who preferred wine, women, and song – and often crime – to study.

Groat: a coin worth four pence.

Groom: a lower-rank servant to a lord. Often a youth, occasionally assistant to a valet, and ranking above a page.

Haberdasher: a merchant who sold household and personal items such as pins, buckles, hats, and purses.

Hallmote: the manorial court. Royal courts judged tenants accused of murder or felony. Otherwise manor courts had jurisdiction over legal matters concerning villagers. Villeins accused of homicide might also be tried in a manor court.

Hamsoken: breaking and entering.

Hippocras: spiced wine. Sugar, cinnamon, ginger, cloves, and nutmeg were often in the mix. Usually served at the end of a meal.

Hocktide: the Sunday after Easter. A time of paying rents and taxes, therefore getting out of hock.

Hosteller: also called the guest master. The monastic official in charge of providing for abbey guests.

King's Eyre: a royal circuit court, generally presided over by a traveling judge.

Kirtle: the basic medieval undershirt.

Kyrtyn: a spiced cream sauce of flour, ginger, cinnamon, and saffron beaten into cream and boiled, then poured over fish or chicken.

Leach Lombard: a dish of ground pork, eggs, raisins, currants, and dates, with spices added. The mixture was boiled in a sack until set, then sliced for serving.

Liripipe: a fashionably long tail attached to a man's cap and worn wrapped about the head.

Lych gate: a roofed gate to a churchyard under which the deceased rested during the initial part of a burial service.

Manchets: bread made from wheat flour, salt, sugar, and yeast and generally baked into balls.

Marshalsea: the stables and associated accoutrements.

Martinmas: November 11. The traditional date to slaughter animals for winter food.

Maslin: bread made from a mixture of grains, commonly wheat and rye or barley and rye.

Michaelmas Term: the academic term from September to Christmas.

Midsummer's day: June 24.

Noble: the first English gold coin produced in quantity, in 1344. Its value was six shillings and eight pence, or eighty pence – one-third of a pound.

Novice: a probationary member of a monastic community. The novice's period of instruction and testing usually lasted for one year.

Page: a young male servant, often a youth learning the arts of chivalry before becoming a squire.

Palfrey: a riding horse with a comfortable gait.

Particolored: of differing colors – often used to describe chauces when each leg is of a different color.

Pork in egurdouce: pork served with a syrup made of ground almonds, currants, dates, wine vinegar, sugar or honey, and spices.

Pottage of whelks: whelks boiled and served in a stock of almond milk, breadcrumbs, and spices.

Reeve: the most important manorial official, although he did not outrank the bailiff. Elected by tenants from among themselves, often the best husbandman. He was responsible for fields, buildings, and enforcing labor service.

Remove: a dinner course.

Rogation Sunday: five weeks after Easter. A time of asking God to bless the new growing season, accompanied by a parade around the village. Monday, Tuesday, and Wednesday after Rogation Sunday were called "gang days."

Runcie: a common horse of a lower grade than a palfrey, often used as a cart horse.

Sacrist: the monastic official responsible for the upkeep of the church and vestments and also timekeeping.

St. Beornwald's Church: today the Church of St. Mary the Virgin in Bampton, in the fourteenth century it was dedicated to an obscure Saxon saint enshrined in the church. Church scenes in the *Downton Abbey* TV series were filmed there.

St. John's Day: June 24.

Shilling: equivalent to twelve pence. Twenty shillings equaled one pound, although in the fourteenth century there were no one shilling or one pound coins.

Sinister: the left hand or left direction.

Solar: a small private room, more easily heated than the great hall, where lords often preferred to spend time, especially in winter.

Stationer: a merchant who sold parchment, vellum, ink, and books.

Statute of Laborers: following the first attack of plague in 1348–49, laborers realized that because so many workers had died their labor was in short supply and so demanded higher wages. In 1351 parliament set wages at the 1347 level. Like most attempts to legislate against the law of supply and demand the statute was generally a failure.

Stewed herrings: herring stuffed with a mixture of breadcrumbs, parsley, thyme, black pepper, currants, sugar, and onion, all chopped fine, then boiled.

Stockfish: the cheapest salted fish, usually cod or haddock.

Stone: fourteen pounds.

Tenant: a free peasant who rented land from his lord. He could pay his rent in labor or, more likely by the fourteenth century, in cash.

Toft: land surrounding a house. In the medieval period often used for growing vegetables.

Trephine: a surgical tool used in trepanning – the removal of a circle of bone from the skull. Usually done to relieve headaches, it sometimes succeeded.

Trinity Term: the third term of the academic year, from mid-April to the end of June.

Tun: a large cask, especially for wine, holding up to 250 gallons. A ship's "tunnage" did not refer to the weight it could carry but to the number of tuns which could be loaded.

Villein: a non-free peasant. He could not leave his land or service to his lord, or sell animals without permission. But if he could escape his manor for a year and a day he would be free.

Void: dessert – often sugared fruits and wine.

Wattles: interlaced sticks used as a foundation and support for daub in plastering a wall.

Week-work: the two or three days of work per week (more during harvest) owed by a villein to his lord.

Weld: a plant from which yellow dye was made.

Winchester geese: prostitutes licensed and taxed by the Bishop of Winchester to ply their trade in his enclave of Southwark.

Woad: a plant whose leaves produced a blue dye.

Yardland: thirty acres. Also called a virgate. In northern England often called an oxgang.

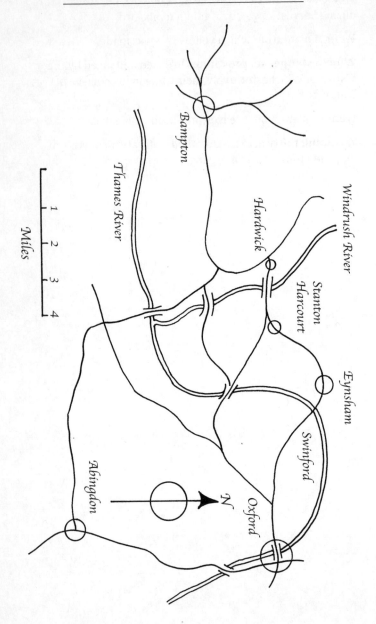

Chapter 1

Plague has made travel somewhat safer. Many folk have died of the great pestilence in the past twenty-some years, so that those who yet live can find employment where they will and have no need to rob other men upon the roads and risk a hempen noose. Safer, aye, but not always safe. There will ever be those who prefer to live by the sweat of another man's brow. Hubert Shillside, Bampton's haberdasher and coroner, learned too late that this was so.

'Twas Good Friday, the fourth day of April, in the year of our Lord 1371, that I learned of Shillside's unwanted discovery. I attended the Church of St. Beornwald alone that day, to see and honor the host as it was placed into the Easter Sepulcher. My Kate had given birth two weeks earlier to our son, whom we named John, in honor of the scholar John Wycliffe, who had been my master at Balliol College twelve years past. So Kate remained at Galen House, with Bessie and the babe, until the time for her churching, and I kept house, boiled pottage for our dinners, bought bread from the baker and ale from his wife, and waited impatiently for her confinement to be past.

I cannot enter the church porch but that my eyes stray to the turf near the west end of the churchyard, where Kate saw our infant daughter, Sybil, placed in her small grave eight months past, whilst I was away in France, bid to accompany my employer, Lord Gilbert Talbot, at the siege and recapture of Limoges.

Perhaps one day I will enter the church porch and not remember the child. I pray not. She has gone before her mother and me, escaping early from the land of death and exchanging it for the land of eternal life.

Father Simon dismissed the congregation after the velvet curtain was drawn across the opening to the Easter Sepulcher. With other Bampton residents – all of us somber, as the remembrance of the Lord Christ's sacrifice to free men from the penalty of their sins came fresh to mind – I departed the church and stepped from the porch into a cold, misty rain. 'Twas appropriate to the day. Good Friday should not be warm and cloudless. Sunshine should be reserved for Easter Sunday.

Halfway from the porch to the lych gate I felt a tug upon my sleeve and heard my name called. 'Twas Will Shillside who accosted me.

"My father has not returned from Oxford," he said. I had not known he had traveled there.

"He went there on business?" I asked.

"Aye. Departed on Tuesday. Was to return to Bampton last eve. Thought perhaps he'd become weary, carryin' a sack full of goods, an' sought lodging for the night, mayhap at the abbey in Eynsham."

"If he did so," I replied, "he would surely have returned by now."

"Aye. That's why I'm troubled."

Will Shillside was a youth of twenty or so years, his beard in the process of changing from gossamer threads to bristles, and his form filling out from his youthful appearance of knees and feet, hands and elbows, threaded together by scrawny arms and legs. Last June he had wed Alice atte Bridge, and it was become clear that Hubert Shillside would be a grandfather before this summer passed. Depending upon what may have befallen him upon the road to or from Oxford.

"What business had he in Oxford?" I asked.

"He travels there for the goods he sells here. I told him I would go, but he insisted that I am unskilled in business matters and would be gulled by the men of Oxford who supply the stuff we sell."

"Pins and buttons and buckles and such," I said.

"Aye. And ribbons and spools of linen and silken thread, this trip."

"Oh, aye. I did mention to your father some weeks past that my supply of silken thread is near depleted."

Silken thread is of value to me in my service as surgeon to the folk of Bampton and nearby places. I trained for one year in Paris, returned to Oxford, and found employment as both surgeon and bailiff to Lord Gilbert Talbot, lord of the manor of Bampton and its castle. When folk lacerate themselves at their work, or drop stones or beams or axes upon their toes, silken thread is useful to stitch them back together again.

But it was as bailiff that Will Shillside sought me to report his father missing upon the road to Oxford. 'Tis a bailiff's duty to see to the welfare of those of his bailiwick. 'Tis a great misfortune, for those of us who do so, that many bailiffs do not.

It was too late to set out that day for Oxford. If Shillside had stumbled under his load and fallen into a ditch it would soon be too dark to see his prostrate form. And if he had toppled and struck his head against a rock and was insensible, he would not hear and respond if we called to him. I told Will that he should come to the castle at dawn. I would gather a few of Lord Gilbert's grooms and instruct the marshal to have palfreys ready. Beasts would speed the search, and several pairs of eyes and ears would be better than two.

Saturday morn dawned clear but cold. I consumed a maslin loaf to break my fast, and a cup of ale, and told my Kate that, depending upon the success or failure of the search, I might return to Galen House yet this day, or on the morrow, or perhaps not. She nodded and kissed me farewell, being well accustomed to a bailiff's tangled schedule. I left her with some guilt vexing me. I had a duty to her, but also to Lord Gilbert Talbot and the folk of his manor at Bampton.

I wrapped my fur coat about me and set off down Church View Street for Bampton Castle. Will Shillside, his face drawn with worry, stood before the gatehouse awaiting me. I came in hope that his father might have arrived home in the night, but one glance at the dark circles under Will's eyes told me this was not so.

Arthur and Uctred, grooms in Lord Gilbert's service, had proven useful companions before when my service as Lord

Gilbert's bailiff required assistance. So I had told them to be ready with palfreys saddled as soon as daylight would make a search possible.

Lord Gilbert was not in residence at Bampton Castle. He had spent most of the winter at Goodrich Castle, as was his custom. Without the master in residence, life for a groom of Bampton Castle was tedious. A search for a missing haberdasher would enliven dull days.

Several ways lead from Bampton to Oxford. It would take many days to search them all, but Will assured me his father always traveled by way of Eynsham, crossing the river at Swinford. We four did likewise, calling out Shillside's name every hundred paces or so, and keeping eyes upon the verge. We got no response to our shouts, nor saw any sign of a man lying ill or injured near the road.

We passed Osney Abbey and entered Oxford across Bookbinder's Bridge. I asked Will where his father was accustomed to do business in Oxford.

"Martyn Hendy is our usual supplier. Shop is on Fish Street."

We went there. Arthur and Uctred remained with the beasts whilst Will and I sought the proprietor. Hendy is a moon-faced fellow, with an equally circular belly. His business prospers, I think. He remembered Will from past visits, when he had accompanied his father. His greeting brought us no joy.

"Ah, Will... is your father well? He has sent you to do his business rather than attend himself, I see."

"Has my father not called here a few days past?" Will asked.

"Your father? Here, in Oxford? Nay, I've not seen 'im."

Will looked to me with alarm writ across his face. Hendy saw, and spoke.

"Perhaps he has taken his custom elsewhere. Although he'd not get a fairer price than from me."

"Father did not speak of taking his business to another," Will said, "but perhaps he did so."

"Why do you ask this?" Hendy asked.

"Hubert Shillside was to return to Bampton Thursday,"

I said. "He did not, so I and two others have come with Will seeking him. Where might he have sought supplies if he did not do so here?"

Hendy directed us to three other Oxford merchants who dealt in buttons and buckles and pins and thread and such stuff. We received from these burghers the same answers we had from Hendy. Hubert Shillside had not visited the proprietors. There were no other establishments in Oxford dealing with the kind of goods Shillside wished to purchase. Something had apparently happened to the man while he walked to Oxford four days past. What that might be did not bear thinking about. But bailiffs are employed to consider such things. I must soon earn my wages.

Four men might search for another between Bampton and Oxford for a fortnight and not find him. If Shillside had met with felons who demanded his purse and then slew him, his corpse might be hid in some wood or dumped in the Thames if he was attacked near the river. We might never find the man. I did not say this to Will, but I did study the river as we recrossed Bookbinder's Bridge.

We had passed Osney Abbey when Will said what we all were thinking.

"He's slain, I fear. Some men have seized him and slain him for his purse."

"How much coin did he travel with?" I asked.

"Father usually purchased ten or so shillings' worth of goods. He said to buy less meant walking to Oxford more often."

"Did he speak to others of his journey? That he would set out for Oxford Tuesday morn?"

"Don't know. Might've, I suppose."

We splashed across the Thames at Swinford and a short time later approached the gates of Eynsham Abbey. The days were growing longer. If we pressed our beasts we might reach Bampton by nightfall, but this would be cruel to animals which had already borne us more than twenty miles this day. And I thought the abbot might assist me if he learned of my search for a missing man and his missing shillings.

Abbot Gerleys owes his position, to some extent, to me. A few years past, whilst I sought the felon who had slain a novice of the abbey, I discovered a heresy among a few of the monks. The leader of this heretical sect was the prior, Philip Thorpe, and but for my learning of his heresy he would likely have become the next abbot of the house. But Philip was persuaded to transfer to Dunfermline Abbey in Scotland, where winter lasts 'til May and each frigid morning will remind him of his sin, and Brother Gerleys became abbot upon the death of the elderly Abbot Thurstan.

The abbey hosteller recognized me, sent for two lay brothers to care for our beasts, and led us to the guest house with a promise of loaves, cheese, and ale soon to arrive. I told the monk I sought conversation with Abbot Gerleys, and soon after our meal arrived the abbot did too.

This was an honor I did not expect. When a man wishes to speak to an abbot it is he who must, if granted permission, call upon the abbot. Will and Arthur and Uctred were suitably impressed that a man whose presence was required when King Edward called a parliament would deign to seek his humble visitors.

Abbot Gerleys requested more ale be brought, and seated himself across the table from me. When I had last seen him he was a spare, slender, almost emaciated monk. His post evidently suited him, for his cheeks were now rounded and his habit offered a slight bulge where it once had draped flat across his stomach.

"How may I assist Lord Gilbert's bailiff?" he said.

I told the abbot of our journey to Oxford and the reason for it. He listened silently, intent, his brow furrowed and lips drawn thin.

"We four," I concluded, "will continue the search for Will's father on Monday, when we return to Bampton. But I have small hope of success. 'Tis a busy season, I know, but if you could assign some lay brothers to leave the abbey and search other roads and byways nearby I would be much obliged to you."

"It will be done," Abbot Gerleys replied, "and not only for your need. There is much amiss hereabouts. Word has come to me that men have made hamsoken on householders in villages nearby. Two of these attacks happened in abbey manors. A man was beaten nearly to death in Appleton when he objected to having his oxen taken, and a man from Wytham has gone missing."

"Was he upon the roads – a traveler?" I asked.

"Aye. Not fleeing a harridan wife, so I'm told, but taking sacks of barley to Abingdon a fortnight past. Man, horse, cart, and barley have disappeared."

This was not good to learn. Nothing of the sort had happened near Bampton, at least not that I had heard – and bailiffs are expected to hear of such things – but if theft and murder are but ten or so miles away 'tis likely the affliction will spread, as contagion surely passes from the ill to the healthy. Why is it, I wonder, that good health does not spread from the vigorous to the sickly, but only the other way round?

I would have preferred to celebrate the feast of the resurrection in Bampton, at the Church of St. Beornwald, even if my Kate could not accompany me, but duty and desire are oft in conflict. I and my companions heard Easter Mass at the abbey church, rested our beasts and, after a dinner of roasted capon and loaves with honeyed butter, wandered the roads about Eynsham searching for Hubert Shillside. I did not expect to find him in a place with so many folk abroad, who would already have discovered a man injured or dead near to a road, and did not. But Will could not remain idle in the abbey guest house whilst his father might be somewhere near and in distress. So we poked into hedges and climbed over walls and prowled forests with no result but for a sting from young nettles growing alongside the stone wall enclosing an abbey field.

We broke our fast next morning with loaves fresh from the abbey oven and cups of excellent ale. I saw Abbot Gerleys speaking to a band of lay brothers while others brought our mounts to us, gesturing to north and south, east and west as he spoke. "Here are the men who will seek your father," I said to Will.

The lad had not slept well. His pallor and bloodshot eyes gave him the appearance of a man twice, nay, three times his age.

The abbot concluded his instructions and sent the searchers off, two by two. I thanked him for this aid, bidding him send word to Bampton if his monks found any clue to Hubert Shillside's disappearance, then prodded my palfrey through the abbey gate.

Men, women, even children were busy in the fields this day. Some strips had not yet been plowed for spring crops, so teams of oxen and horses were at work turning the soil. In another field several women were at work with dibble sticks, planting peas and beans.

Other fields were being sown to oats or barley or perhaps dredge, and small boys found employment slinging stones and clods at birds who would consume the seed before harrows could cover it with soil.

Several places along the road I stopped and called to laborers, asking them to keep watch for any traveler they might find along the way who had been injured or assaulted. Always these folk readily agreed, tugging a forelock in appreciation of my status as told them by my fur coat. This garment had been of value two days past, but was now too warm. The spring sun warmed our travel, if not our hearts.

We reached Bampton shortly after noon, having seen no sign of Hubert Shillside nor speaking to any folk who had.

Wednesday, about the sixth hour, two of Abbot Gerleys' lay brothers rapped upon the door of Galen House. A corpse was found, they said, stripped of clothing and shoes, in a wood between Eynsham and Farmoor. The body rested now before the altar of the abbey church, and Abbot Gerleys desired me to attend him forthwith to identify the man, for the corpse was putrid and beginning to stink, which interfered with the monks' observance of canonical hours. I thought the dead man must be Hubert Shillside, struck down by robbers. Not so.

Chapter 2

The corpse lay upon a catafalque, covered with a black linen shroud which the abbey must keep for just such a purpose. Abbot Gerleys drew back the shroud from the dead man's head and I knew before the face was uncovered that 'twas not Hubert Shillside whose corpse lay here. Shillside was bald, or nearly so, with a rim of brown hair laced with silver about his ears. The man whose form now lay in the abbey church had a thick shock of yellow hair.

I had not told Will Shillside of the abbey corpse, unwilling to have the lad look on his father's decomposing body. I could identify the man and return him to Bampton to rest in the village churchyard without requiring Will's involvement in the identification. So I had brought with me to Eynsham only Arthur, who rode upon a cart drawn by a runcie whilst I rode a castle palfrey. A cart would be needed, I had thought, to return Hubert Shillside's corpse to his son.

"Is this the man?" Abbot Gerleys asked.

"Nay. Did you say a man has gone missing from Wytham?"

"Aye. Wytham is less than a mile from the wood where this fellow was found."

"One of your lay brothers found this man?"

"Nay. They have been seeking your missing man along the roads and venturing into woods and fields along the highways, but 'twas an abbey verderer who found this fellow. He was deep in Wytham Wood, marking oaks suitable for the beams needed when we build our new barn, when he discovered the corpse."

"Not near the road to Abingdon?"

"Nearly a mile from that way."

When I did not immediately reply Abbot Gerleys continued. "What are you thinking?"

"That to carry a man you have just slain for a mile through a greenwood is a thing most felons would find objectionable."

25

"Why so?"

"You have taken all he possesses, even his clothes, it seems, and if no witnesses saw the crime you will not be identified. Why would you then care if the corpse be found? Why go to the trouble of disposing of your victim in the middle of a wood? It seems to me the felons, if they attacked a man upon the road and slew him, would be content to drag him into the undergrowth and there scatter some of last year's fallen leaves over him 'til worms and carrion crows have done their work and the remains are no more than a pile of bones."

"Still, this may be the man missing from Wytham."

"Aye, it may be so. But I think the fellow was not a traveler upon the roads but caught in the woods at some business, and slain there, where he was found. How did the man die? Is there a wound?"

"There is," the abbot said, and drew the shroud down to the dead man's belly, swollen with decomposition.

I saw a wound just under the heart where the fellow had been stabbed. The cut was large, made by a sword, or perhaps a large dagger twisted when the thrust entered the man's body. Here was no accidental stroke made by a thief as his victim gave up his property. This puncture was deliberate, accurate. Its intent was to kill, not to maim. If the same men who slew this fellow accosted Hubert Shillside along the road, he was likely dealt with in a similar fashion. I said this to Abbot Gerleys.

"Men?" he said. "You believe that more than one man is responsible for this death?"

"Would one man drag his victim so far from a road, and so deep into a wood, if that is what happened?"

"They would not," he agreed. "Perhaps even more than two men did this murder. If the man was not slain where he was found."

"And you said men have made hamsoken on homes hereabouts?"

"Aye. Often upon a Sunday, when folk are at mass. They return from the church to find their homes plundered. You suppose the same felons who did this murder are those who are looting houses?"

"Did these robberies begin recently?" I asked.

"Aye, they did. About the time the man from Wytham went missing, or perhaps a fortnight earlier."

Abbot Gerleys said he would immediately send lay brothers to Wytham, there to seek the wife of the man missing from the place, and bring her to Eynsham. She could tell us if 'twas her husband whose corpse rested before the altar. I could see the abbot dearly wished the dead man out of his church. But he also promised Hubert Shillside would not be forgotten. The brothers would continue to prowl roads and fields and forest in search of him. Seeking his corpse, that is, for I felt sure nothing more remained of my friend.

Arthur and I returned to Bampton before dark. Kate greeted me with a kiss, the babe upon her hip and Bessie at her side. I was much pleased to see all three. "Was it Hubert, then, found dead in the wood?" she asked.

"Nay. Some other. Probably a prosperous tenant of Wytham who disappeared whilst taking sacks of barley to Abingdon."

"Probably?"

"Abbot Gerleys has sent for the man's wife, to identify the corpse. But the dead man was not Shillside, so whatever happened to him is not of my bailiwick."

So I thought.

Will Shillside came to me Saturday morning to ask if any news had arrived from the abbey. None had but for the corpse which was not his father, and I had related that news to him on Thursday morn. Each day since, he said, he had walked roads and lanes to the east of Bampton seeking his father. With no success. I felt guilty that I also had failed to discover his father, so, after partaking of a maslin loaf and ale, I joined him in his continuing search that day.

He had already traveled the road to Yelford and Hardwick, but had resolved to search that way again. This was the route we four had followed to Eynsham and Oxford when the search for Shillside began, so 'twould be the third time the route had been examined. I thought this a waste of time, believing that the surest hope of finding the missing haberdasher would be through the efforts of the brothers of Eynsham Abbey. But Will is young, and the young are oft impatient. He no longer hoped to find his father alive, I'm sure; to find him and see that he was interred in hallowed ground was now his purpose.

The day had dawned clear, with a warm sun to drive away our low spirits. But before we reached Yelford low clouds swept in from the north and so we plodded on toward Hardwick with soul and eyes both downcast. We searched silently. There was no point in calling Shillside's name. If he had lain somewhere along the verge for more than a week he would be in no condition to answer. When we saw folk at work in roadside fields we stopped to seek knowledge of them. Some of these we had questioned on our return from Oxford a week past. They knew nothing then and knew nothing now.

I was ready to quit the search at Hardwick and return to Bampton, but Will prevailed on me to walk just a little way farther. To the bridge over Windrush stream, he pleaded. I agreed.

As we approached the bridge, half a mile beyond Hardwick, I saw two black-clad figures approaching from the east. Will and I met the fellows at the bridge. They were Eynsham brothers sent this way by Abbot Gerleys, seeking but not finding.

We stood together on the bridge advising each other of our lack of success in discovering Hubert Shillside. I spoke of the corpse I had seen in the abbey church three days past, and asked if the dead man had been returned to Wytham.

"Wasn't 'im," one of the monks said.

"What? The dead man found in the wood – the one I saw before your altar – was not the man missing from Wytham?"

"'At's right. Wife come to the abbey to fetch 'im 'ome, saw it wasn't 'er husband, an' swooned to the tiles."

"Who was it then," I asked, "the man you found dead in the wood?"

"No man knows. Must be another man missin' from hereabouts what nobody knows of. Couldn't leave 'im before the altar no longer. Abbot Gerleys 'ad 'im buried yesterday in St. Leonard's churchyard."

During this conversation I had glanced into the Windrush several times. I cannot cross a bridge without pausing to gaze into the stream. Spring rains had deepened the river and increased its flow. I could not see to the streambed from the center of the bridge.

Our friends turned from the bridge to return to the abbey, their search completed for the day. I bid them "Good day," asked them to commend me to Abbot Gerleys, then stepped forward to follow them down from the bridge. There was nothing more to be done. I might as well go home to Bampton.

As I set about doing so my eyes lingered upon an object twisting gently in the flow of water about fifty paces or so downstream of the bridge. I assumed it to be a branch of a tree fallen into the stream, but something caused me to halt and view the object more closely.

It was raised above the water nearly the length of my hand and wrist, and was brown, as a fallen limb would be, but had a shape unlike that of a tree branch. The object seemed like an ankle garbed in brown chauces, ending in a foot within a shoe.

Will had looked upon the river and its banks while I spoke to the brothers, and now walked ahead of me, but saw, or felt, that I was no longer close behind him. He turned, saw me staring downstream, and followed my gaze. He apparently noticed nothing to capture his attention, so asked what caused me to peer into the distant flow.

"Come," I said, hastening from the bridge to the bank, past the end of a low stone wall which, terminating at the river's edge, ran thence through the tall grass of a meadow. From a different angle the object which had seized my attention assumed more the appearance of a branch swept down the river until it fetched up against some impediment to its farther progress.

But when we came close I saw the thing had never been part of a tree. Will recognized this also, and I heard him catch his breath as he realized what lay in the Windrush.

Neither of us spoke as we hurried along the riverbank. Neither of us wanted to acknowledge that some man lay hidden in the river but for a protruding ankle and foot. Sheep pastured in the meadow lifted their heads to watch as we stumbled through the grass. Lambs nursed enthusiastically, their tails thumping.

Will hurried ahead of me, and when we reached the section of riverbank closest to the drowned man – for it was now clear this was what we had found – he crossed himself, then stepped into the knee-deep water to tug at the protruding foot.

There seemed some impediment to Will's effort to draw the corpse from the river. He pulled upon the foot with no immediate success. Then suddenly the hindrance gave way and Will staggered back, struggling to keep his footing, grabbing at a tuft of grass with one hand but stubbornly refusing to release the corpse from the other's grasp.

I leaned down to assist the lad and took hold of a hand now floating free of whatever restraint had held it fast in the current. Will regained his feet, and together we hauled the body from the river. I was closest to the dead man's face, and so as the visage came from the water saw sooner than Will that we had found his father.

All this time, hurrying from the bridge, to laying the corpse in the meadow grass, we had not spoken. Will broke the silence.

"I've crossed this bridge, seekin' 'im, three times, yet never thought to examine the river. Wonder why 'e fell in. Wasn't tottering on 'is feet as aged men often are. Not that old."

Will's first thoughts were of mischance, not felony, and I might have shared them but that I noticed two leather thongs wrapped at one end about Shillside's belt but at the other terminating in freshly cut ends. The haberdasher's purse was gone.

I picked up the cut ends and Will seized upon my discovery.

"Gone. You think 'e might've lost it struggling in the river? Mayhap it caught upon some sunken log."

"Nay. Look here. The straps have been cut cleanly. Had the purse been torn from him the ends would be tattered, frayed."

"Robbed and slain, then?"

"Aye, so I believe. You must hurry back to Bampton and return with a horse and cart so we may take your father home. Go to the castle. Seek Arthur and tell him what we need. Hurry. We want to be home before nightfall. I will remain with your father."

I sent Will, rather than going myself, for several reasons. Will was younger, and fleet of foot. As I once had been, but Kate's cookery had slowed me somewhat. The reverse was surely not true. The meals I had been preparing since John's birth would not cause Kate to let out the seams of her cotehardie. Will would not have been well served had I left him beside the river to stare into the bloated face of his dead father whilst I sought help. And while Will was away I intended to examine the corpse to learn, if I could, what had caused this death. Did Hubert drown, or was he dead when he entered the river?

My first thought was that men had accosted Shillside upon or near the bridge, stolen his purse, and then thrown him into the river so they might make good their escape whilst he struggled to save himself. The man could not swim, of this I was quite certain. I can, for I lived as a child near a river in Lancashire where my three older brothers thought it great sport to toss me in and watch me splash to the riverbank, but I know of few other men who can do so.

The corpse lay as we had drawn it from the Windrush, face up, arms splayed out to each side. Shillside had been in the river for more than a week, I assumed. His features were swollen, the skin white and wrinkled. I examined the face, and then his clothing, seeking some sign of a stroke or thrust which might have slain the man or rendered him senseless.

I found such a wound. A small tear in Shillside's cotehardie caught my eye. No blood stained the perforation. If the man was stabbed the river had long since washed the blood from kirtle and cotehardie.

And stabbed he was. I drew aside his clothing and saw a laceration upon Shillside's breast. The blade which made it would have penetrated his heart, given the location of the wound.

31

Against the pale skin I saw some dark object within the cut. I placed a finger against the wound and felt some unyielding thing where such should not have been. Immersion in the Windrush had puckered the cut. I spread the laceration and saw embedded in Shillside's chest the broken blade of a dagger.

I grasped the weapon and attempted to pull it free but it was stuck fast between two ribs. How to extract the dagger puzzled me, as I had with me no tools, nothing with which to grasp the broken blade.

I did have my dagger. I pushed it into the wound and pried the blade free. Shillside would not mind.

The broken dagger was of the meaner sort and poorly made. No wealthy man had owned such a weapon. The broken segment was the length of my first finger, long enough to pierce Shillside's heart before it snapped as he struggled against it. I did not know if this fragment could lead me to a felon, but placed it in my pouch for safekeeping. Just in case.

But the manner of Shillside's death was of little consequence. He was dead, slain for his coins, and 'twas my duty to discover who had done the felony and see them sent to the scaffold for their crime. Or crimes. What of the unidentified corpse I had seen before the altar of Eynsham Abbey church? Or the missing man from Wytham? Did the same men slay these also?

The grass near the river had grown vigorously with warming spring days and plentiful rain. So it was that, my examination of the corpse complete, I could sit and be nearly obscured from view. I waited for Will and Arthur to appear, idly watched birds flitting about, saw a fish leap in the river, and twice observed travelers cross the bridge, intent upon a destination. They crossed without glancing upstream or down. And had they glanced in my direction the grass would have hidden my presence to all but the most intent observer.

The sun was low in the western sky before Arthur and Will appeared on the road from Hardwick. I stood, brushed last year's leaves and blades of brown grass from my chauces, and waited for them to approach.

The stone wall lining the road ended at the bridge timbers, so horse and cart could not be brought near to Shillside's corpse. Arthur tied the runcie to a sapling growing by the juncture of wall and bridge, then he and Will edged past the end of the wall.

We three carried the corpse back to the bridge, but as we reached the cart a movement caught my eye. Some distance to the east, across the bridge and three or four hundred paces beyond, four black-garbed figures stood in the road. I took them for brothers from the abbey, seeking yet for Hubert Shillside.

The abbey should be told that he was found; Eynsham's men would be better employed in the work of preparing abbey soil and planting than in seeking a corpse. Seeing opportunity to send word that we no longer needed the services of Abbot Gerleys' community, I waved an arm above my head whilst Arthur and Will set the corpse into the cart, and trotted across the bridge toward the distant figures.

What happened next surprised me. The black-clad men seemed to take counsel of one another, glanced in my direction, then hurried away toward Eynsham.

Had the fellows seen me? Or had they not understood my gesture? They had seemingly been approaching the bridge from the east. They must have had some purpose in mind. What could it have been that they were dissuaded from it when they saw me motion to them?

Whatever the reason, their hasty withdrawal meant I must travel this way again Monday. Perhaps by then Abbot Gerleys would have news of the crimes committed near to Eynsham.

St. Paul told us, in his letter to the believers in Philippi, that the followers of the Lord Christ must not be anxious about anything. The apostle had no wife or babes to concern him. Perhaps he, like me, would have worried more if he had had souls in his charge, had lost one of them to the churchyard, and been responsible for another but a fortnight or so old.

Such thoughts occupy me more often since returning from France and discovering Sybil dead. I cannot see Kate or Bessie or John without concern that they might also succumb to some illness.

Sunday, after mass, we buried Hubert Shillside in the churchyard of St. Beornwald's Church. Arthur attended, and I bade him have our palfreys ready for Eynsham next morn, to take word of our grisly discovery and call off their search. Had I taken the apostle's advice I might have traveled alone, dismissing my apprehension at journeying unaccompanied, trusting the Lord Christ to deliver me from cut-purses and every kind of violence. But even holy writ must be applied with common sense. The injunction that Christian men should not worry does not mean they should foolishly invite the attention of murderous malefactors.

This day was Hocktide, when 'twas my duty after dinner to collect rents and fines due Lord Gilbert. Men do not find much pleasure in the obligation though Hock Monday and Hock Tuesday bring some cheer, offering a scarce chance to play and make merry. Unless you are Hubert Shillside.

Chapter 3

Monday dawned cloudy, cheerless, and threatened rain. When skies over England threaten rain they generally make good the warning. Hocktide festivities would be dampened, I feared. A soft mist became a gentle rain before Arthur and I reached Yelford, and we were soaked, teeth chattering, when we arrived at Eynsham.

The guest master again sent for lay brothers to care for our beasts, and another took us to the guest house, where we found a welcome blaze in the fireplace where we could warm ourselves and dry our sodden clothes.

Arthur and I were warmed and dry, or nearly so, when Abbot Gerleys entered the guest house. The abbot was a young man for such a post, and ceremony seemed to mean little to him. Else he would have required of me that I attend him in his lodgings rather than sought me.

"We have had no success in finding your haberdasher," the abbot began.

"He is found," I replied. "You may end the search."

I then told him of discovering Hubert Shillside's corpse, and seeing from a distance brothers of the abbey approach the bridge over the Windrush, then turn away.

"I would have sent word with them that the man was found," I said, "but they hastened away and, as 'twas become late in the day, I wished to make for Bampton."

"Lay brothers?" the abbot said.

"Aye. Four. They took counsel of each other when they saw me, then hastened back toward Eynsham."

"I sent four lay brothers to search for your man on Saturday, but only two sought him toward Hardwick. The others I sent to Cassington and Yarnton."

"Only two toward Hardwick? Perhaps they found the others you sent to Cassington. I met the two you sent toward Hardwick

35

upon the Windrush Bridge, just before I found Hubert Shillside. They left me there to return here."

Abbot Gerleys stood, went to the guest house door, and called to a monk who stood outside. "Find Gaston and Ralph, and fetch them here."

I heard the man accept this assignment, and the abbot returned to his bench. "What of the corpse your verderer found in Wytham Wood?" I asked. "Has the man been identified?"

"Nay. The man we found we cannot name, and the man we know has gone missing is not to be found. But another evil has come upon a nearby village since we last spoke. A tenant of Church Hanborough sent his daughter to plant peas in a new plowed field last Wednesday. When she did not return for her dinner he sought her. She was not to be found. Only her dibble stick and bag of seed were in the field. Many footprints, he said, were there in the soft ground, and led to a road, much traveled, where they could no longer be followed."

"The lass was taken?" I said. "How old was she?"

"Fifteen, I believe he said."

"And now she is missing?"

"Nay. The father and others of the village sought her that day 'til dark, and intended to resume the hunt next morn, but as the dawn came the lass returned to her home."

"What? Had she run off... with a lad, mayhap?"

"Nay. Nothing of the sort. Men plucked her from the field, she said, had their way with her, then set her free."

"And her father came to you seeking justice?"

"Aye. The village bailiff has sent men to search for the felons, but he has had no success." Abbot Gerleys shook his head as he considered the outrage. "She was a quiet lass, I'm told, and since that day has not been seen out of doors. Where will she now find a husband? One may hope that her father is prosperous enough that he can provide a substantial dowry. Or perhaps some widower with children to rear will have her."

A thought came to me. "How many men took the lass?" I asked.

"Four, the father said."

"Were they clad as scholars or lay brothers or monks, in black gowns?"

"Hmmm. Didn't think to ask... but I will. You think they might be the four you saw upon the road when you found your haberdasher?"

"It had occurred to me."

"Worth pursuing, if it turns out so to be."

"Perhaps worth pursuing even if the assailants wore green and brown and such. Men may change their clothing to suit their labor... or their felony."

"Just so. Ah, here are Gaston and Ralph."

I recognized as the men I had last seen upon the Windrush Bridge the sturdy, well-fed lay brothers of thirty or so years who now entered the guest house and stood, awaiting instruction.

"I sent you to search for a missing man Saturday," Abbot Gerleys said. "Told you to explore the road to Hardwick. You did not report back to me. Did you complete the search?"

"Aye, m'lord Abbot," one said. "You was with Brother Prior when we returned, an' we found nothing, so had no report."

"Did any others accompany you that I know not of?"

"Nay. Just me an' Gaston."

"When you found no man injured or ill or dead on the way I sent you, did you join with Calkin or Richard upon your return?"

"Nay. No time for seekin' the way to Cassington. 'Twas near to dark when we returned from Hardwick."

Abbot Gerleys looked to me, a silent offer to add questions of my own for Ralph and Gaston. I had none, and shook my head to indicate so. The abbot told the lay brothers that the man they had sought for many days was found, so they could resume work in the abbey fields on the morrow. The announcement seemed to bring the fellows little joy. They no doubt preferred a leisurely stroll along pleasant lanes to plowing and planting and mucking out.

When Ralph and Gaston had gone, Abbot Gerleys turned to me and spoke. "The black-clad men you saw, who could they have been? Oxford scholars, mayhap?"

"Perhaps, but why would they seek to avoid me?"

"Could it be they thought you wanted to lure them into a trap? Word has likely reached Oxford of the felonies plaguing this place. Traveling scholars might be cautious of a man upon the road who seemed too eager to meet with them."

I agreed this might be so. "But I would like to know from the lass who was taken from her work in the pea field what clothing her abductors wore."

"I will send lay brothers to her house on the morrow, and next day send them to you with the answer."

"No need to do so if they wore black gowns. If no men come to me from the abbey on Wednesday, I'll take it that the fellows wore black. Send word only if they wore layman's garb. And, if the lass can remember, ask the colors of their cotehardies and caps." Even as I said it I realized that these details might not have been the first thing on her mind. But we had to enquire.

Wednesday, about noon, Ralph and Gaston rapped upon Galen House door. Their message from Abbot Gerleys was delivered by their presence, before they spoke. The men who attacked the lass near to Church Hanborough had not been clothed as scholars or monks or lay brothers.

"Lass couldn't recall much," Gaston replied to my question about the garb of the assailants. "Said as one wore a blue cap, another a green cotehardie. Couldn't remember much else, but they was beardless."

Even should the rogues be found, 'twould be difficult to grant the lass justice. Galen taught that a woman will not be found with child if she is ravished against her will. If she becomes pregnant that will be considered evidence that she gave consent. Of course, if a lass claims that she was assaulted but does not conceive, the man accused can protest that the woman lies, and who can know who speaks true? I wonder if the great physician of antiquity might have been mistaken?

Kate had prepared a porre of peas and apple moyle for our dinner. 'Twas enough to feed us and two lay brothers. And we had three maslin loaves fresh that morn from the baker.

"Abbot Gerleys told us," Gaston said between mouthfuls of bread and pottage, "that you saw four men on the road near to the Windrush Bridge when you found your missing man, an' they turned from you when you would have spoken to them."

"Aye. They hastened away when they saw me upon the bridge. When you left me upon the bridge that day to return to Eynsham did you meet others upon the road? Four others?"

"Nay. Seems odd, though. Four men attacked the lass, an' four men wished to keep away from you."

"Four against one," Ralph said. "Why would four men fear one upon the road?"

"Mayhap they saw my companions. The dead man's son was there, and also a groom to Lord Gilbert Talbot."

"Ah... four against three. Men intent upon evil might seek better odds, I think," Gaston said, then licked his lips noisily. Children are mimics. Bessie watched him do this, then did likewise, concluding the exercise with a satisfied grin. I glanced to Kate. Her lips were thin. She was displeased that a man of the abbey was providing such a poor example of manners to our daughter. There would be words, I thought, after the lay brothers' departure.

Ralph and Gaston were no more than ten paces from our door when I heard a wail from our chamber. John had awakened in his crib and was demanding to be fed. Kate hurried up the stairs and so I escaped censure for my guest's misbehavior, calling after her that I had business at the castle.

A bailiff can always find business at his lord's residence, be it a simple manor house or a great lord's castle. But upon this occasion I found duty to perform before I reached the castle.

I had crossed the bridge over Shill Brook, passing the lane to the Weald, when I heard a man call my name. I glanced down the path and saw Father Thomas waving vigorously and heard him call out again. I halted my journey to the castle and waited for him to come puffing, red in the face, to me.

"Ah, Master Hugh," he wheezed. "You are well met. I have

just come from Alain Gower," he said, glancing over his shoulder at the row of houses lining the lane to the Weald.

Alain is one of the more prosperous residents of the Weald, but as folk there are tenants of the Bishop of Exeter and not of my bailiwick I do not know the man well.

"He was robbed last night," Father Thomas continued. "Men slashed the skin of a window and entered silently, whilst he and Margery and their babes were asleep."

"Did Alain not awaken during the theft?"

"Aye, he did. One of the brigands kicked a table in the dark. Alain sat up in his bed and received a blow across his pate. This awakened Margery, but she could do nothing."

"What was taken?" I asked.

"Two pewter cups, a silver spoon given to Margery as a bridal gift, a glazed pot, and two candlesticks."

"Silver?"

"Nay. Alain is prosperous, but not so that he can light his house with candles in silver candlesticks. Pewter."

"His is the largest house in the Weald, is it not?"

"Aye. No doubt why the thieves made him their target. No sense risking a noose robbing the house of a poor man who will possess little worth stealing.

"I was about to seek you," the priest continued. "Happy thing that you were passing this way."

I said nothing, but waited for Father Thomas to say what I had already guessed.

"The Weald has no bailiff. We get by with but a reeve. The bishop has decided that, as St. Beornwald's Church has three vicars, one of us can do the work of a bailiff. For collecting the bishop's rents such an arrangement is satisfactory, but neither I nor Father Simon nor Father Ralph are suited for the work of apprehending felons.

"And," he continued, "as Lord Gilbert's lands are greater and his tenants more numerous than the bishop's, 'tis likely that the guilty are of your bailiwick."

"Hubert Shillside was of my bailiwick," I said.

"Aye. Have you found who slew him?"

"Nay, and that work must consume my time – more so than stolen candlesticks."

"Indeed," Father Thomas conceded. "But do not forget Alain and his loss."

I promised I would not, but I felt little interest in seeking a miscreant in the Weald. Then, as I crossed the moat and entered Bampton Castle, it occurred to me that the hamsoken made on homes in villages near Eynsham had now come to Bampton. Did four men assault Alain, I wondered? There was but one way to discover if 'twas so.

Chapter 4

"Don't know... Dark, wasn't it," Alain said when I asked the number of his assailants.

"And your head: did the blow leave you with a tender skull?"

"Aye. 'Ad me nightcap on, so softened the blow a bit. Margery says I was laid senseless for near an hour."

I turned to the woman, a well-fed example of a prosperous tenant's wife, and asked if she saw the thieves leave the Weald.

"Aye. Went toward Mill Street, last I seen of 'em."

"Did they carry more loot than what they stole from you?"

"Couldn't tell. No moon."

"Was there enough light that you could see how many men fled from your house?"

"More'n two, I'm sure."

"How were they clothed?"

"Too dark to tell. All seems black on such a night."

"'Twas Walter Mapes an' 'is lads," Alain said.

"You are sure of this? Did you recognize them? Did you tell Father Thomas of this?"

"Nay. But they've set themselves against me since I accused Walter of stealin' my furrow three years past at the bishop's hallmote."

"You prevailed in the dispute?"

"Aye."

"Did you tell Father Thomas of your suspicion?"

"Nay. He'd do naught but ask Walter, an' he'd deny 'twas so, an' there'd be an end to my complaint."

"What do you intend?"

"That's the business of us in t'Weald. You've no reason to concern yourself, bein' Lord Gilbert's man."

Alain turned from me and I saw him grimace as he did so. His head caused him more grief than he wished known, I think.

"I have physics which will dull your pain," I said.

"Nothin' I can't endure," he said, turning to the window his intruders had sliced away. He did not wish any further conversation regarding his loss, and when a victim of another man's misdeeds maintains silence there is little a constable or bailiff can do to amend the matter.

But Father Thomas should know of Alain's accusation. Quarrels between neighbors may grow. Folk who know both parties to such a dispute will choose sides. There was already one cracked skull in the Weald. The vicars of St. Beornwald's Church would not wish to learn of another.

"Walter Mapes?" Father Thomas said when I told him of Alain's accusation. "I can believe that of him. Wonder why Alain would speak of his suspicion to you but not to me?"

"Because I have no authority over him. You do, and can forestall his revenge."

"Oh... aye. And this I must do, else the cycle of reprisal will continue."

"Walter did steal a furrow of Alain?"

"Aye, he did. No doubt of it. Walter will steal anything he can."

"Alain claimed his attackers were Walter and his sons. How many lads has he?"

"Five, and three maids. Odd thing about Walter and his wife. For all his misdemeanors the Lord Christ has blessed him with healthy children. Not one lost to the churchyard."

I considered Sybil, and thought here was another question for the Lord Christ when I saw Him beyond my grave.

"Perhaps 'tis his wife who merits the Savior's favor," I said.

"May be. She has suffered enough as Walter's wife without enduring the loss of babes. As for his sons, oldest is twenty, perhaps. He's named Walter, also. Then Thomas, eighteen, I'd guess, an' Janyn would be sixteen, thereabouts. Other two sons would be too young for hamsoken."

The four men I saw from the Windrush Bridge stood too far away to identify, but three of them could surely have been lads just growing to manhood. Did they know who it was that signaled to them, and fear that if I came close enough I would recognize them as from the Weald? How would Walter Mapes get the black gowns of scholars, or monks' habits? And did Hubert Shillside speak to the wrong man about traveling to Oxford, so that talk of his journey spread to the Weald?

If so, could the murder and robbery of Hubert Shillside be tied to the thefts about Eynsham? Would Walter Mapes travel so far to do such felonies? I decided to seek the fellow and discover what I might.

I learned little. Mapes' house is mean and proclaims poverty from every beam and stalk of moldy thatching. Three small children, a lass and two lads, worked in the toft with crude hoes, chopping out weeds to ready the plot for a late planting of onions and cabbages and such. They peered mistrustfully at my approach, prepared to run to the hovel if I seemed a threat.

"Ain't 'ere," an emaciated woman said when a rap upon her doorpost brought her to the light. "Be plantin' dredge in yon field."

The woman pointed over my shoulder. Beyond the house and barn which occupied the opposite side of the lane I saw three figures, sacks slung across their backs, strewing seed upon a new-plowed strip. I bid the woman "Good day," crossed the lane, and approached the planters.

I recognized the oldest of the three as one I had seen about Bampton, and assumed him to be the elder Walter. So he was. He ceased his labor as I came near and awaited my explanation for interrupting his work.

"Good day. I am Lord Gilbert's bailiff, Hugh de Singleton."

"I know who you are," Walter replied. "What does Lord Gilbert's bailiff want w'me?"

"Father Thomas asked me to seek who has done hamsoken to Alain Gower."

Walter turned from me and spat upon the ground. The two younger men – his sons, I assumed – looked from me to their father with dull-eyed expressions. Hamsoken in their neighborhood seemed to arouse no interest in them. Perhaps they had not robbed Alain Gower of his possessions. I saw no guilt in their eyes. They could surely have little anxiety that the same misfortune might occur to their own household. One glance at the exterior of the house would tell a man 'twas unlikely there would be anything inside worth the risk of a noose.

"Someone has stolen goods of Alain? He has enough to spare," Walter said. "Won't miss the loss. Did Alain send you to me?"

"You dislike him, I am told."

The man pursed his lips. "So do most folk in the Weald."

"Why so?" I asked.

"Got more lands of the bishop than most. Near two yardlands. Hires servants. Thinks 'is shillings makes 'im a better man than us with less coin."

"You stole a furrow of him."

"So the priests said. Wouldn't 'ave missed it, even if I had."

Who, I wondered, was most disliked in the Weald? Would it be the honest man whose wealth was greater than others', and was therefore envied, or the poor man all knew was a thief?

I had no answer. Whilst I thought on it Walter reached into his sack, turned away, and continued casting seed upon the fresh-turned earth. His lads did likewise.

Walter glanced back over his shoulder, saw that I was not leaving the field, and spoke again. "We of the Weald don't need Lord Gilbert's bailiff meddlin' in our affairs. We deal with our own troubles."

This was what Alain Gower had said. I foresaw much discord in the Weald if the inhabitants picked sides in a disagreement between Alain and Walter. And likely such conflict would spill over to embrace Lord Gilbert's lands and tenants, whereupon I would be called to end a conflict I had no authority to halt as it began.

If Walter had indeed robbed Alain, the stolen items would likely be found somewhere within Walter's house or dilapidated barn. I returned to Father Thomas and voiced to him my fear of a conflict in the bishop's demesne. I suggested that he, Father Simon, and Father Ralph and their clerks descend unannounced upon Walter Mapes' house and seek there for Alain Gower's stolen property. If the goods were found Alain's accusation would be proved and his possessions returned to him. If the stolen items were not in Walter's possession, what then? Would that be proof that he was not the thief, or only that he was skilled at concealing his wrongdoing?

Father Thomas took my advice. I returned to Galen House, found my Kate had forgotten her pique at the unmannerly lay brother, and less than an hour later I saw through a window the three priests and their clerks hastening down Church View Street toward the Weald.

Shortly before dark I heard a rapping on Galen House door and opened it to find Father Thomas. A search of Walter Mapes' property, he said, found nothing matching any description of Alain Gower's stolen possessions. Alain was told this, but seemed unconvinced, so was also warned against vengeance. The vicar seemed unsure the admonition would be heeded.

When Bessie and John were put to bed Kate and I sat before the embers of our dying fire and discussed the matters vexing me: how to discover who had robbed and slain Hubert Shillside; whether or not his death had to do with other felonies committed near to Eynsham; if those who did hamsoken in the Weald might be the same scoundrels causing distress and death a few miles to the east; and if Walter Mapes might have known of Shillside's journey to Oxford with a heavy purse hung from his belt.

Discussing irksome matters with Kate often opens my mind, but not so this evening. No overlooked clue came to me, no insight where before there had been obscurity.

Next morn I went early to the castle, found Arthur, and told him to prepare two palfreys. We would return to the Windrush Bridge, I said, and seek information of folk from Hardwick and Stanton Harcourt of black-garbed men they might have seen.

As monks are not commonly allowed to leave their monastery the men I saw would not likely have been black-robed Benedictines. Lay brothers may travel, and Oxford scholars are occasionally upon the roads.

If scholars from Oxford or lay brothers had approached that day, where was it they were going? The destination must not have been important, as they turned and fled quickly when they saw me. Or perhaps the destination was important, but not so much as safety. What was it, then, about my appearance which caused the four to feel imperiled? Were they innocent travelers fearful of an unknown man standing in their path, or felons fearful of discovery? Fear surely had something to do with their withdrawal.

The great plague and its return has much reduced Hardwick. Half the houses are empty, roofs fallen in, and daub dropping away from rotting wattles. Even in such a stricken place men and women who have survived must plow and plant if they wish to live until plague or some other malady may return to take them also to the churchyard.

The manor house looked equally neglected. When I rapped on the door it rattled loosely upon its hinges. If the village had ever supported a smith it no longer did. The hinges proclaimed it so.

A servant lad of ten or so years answered my knock on the insubstantial door and in response to my question directed me to the rear of the toft. There I found the lord of the manor directing two men in the repair of his dovecote. The doves, of course, had fled, and were no doubt at the moment pecking at the grains of corn his tenants had recently sown. 'Tis no wonder tenants and villeins have no love for such fowl.

But for his directions to his workers and their obedience I might not have identified the lord from his men. All three wore simple brown cotehardies and their chauces were of the meanest sort; no fine linen here.

The three stopped their work as Arthur and I approached, and eyed us warily. Arthur's approach will do that to other men, even if he is smiling and of benign countenance. I am a slender fellow and even Kate's egg leaches and roasted capons have added but little flesh to my bones. So my appearance does not cause apprehension in most men. Arthur, on the other hand, is assembled like a tun set upon two beech stumps. His frown will cause most men to seek ways to avoid him, and even when his expression is benevolent strangers seem eager to keep from his company. This feature has proven helpful in past encounters with men who might otherwise have tried to escape the consequences of their felonies.

I greeted the three fellows, asking after any black-robed men seen in the vicinity. The men looked to each other, shook their heads, and denied seeing such persons near to Hardwick. I detected no guile in their eyes or words, and a brief examination of the village told why 'twas likely no thieves had been observed in the place. Hardwick's appearance shouted that here would be no valuable loot. Even the church, standing alone at the north end of the village, told of poverty. Folk of Hardwick would more likely be thieves than thieved upon.

Arthur and I mounted the palfreys and departed Hardwick, pleased to be away from a place of such destitution. Stanton Harcourt is little more than a mile from Hardwick, but might well have been another world. There were empty houses in Stanton Harcourt, as in every English village and town, but those still occupied seemed prosperous enough, as did the village church.

I sought the manor house and the lord, Sir Thomas Harcourt. He was at home and taking his dinner. A servant answered my knock upon the manor house door, called to his master, and the man appeared, not pleased, I think, to be called from his table.

I introduced myself and my purpose, and at the mention of Lord Gilbert the fellow's frown softened. 'Tis always better for such a knight to be known to a great lord like my employer as a man who will further the lord's cause than as one who obstructs it.

"How may I serve Lord Gilbert's bailiff?" Sir Thomas said. As the man spoke I saw he had one cheek swollen. I took it at first for a mouthful of food, but not so. He spoke clearly, and closer observation showed the bulging cheek was reddened.

I asked of black-robed men. Had any been seen recently hereabouts, particularly Saturday last?

"Nay," Sir Thomas replied. "Only man likely to be seen here wearing black is Edmund... my younger son. Studies at Queen's Hall, does Edmund."

This was a common enough undertaking for younger sons of knights and gentlemen. Even for the younger sons of prosperous burghers. Second, third, fourth sons will not inherit a father's lands, so must seek their own way in the world, or wed a lass who has no brothers and stands to succeed to a father's estates. I found myself at Oxford many years past for this reason, being the youngest son of a minor knight of Little Singleton, in Lancashire.

"Does Edmund bring lads here from Oxford to enjoy your table?"

"Aye," the knight smiled. "He does. Told him to be less profligate of my good will. He'd have half of Queen's Hall dining in my hall did I not put my foot down."

"When was your son last here with friends?"

The frown reappeared upon Sir Thomas's face. "Why do you wish to know? And why do you ask of men garbed in black last Saturday?"

"Has any house of Stanton Harcourt suffered hamsoken recently?" I asked.

"Nay, though other villages have. The felons have not struck here. What has this to do with men wearing black gowns?"

"Perhaps nothing," I said. "A fortnight and more past, a merchant of Bampton traveled to Oxford with a heavy purse. He did not return, nor was he seen in Oxford at the place where he commonly went to complete his business, or any other."

"Never got there, eh?" Sir Thomas said.

"Just so. Lay brothers of Eynsham Abbey went out to search the roads and lanes for him, and I and the man's son did likewise. We found him last Saturday, in the Windrush stream, between here and Hardwick."

"Drowned?"

"Assaulted, robbed, stabbed, and his purse cut free."

"Men garbed in black did this?"

49

"No man knows. An hour or so after he was found I saw four black-clad men approach the bridge from this direction. When they saw I had noticed their approach they halted, then hurried away."

Throughout our conversation Sir Thomas had put a hand to his swollen cheek and rubbed it tenderly. "So you ask about such men, to learn what they were about, and find why they fled from you and the Windrush Bridge?" he said.

"Aye. You are in pain?"

"I am. Toothache. Can eat naught but the smoothest pottage for more than a fortnight."

"Perhaps I may ease your discomfort."

"What? A bailiff remedy my toothache?"

"I am also a surgeon… trained in Paris."

"Oh. Have you dealt with men's aching teeth?"

"I have."

"What is to be done? Last week I rode to Oxford and sought a physician."

"His remedy was not successful?"

"Nay. Said the ache was caused by tiny worms boring into a man's tooth. Held the flame of a mutton fat candle so close to the tooth as could be. Said that would drive out the worms. Burned my cheek. Have yet the blister."

"And also the toothache?" I said.

"Aye. Would you try again the same cure?"

"Nay. What the leech did is common enough, but unlikely to end your pain."

"But the fellow said 'twas sure to dispel my ache."

"Of course. Would you expect him to say, 'Pay me six pence and I will provide a treatment which will do you no good'?"

Sir Thomas grunted, seeing the force of my point. "What do you suggest, then?"

"If the ache has persisted for a fortnight the tooth likely must be drawn. Come outside, where the light is stronger, and I will examine the tooth and tell you what course to pursue."

With Arthur peering over my shoulder I drew back Sir

Thomas's lips. I hoped his sore tooth was an upper, as these have but one root and are easier to draw, but not so. A swollen, reddened gum told of the troublesome tooth, which I could see was cracked and blackened at one corner. I have oft wondered why it seems that nobles and gentlemen are more likely to have rotten teeth than their tenants and villeins.

"You see it?" Sir Thomas mumbled as my fingers pried his cheek from the offending tooth.

"Aye. It must be drawn. It is broken and rotten. No candle flame will make it whole. My instruments are in Bampton. I will return tomorrow with the tools I need, if you wish me to deal with your affliction."

"You are certain there is no other cure?"

"Aye. Should you slash your arm it may be stitched together and in a month or so be good as new, or nearly so. But when a tooth is rotten no repair is possible.

"Meanwhile, ask of your bailiff and tenants if they have seen men about the roads garbed as scholars or lay brothers or such."

"I will do so," he agreed.

Chapter 5

As there are several palfreys in Lord Gilbert's marshalsea, some surely in need of exercise, I told Arthur to have two beasts ready on the morrow. He smiled approval of my proposal, having short legs ill-suited for walking any distance. Stanton Harcourt is no great journey from Bampton, but Arthur prefers to exercise his stubby legs no more than necessary.

Next morning I placed pliers and a vial of crushed hemp seeds into a sack, broke my fast with a maslin loaf and ale, and set off for the castle. I told Kate I did not expect to return 'til the morrow, it being my intention to travel on from Stanton Harcourt to Oxford, there to seek her father for several gatherings of parchment and a pot of ink. Robert Caxton is a stationer, and for my service extracting a festering splinter from his back some years past he promised as much parchment as I might ever need. I thought the death of Hubert Shillside might be a tale worth recording.

"Do not trouble Father for ink," Kate said. "Remember when we first met I was making ink in Father's shop. I will make what you require. The oak apples we collected last autumn are dry and ready to be crushed."

Little more than an hour later Arthur and I entered Stanton Harcourt and tied our palfreys to a rail before the manor house. We were expected. The servant opened the door to us before we reached it, and behind him stood Sir Thomas, eager to have his ache dealt with.

I told the knight to have his servant bring a cup of ale and another of wine. And also a clean fragment of cloth. Linen or wool from a discarded garment would suffice. Into the ale I emptied the vial of crushed hemp seeds. It is my experience that consuming such as hemp and lettuce seeds and the dried sap of lettuce will dull a man's pain an hour or so after they are consumed. My supply of lettuce seeds was exhausted, no more to be had 'til the summer's new growth should mature, so the crushed hemp seeds must suffice.

Sir Thomas sat upon a bench whilst I waited for the hemp seeds to do their work. When he began to nod, nearly tumbling from his bench, I told Arthur to help the man to his toft. I carried the bench.

There, in the sunlight, I had Sir Thomas lay upon his back, open his mouth, and with the pliers I grasped the rotten tooth. I was some concerned that, because it was cracked, the tooth might not emerge whole.

I have not drawn many teeth. Most folk prefer a rotten tooth to fall out on its own rather than pay me to extract it, so long as their discomfort is bearable. But when I have been called upon to remove a tooth I have learned that temporizing is harmful to the sufferer. Faint-hearted use of the pliers will not reduce his pain. I grasped the offending tooth firmly, then twisted and yanked at the same time. The tooth came free of his jaw with a gush of blood.

I stuffed the linen fragment into the knight's mouth to staunch the flow of blood, then bade Arthur assist the fellow to rise. Sir Thomas swayed on the bench, the hemp seeds requiring several hours to lose their potency. I sent the servant to bring the cup of wine and told Sir Thomas to use this for rinsing his mouth. Cleansing a wound with wine is effective at assisting healing, although no man knows why this is so. As drawing a tooth creates a wound within a man's mouth, it seems to me that passing wine over the injury may serve also to speed recovery.

Sir Thomas took a mouthful of wine, swirled it about his mouth, then spat it upon the ground. I watched as, with his tongue, he tentatively explored the place where the tooth had been. The tooth was yet firmly in the jaws of my pliers, and he reached for it.

"Such a small thing to cause such great pain," he said.

"Rinse your mouth again in an hour or so, and again before you seek your bed," I said. "And once or twice on the morrow.

"Now, on another matter, have you spoken to your bailiff

or tenants about strangers wearing scholars' robes seen hereabouts?"

"Aye. Only Edmund and friends who sometimes accompany him – none other."

"Keep a watch for men unknown to the village, even if they are clothed in common dress. A lass was assaulted near to Church Hanborough. The felons did not wear scholars' attire."

"How many?" Sir Thomas asked.

"Four, the lass thought."

"Coincidence, perhaps, that you saw four upon the Hardwick road?"

"Aye, perhaps."

I collected my fee of four pence, then Arthur and I set out for Oxford. We passed Eynsham Abbey without stopping to learn if any new felonies were reported. I thought to spend the night there upon our return, so could learn then if 'twas so.

Just beyond Bookbinder's Bridge, Oxford Castle, and the Franciscan friary is an open area where traveling players and such like entertainers seek attention and custom. As Arthur and I approached the place, I saw a crowd gathered to watch some performance. From the advantage of horseback I could see over the heads of the spectators, as could Arthur. I gave my attention to the players and thought one seemed familiar. Evidently Arthur did too, for he said, "'Tis Hamo the tanner."

Indeed it was. His band was larger than when I had first met the fellow. Then he had but one contortionist, a lass. Now there were two, one a limber lad. His son was yet the knife-thrower. A juggler was new to the troupe since I had last seen a performance, and Hamo yet wrestled those who would challenge him, as before. And now he had another, I learned later, who wrestled smaller men so that an onlooker, challenged to wrestle for the six pence which Hamo offered to any who could best him, might contend with an opponent nearer his own size and weight. Hamo was assembled like Arthur, and few men would accept a challenge to wrestle him when he outweighed most by two or three stone.

I watched as his troupe went amongst the crowd seeking wagers, while a strapping youth prepared to seek six pence of Hamo.

"Why did you never challenge Hamo?" I asked Arthur as we watched the preparations. "You are as strong as he."

"Aye. Likely. Mayhap stronger. But Hamo knows how to use his strength."

I peered at Arthur quizzically, unsure of his meaning.

"See that lad about to challenge Hamo? He's half Hamo's age, an' robust as an ox, but Hamo will vanquish 'im in a trice. Someday, I suppose," Arthur continued, "Hamo's years will tell against 'im, and a younger man whose bones do not yet ache will best 'im."

"But not yet?"

"Nay, not yet."

Hamo's son clapped his hands and the antagonists circled each other. The youthful challenger thought he saw an opening and plunged toward Hamo. The crowd roared, some in approval, some not, depending upon their wagers.

For all his bulk Hamo can move quickly. He stepped to one side, tripped the lad as he charged, delivered a blow with his forearm to the back of the challenger's neck, then fell upon the fellow as he rolled in the dust. Hamo grasped an arm, twisted it behind the youth's back, and the lad responded with a yelp of pain. Hamo demanded that the fellow submit, and twisted the arm further to make his point. The lad screamed out that he would yield, and in less time than it took to write of the combat Hamo stood, triumphant.

"You see," Arthur said. "Even a scrawny fellow like you could defeat a stronger man if you could put him face first on the ground an' get an arm behind 'is back. Takes no great strength to wrench a man's arm like that, once you've got it so behind 'im."

"If you know these tricks, why not try yourself against Hamo?"

"Knowin' an' doin' is different. Perhaps now that 'e's older I might 'ave a chance against 'im. 'Course, I'm older, too. Call it a draw."

As this conversation ended I saw Hamo Tanner plunge through the crowd in our direction. I caught his eye and he grinned broadly in reply. When Hamo wishes to make his way through a throng he does so. Few men will hold their place to impede him.

"Master Hugh... Arthur! You are well met! Wait 'til we've collected our winnings. I must speak to you."

Hamo's earnest request piqued my curiosity. I wondered what urgent matter required my attention.

Hamo and his troupe passed through the crowd, collecting pennies from those he had entertained and others who had wagered that the brawny youth could vanquish Hamo. From the time taken to collect the winnings I believe that Hamo did profitable business this day.

Arthur and I dismounted, waiting for the wrestler to gather his gains. While he and his troupe were at this business I watched as several men hurried from the place, no doubt having wagered mistakenly and now eager to lose themselves amongst the folk on Great Bailey Street.

When Hamo had finished fattening his purse he approached, held the leather pouch before him, and grinned.

"We will dine well this day." From his appearance I doubt not that Hamo dines well most days. "Join me at yon inn. I have a matter to discuss with you. It concerns one of my men."

Arthur and I followed Hamo to the Black Boar and tied our beasts to the rail before the place. 'Twas a fast day. The inn served a pottage of whelks for our dinner, with loaves and ale. Hamo motioned to a bench in a quiet corner. Well, not quiet, but perhaps quieter.

"I'd like you to take a look at Will," Hamo said. "We was attacked upon the way to Oxford yesterday an' Will received a slash upon his arm. Don't seem bad. I was gonna seek a leech today an' have it seen to. But you're 'ere, an' I'd have you deal with the wound."

"I have no instruments with me... no needle nor silk thread with which to close a wound."

"Can these things not be had in Oxford?"

"Aye, they can, but Will could seek care for his wound from some other. Oxford is filled to brimming with physicians, and surgeons as well."

"S'pose so, but I've not seen their work, an' I have yours. Men may die of lesser cuts, an' if the injury be not mended proper, mayhap 'e'll not be able to wrestle again, an' I'll need to find another small man who can take on men of 'is size an' not be bested."

"Very well. There are haberdashers in Oxford who sell silken thread and needles which will serve. And I'll need wine to cleanse the wound. Where is the man?"

"Will!" The tanner called out over the din. I saw a small fellow look up from his ale and rise from his bench in response to Hamo's bellow. He held his right arm stiffly, as if it was encased in plaster.

"Here is Master Hugh, the surgeon you've heard me speak of. When we finish our meal we can retire to our chamber for Master Hugh to attend to your wound."

The Black Boar is a thriving establishment, constructed about a central court with stables at the rear, the front and sides two stories high. A central passage allows entrance to the enclosed yard. Hamo Tanner's business evidently prospered, that he could hire a room in such a hostelry.

We completed the meal and entered the enclosed yard whence the stairway climbed to the upper floor and chambers. Before we ascended, Hamo told his son to see to the beasts and carts. Beasts! Two or more. When I first met Hamo he owned but one horse, and that won in a wager.

When we had entered the privacy of the chamber Hamo occupied, he directed his injured wrestler to remove his cotehardie and kirtle so that I could examine the cut.

"Wrapped the sleeve of an old kirtle about it yesterday, after we was set upon," Hamo said.

The threadbare linen was stained and stiff with dried blood. I asked for another such cloth, for I knew when I drew back the bloodied wrapping from the cut, a fresh issue of gore would flow.

The injured man was small, but not puny. The slashed forearm was as large around as my bicep, and, as I expected, a small stream of blood flowed when I loosened the winding.

The laceration was more serious than Hamo had led me to believe. It extended nearly from elbow to wrist, and was deep enough that I thought, but for the blood, I might see bone.

"Can you stitch me up?" Will said. "Or am I to meet the Lord Christ with but one good arm?"

"We will all meet the Lord Christ," I said. "But not necessarily soon. I can deal with this cut."

"Will I wrestle again?"

The man was no doubt concerned for his livelihood. Hamo would not keep him on if he could not contribute to his keep.

"Not for many weeks. Perhaps by Midsummer's Day."

I saw the man's countenance fall. I guessed he feared that, even if his infirmity proved temporary, Hamo would replace him. The tanner was silent, which did nothing to reassure Will.

"There is a haberdasher on Fish Street who'll have the needle and silk thread I need. 'Tis not far. Meanwhile, whilst I am away, get a cup of wine from the innkeeper."

Hamo raised his eyebrows at this request. Evidently his prosperity did not encompass paying for wine at midday. Or perhaps at any time.

"To cleanse the wound," I said, and with Arthur thumping down the stairs behind me I descended to the yard and thence to the street.

Martyn Hendy took one glance in our direction as we entered his shop and before I could speak said, "Ain't seen Hubert since you was 'ere seekin' 'im. He ever return to Bampton?"

"Aye," I said. "He now resides in the churchyard."

"Dead?" Hendy gasped, and crossed himself.

"Aye. Slain for his purse."

"'Tis why he never arrived, then."

"That would be the right of it. His son, I believe, will continue the business. Bampton needs a haberdasher and no man is so well suited to continue the trade as Will. You will see him soon, I think, as he must replenish his father's reduced store."

"Best he not travel alone. I'd not like to lose another customer."

"Indeed," I said, and nodding in agreement I came to my business. "I need a needle – the finest you have – and a spool of silken thread."

"Ah," Hendy grinned. "Some man has been at the wrong end of a blade."

"Just so."

The haberdasher went to a shelf and lifted down a tiny wooden box. "Here are three of my finest. From Milan, where the craft is best. Will you have all three, or but one? Five pence for one, a shilling for all."

The needles were narrow indeed, so much so that I first asked for the spool of silk to be sure I could thread the eye of such a needle. I could; just.

"I'll have all three," I replied. "And the spool."

I paid Hendy a shilling and four pence and hastened back to the Black Boar.

"You'll lose money at this," Arthur said between breaths as we hurried to the inn. For all his strength, Arthur is no longer young.

"The needles will serve many years," I replied, "and Hamo will not begrudge my fee if I am able to restore his man."

I was, and he did not.

At the upper chamber of the inn I bathed the gash with wine, stood in the sunlight of an open window – even then peering close – to thread the needle, then went to work stitching up the wounded wrestler. He did not quail at the pricks. As I did so I asked of the injury – how it had happened.

"We spent two days in Abingdon," Hamo began, "then set out for Oxford. We always gather plenty of coin in Oxford."

I believed that. Young scholars, even those with a thin purse, do not always exhibit good judgment when a wager is presented to them. Greed has been the downfall of many, be they commoners or kings.

"We was perhaps halfway 'ere when we was set upon. Mayhap wouldn't have been, had we stuck together."

"You traveled divided, in two parties?"

"Aye. One of our beasts has a sore hoof – you know anything about such matters?"

I shook my head.

"Nay. You'd likely not. So we who rode on the carts traveled slow, while Will, Roger, an' Giles walked on ahead. They disappeared beyond a bend in the road, when we with the carts was a hundred paces or more behind. I heard a tumult ahead, which upon the road can mean no good thing, so cracked the whip an' hurried on to see what was the trouble. Met Will an' Roger an' Giles runnin' to us, with three men close behind. When the scoundrels saw us with the carts they turned on their heels an' ran across a meadow to a greenwood."

"Three men attacked? Not four?"

"Nay, only three. Wanted nothin' to do with us when they saw we outnumbered them."

"What did they wear?"

"Odd you should ask. Wore black, like the scholars hereabouts, or monks' habits."

I spoke to Will. "You saw them close. Were the assailants young men, or older?"

"Young, they was. But old enough to parry a blade an' give me a thrust when I fought 'em."

"They demanded your purses?" I asked.

"They did. Hid themselves in bushes beside the road. Whoso owns the fields there should be fined for not keepin' the verge clear. The sheriff must hear of this."

Indeed, the Statute of Winchester requires manorial lords to clear brush and undergrowth back from roads to a distance of seventy-five or so paces, excepting only great oaks and greenwoods, exactly so felons may not conceal themselves and surprise unwary travelers.

"The slash is to your right arm," I said to Will. "Was the man who delivered the wound left-handed?"

"Aye, so he was."

I made fourteen stitches in Will's lacerated right forearm, then bathed the cut again with wine and pronounced the work complete.

"Is there no salve?" Will asked.

I explained that I favor the practice of Henri de Mondeville, father of French surgery. Treating wounded soldiers of the king of France, he discovered that cuts left open to the air, wrapped but lightly and washed only with wine, healed better than slashes covered over with ointments.

"If your travels take you near Bampton about Rogation Sunday, seek me and I will remove the stitches. But if you are elsewhere, a sharp blade will slice through the silk, and the cut threads may be pulled free. On no account, even after the stitches are removed, must you wrestle again, or do any other heavy toil with that arm, 'til St. John's Day, else the wound may open and be more troublesome to close than at the first."

Neither Will nor Hamo seemed troubled by my admonition. I believe they expected the warning. Arthur and I bid the tanner farewell and led our beasts through Oxford's crowded streets to Holywell Street and Robert Caxton's stationery shop.

Chapter 6

When I last saw my father-in-law I had been surprised at how much he had aged. In the intervening months the process had accelerated. He greeted me with a smile upon his face but his countenance was grey, and deeply lined. He walked bent at the waist, as if the splinter I had drawn from his back remained and vexed him.

Caxton was eager to learn of his new grandson, yet still saddened to think of Sybil. He would take joy in Bessie, I felt sure, if he could lay eyes upon her.

"I am in need of more parchment," I said. "Three gatherings, I think. But this time I shall pay. You have more than discharged the cost of the surgery I performed upon your back. How much do you receive for a gathering?"

"Not so much as years past. Three pence only. There are fewer scholars since plague has returned, so fewer masters and doctors to write their thoughts. Near as many sheep, though, so a hide is worth half what it brought twenty years ago. What brings you to Oxford? What will you write?"

I told my father-in-law of Hubert Shillside's death, and of the felonies in villages and upon the roads near Eynsham and Abingdon.

Caxton listened carefully to my tale. "'Tis an evil world," he said when I had done. "'Tis a wonder the Lord Christ does not return and put an end to all the wickedness."

"Perhaps He is more patient than we," I replied.

"Patient, you think? How so?"

"When He returns 'twill be too late for malefactors to repent of their sins. So long as He delays, transgressors have yet opportunity to mend their ways."

"But then a new generation of wicked men will replace the one we already have," Caxton said. "Will the Lord Christ's patience never wear thin?"

"Aye, surely. But we must not dally," I said.

"You return to Bampton this day?"

"Nay. Only so far as Eynsham. We will stay the night at the abbey, and I will seek news of the abbot, lest any more felonies have occurred."

It was near dark, and the porter about to close the abbey gate, when we reached Eynsham Abbey. The guest master again showed us to the guest chamber, sent for lay brothers to care for our beasts, and promised a supper would soon be on the table. I asked the monk if I might speak to Abbot Gerleys following the meal, and he promised to arrange it.

He made good his promise of supper, and by the light of three cressets Arthur and I ate our fill of pease pottage and broiled stockfish, barley loaves, and fresh ale.

Arthur was not yet finished with his loaf and ale when the guest master reappeared, instructing me to follow. Abbot Gerleys, he said, was unwell, but would be pleased to speak to me. Arthur seemed pleased to remain at his unfinished task.

I found the abbot sitting at his desk, but clearly in much discomfort. I asked of his symptoms. His ailment was not such as a surgeon could cure.

"Ah... I burn with fever, yet must cover myself in blankets for the chill. Every part of my body aches – head, neck, back. I cough, especially when I lie upon my bed, and my throat is sore so that I can swallow little but ale. 'Tis the ague, I think."

"Have others of the abbey complained of the same afflictions?"

"Aye, several."

"'Tis surely the ague," I agreed.

"And nothing to be done," the abbot said, "but to mend or die. Have you advice to promote the first and avoid the second?"

"When ague afflicts the lungs it can be troublesome," I said.

"Troublesome? You mean deadly?"

"Mayhap. To avoid the lungs filling with fluid 'tis best to stay upright so much as possible. Sleep with several blankets folded under your shoulders, so that you are propped as near to vertical as can be."

"I will do so. Now, to other matters. Have you found the felon who slew your friend?"

"Nay. I've learned of more felonies hereabouts, and a tenant of the Bishop of Exeter was robbed in the night near to Bampton."

"What other felonies?" the abbot asked, roused to apprehension despite his own health concerns.

"A troupe of entertainers traveled yesterday from Abingdon to Oxford and was waylaid upon the road."

"Were any injured or slain? Did the brigands make off with much loot?"

"One man received a slash on his forearm. I stitched him whole this day. The company had got separated upon the road. Three of their men walked ahead, three others and a lass following behind with two carts. When the thieves realized the three they had attacked had companions, they ran off."

"How many assailants?"

"Three, and wearing black robes, as scholars or lay brothers."

Abbot Gerleys listened thoughtfully to my tale. "And one of the three who were set upon received a wound, you say?"

"Aye."

"Here is a puzzle to add to your others, then. Last eve three men came here, requiring lodging for the night. They told Brother Watkin of being attacked upon the road. He thought I should know of it, so brought them to me."

"They traveled from Abingdon?" I guessed.

"Aye. To Stratford, they said."

"A long journey."

"Aye, and they had no horses, but walked. Mayhap they were accosted by the same fellows who wounded the man you aided. But here is the odd thing. One of the three said that the felons ran off when he drew his dagger and wounded one of them."

"Where was this injury? Did your guest say?"

"Aye. Said he pierced the rogue's arm."

Here was disquieting news. Was Hamo Tanner's prosperity due to thieving as well as wrestling and knife-throwing and juggling and the like? 'Twould be a great coincidence if two men received cuts to their arms along the same road, and upon the same day.

"What was their business in Stratford?" I asked.

"They did not say, and I did not ask."

"Were one or two of the men servants to the other?"

"Didn't seem so. They spoke as gentlemen, none taking precedence over the others."

"Odd that gentlemen would travel so far with no pages or grooms to assist, nor any beasts."

"Aye."

"Perhaps they said more to Brother Watkin before or after they spoke to you?"

"I will call for him. 'Tis nearly time for Compline, but he will be free 'til then."

Abbot Gerleys called out to the youthful monk who served him and sent the lad in search of the hosteller. Brother Watkin appeared soon after and Abbot Gerleys bade him sit upon a bench drawn against the wall.

"Master Hugh seeks knowledge of the men who occupied the guest chamber last night," the abbot said.

"What can I tell you?" Brother Watkin said to me.

"Were the men old, or young?"

"Young. Beardless – although one of them seemed recently to have been shaved, as stubble grew about his chin."

"Abbot Gerleys said they spoke as gentlemen."

"Aye. They were not of the commons. Educated fellows, I'd guess."

"And none seemed servant to another?"

"Nay."

"Did they dress well?" I asked.

"Aye. 'Tis no wonder they were set upon. Fine wool cotehardies, and one wore particolored chauces and a bright blue cap with liripipe long enough to wind thrice about his head.

Men garbed in such a fashion will likely possess heavy purses and attract miscreants."

"If so, why walk all that way?" I wondered aloud. "'Tis forty miles, near enough, from here to Stratford. Men who dress well should be able to hire beasts for such a journey, even if they have none of their own – which seems unlikely."

Brother Watkin looked at me and shrugged in reply. He had no answer, nor did Abbot Gerleys. The abbot then spoke.

"The Rule decrees we must offer hospitality to all, regardless of their state, or reason for travel. As there is no point therefore in asking a man's business upon the road, we avoid doing so. You think the fellows did not speak true? That they were not attacked upon the road? That, perhaps, they do not travel so far as Stratford?"

"Someone was waylaid near to Abingdon," I said. "Perhaps the felons attacked twice, with different victims. In the first attempt the culprits wounded one of the troupe of entertainers – the man whose arm I patched – and wore black gowns. At their second try they wore gentlemen's garb and one of the felons received a wound from the travelers who sought refuge here last night."

"You believe it may so have happened?" Abbot Gerleys said.

"Nay... but perchance 'twas so."

Arthur lay wakeful upon his bed when I returned to the guest chamber. He wished to hear of any new thing I had learned of Abbot Gerleys, and it did my own understanding some good to relate to him what the abbot had said.

"Odd business, two men slashed upon the arm, same road, same day," Arthur concluded.

Odd the matter may have been, but not so that considering the matter prevented Arthur falling quickly to sleep once the last cresset was extinguished. Such is always a trial, for if, when we share a chamber, Arthur falls first to sleep his snoring prevents Morpheus from finding me.

I lay upon my bed and considered the felonies I had learned of in the past fortnight. Two men slain, another missing. A lass taken and abused. Hamsoken in many places, even in the Weald, and two men slashed upon the road north from Abingdon. Or perhaps only one man cut. But if only one, who was speaking true? Hamo Tanner and his wrestler, or three traveling gentlemen?

Brother Watkin brought loaves and ale to the guest chamber next morn, and shortly after we set off for Bampton. 'Twas no trouble to return through Stanton Harcourt to learn how Sir Thomas fared without his rotten tooth, so less than an hour after leaving the abbey we drew up before the manor house.

Before I could dismount I saw from the corner of my eye a black-clad form hasten toward me, coming from the church near Sir Thomas Harcourt's manor house and barns. The village priest, no doubt, I thought, and the disagreeable notion occurred to me that since my dealing with the knight's tooth something might have happened to the man requiring the attention of the village priest. This, as it happened, was so, but not in the manner I had feared.

I waited before the manor house hitching rail while Arthur secured our palfreys. It was clear the priest was intent on approaching the dwelling. He did not take his eyes from the place and his path was unswerving.

He paid us no attention as he strode to the door, his face set in a thin-lipped grimace. In his left hand he carried a small sheet of parchment which I could see – for he passed close by me – was written upon.

From around the corner of the church, as the priest hurried past me, another figure appeared. This was a lad of twelve or so years, bare of foot for the day was mild, wearing what seemed to be a father's cast off cotehardie which reached to his ankles. The youth glanced to the manor house, then turned away and sauntered toward a field some distance away where a plow team was at work. A small figure followed the plow, a lad breaking clods with his bare feet, at work alone. Perhaps the lad from the church was to join him. If so, he was in no hurry.

The priest rapped vigorously upon the manor house door, which drew my attention back to him. The servant I had seen before opened to him, and the priest spoke abruptly, with no greeting.

"Fetch your master. There is news." As he said this he waved the parchment in the servant's face.

News of what, I wondered? Arthur surely thought the same, for he glanced to me with raised eyebrows.

The servant hesitated in the doorway for a moment, as if he was about to ask the priest what the news might be, but thought better of it, quickly turned, and disappeared, forgetting his service and leaving the priest standing in the doorway.

Sir Thomas appeared almost immediately. His face was haggard and grey, but I noticed his swollen cheek had now reduced to its proper size.

"Walchin said you have news of Henry," Sir Thomas blurted.

"Aye. Walter Oxlane's lad brought this just minutes past," the priest said, and held the scrap of parchment before him.

Sir Thomas peered at the parchment, then said, "What does it say? You know I do not read well."

The priest cleared his throat, then read the document.

"We have taken Henry, and will hold him until you pay ten pounds for his return. His palfrey is a fine beast. Worth two pounds. We will send word in a week's time where the ransom must be delivered. If you doubt that we hold your heir we will send a finger, wearing his ring, as proof."

I had sidled close to the priest as he read. The demand was written in English, not Latin or French, but was couched in excellent grammar and written in a dexterous hand. Whoever Henry was, he was held by at least one man who could write English well. And if he could do so, it was likely that he could also make himself understood writing in Latin and French. Few men that I know of can write in one of these tongues but not the others. Who but a scholar, or one who had been a scholar in times past, could do so?

"Twelve pounds!" Harcourt exclaimed. "Where am I to find twelve pounds? This is no great estate. In my whole life I've never seen twelve pounds together in one chest."

Twelve pounds gathered together would surely require a chest. No purse, no matter how sturdy, could contain so many pennies and groats and nobles.

Sir Thomas turned and shouted into his house. "Where is Walchin? Ah, there you are. Fetch Oswald, an' be quick about it."

The servant ducked under Sir Thomas's arm and scurried past me. This was Walchin, no doubt, on his way to seek Oswald, whoever that might be.

Sir Thomas watched the groom hurry away, then noticed me standing behind the priest. "Ah, Master Hugh. My tooth no longer aches. How could it? 'Tis gone. My ache now is of another kind."

Sir Thomas saw the puzzled expression upon my face and explained. "My firstborn is taken. You heard just now the demand for his return. Ten pounds! Where am I to find ten pounds? And two for the beast."

"When did this abduction happen?" I asked.

"Yesterday. Henry rode out about the third hour to see how plowing progressed upon my demesne lands, villeins not being eager to complete their week-work when their own fields need attention. He did not return for dinner, so I sent the reeve to seek him. The plow team – not the one you see in yon field, but another beyond that wood to the north – said he'd never arrived.

"I knew something was amiss. Thought perhaps he'd been thrown from his horse an' lay injured, something broken. I sent Oswald, my bailiff, to seek him, but he found nothing. Oswald, the reeve, Walchin, and two others searched fields and forest alongside me 'til after dark. No sign of Henry. Now I know why."

From the corner of my eye I saw the groom reappear with a corpulent fellow I assumed to be Oswald, Stanton Harcourt's bailiff. So he was.

The rotund bailiff came puffing to a halt before Sir Thomas, and the knight told the man of the demand which had just been delivered.

"Taken, eh? There has been much villainy hereabouts of late. Will you pay?"

"The wretches have given me a week. You have seven days to find Henry if you wish to keep your position."

The bailiff stepped back as if slapped. "But... if I am unable to do so..."

"A week. I have spoken to you before about neglecting your duties. I have considered replacing you in the past, as you well know. Fail me in this and I will surely do so."

Here was an argument I had no wish to enter. My only reason for visiting the village had been to learn of Sir Thomas's aching jaw. Now I knew it to be on the mend I was prepared to renew my journey home. But questions occurred to me. Perhaps the scoundrels who held Henry Harcourt were the same who had slain Hubert Shillside and done the other felonies hereabouts.

"'Twas a lad who brought you the message?" I asked the priest, nodding to the parchment in Sir Thomas's hand.

"Aye. Harold Oxlane."

"Was it he I saw a moment ago leaving the church for yonder field, where the plow team is at work?"

"Aye," the priest said. "That's Harold."

"How did the lad come by the parchment?" I asked.

"Only thing he said was a man told him to give me the message. When I read it I came straight to Sir Thomas."

"Perhaps, was he asked, the lad might have more to tell. Come," I said to Oswald, "let's speak to the child."

'Twas less than a quarter-mile from the manor house to the field where the plow team was engaged. Arthur, the bailiff, Sir Thomas, Walchin, and I set out for the partly turned plot. Oswald was soon left puffing behind.

Our group reached the plow team as they were about to turn at the end of a long furrow. This is not an easy thing to do. Four oxen and two horses are not readily shifted, even though the beasts know what is expected of them. The lads following the plow, stepping upon clods to break them, were temporarily at their ease as the plowman and goad man had yet to change places.

"Which is the lad who brought the message?" I asked the priest.

The lads and the plow team had stopped their work to watch our approach. "Harold," the priest called, and a slender youth of twelve or so years looked to us, saw the priest motion to him, and trotted near.

"This man," the priest said, pointing to me, "has questions for you."

I was about to introduce myself to the child as Lord Gilbert's bailiff in Bampton, but thought better of it. I know nothing of Oswald's governance of Stanton Harcourt, but I do know that bailiffs are oft accused of being villainous, thieving, and conniving. This is because many are villainous, thieving, and conniving. Better the lad not know of my position than to fear my response to his answers.

"You were given a message to take to the priest," I said. "Do you know the man who gave it to you?"

"Nay – never seen 'im before."

"Where were you when the fellow appeared?"

"Just there," the lad pointed. "We'd finished a furrow an' was by the wood, turnin' round, when a man stepped from behind the great oak beyond the hedgerow there, called to me, an' give me that parchment."

The youth pointed to the message that Sir Thomas yet held in his hand.

"Was the man young, or old?" I asked.

The lad shrugged. "Not old." To a lad of twelve years any man of more than thirty years is old.

"Twenty years old, perhaps?" I said. "Or mayhap a little older?"

"Aye. Twenty years, or twenty-five."

"Was the fellow bearded?"

"Nay. He'd been shaved but a day or two past."

"What garb did the man wear?"

"A gentleman 'e was. 'Ad a green cotehardie, particolored chauces of green an' yellow, an' a blue cap."

"Was his liripipe long?"

"Aye."

Here was the third time I had recently heard of a felon who wore a blue cap, and the second time the man was identified as wearing particolored chauces.

"Show me the tree where the man appeared."

The lad turned and walked to the verge of the field where a low stone wall divided the plowed field from a greenwood of oak and beech trees.

"Just there." Harold pointed to the trunk of an oak of enough circumference that two men could conceal themselves behind it.

The wall was not in good repair. Some stones had fallen, so it was no more than waist high.

Since the plague, labor to repair fallen walls is in short supply. I found a place free of nettles, having had experience with nettle-crusted walls in the past, and climbed over. The others, but for Oswald, followed.

I advised the group to stay back, then approached the oak cautiously. I could not say what I expected to find, but if I did not search the place I could be sure to find nothing.

The forest soil under the oak was in broken shadows formed by branches and twigs bare of leaves. I peered intently at the leaves covering the ground but could see there nothing of interest. The decaying verdure retained no footprints to follow.

The west side of the oak was in shade, so I nearly missed the wisp of wool caught on a shard of bark. The wool was about waist high, perhaps a bit higher, and when I lifted it from the bark and held it in the sunlight I saw it was green. The man I sought had perhaps leaned upon the tree, awaiting the slow approach of the plow team. Likely he wished for the adults of the plow team not to see him.

I held the wool before the lad and asked if it seemed the same color as the cotehardie worn by the fellow who had delivered to him the message for Sir Thomas.

"Aye, it does... but the message wasn't for Sir Thomas," the lad said. "'E said I was to give it to Father John."

"He named the priest?"

"Aye, 'e did."

Here was interesting information. Sir Thomas had but a few moments earlier asked the priest to read the message to him, admitting that he read poorly. Was this why Harold was told to take the parchment to the priest? Did the rogues who had seized Henry Harcourt know enough of Sir Thomas to send the demand for ransom to him through the priest? And the fellow knew the priest's name. What else did they know of the village, and how had they come to know it?

Sir Thomas reached for the tuft of wool and examined it. "More weld than woad," he said. Indeed this was so, for there was a faint yellow tint to the strands.

Chapter 7

$\mathcal{T}$here was nothing more to be learned from the lad or the oak, and my stomach was growling mightily. I told Oswald I would leave matters in his hands, the tuft of wool also, and if he should learn of anything tying those who took Henry Harcourt to the felons who slew Hubert Shillside I would be pleased to know of it.

Arthur and I mounted our palfreys, bade Sir Thomas farewell, and hurried away to Bampton and a hearty meal. I dismounted at Church View Street, directed Arthur to see to the beasts, and hurried to Galen House with my bundle of parchments.

My Kate is seldom a disappointment. There was, upon our hearth, a kettle of pottage awaiting my return: peas and white beans, thick and bubbling. Alas, no pork, for 'twas a fast day, but maslin loaves fresh from the baker and fresh ale from the baker's wife. I was well content.

Kate wished to know of my travel to Oxford, so I told her how I'd met up with Hamo Tanner and his troupe and her father, described the two versions of conflict on the road from Abingdon to Oxford, and recounted all about the abduction of poor Henry Harcourt – complete with the grisly threat of sending on a severed finger.

"Odd that the villains who do these felonies seem unalike," I said. Some of the rogues wear black, as do monks or lay brothers or scholars, and others are clothed as young gentlemen."

"Men may change their garb," Kate replied, "depending upon how they might wish to appear.

And how does my father?"

"He grows frail," I said. "There is a pallor about his face, and he walks bent from the waist, as if his back pains him."

"You think the wound from that splinter you removed still troubles him?"

"Nay. When folk become aged they seem oft unable to stand upright, especially crones. Why this is so no man knows, but observation proves it so."

"You believe he will die soon?"

"Aye. I do. And his business is in decline. So many deaths in the past twenty years means fewer scholars and fewer books and less call for parchment and ink."

Kate's face grew somber as I spoke. "I wish he might see Bessie and John before he meets the Lord Christ," she said softly.

"I have thought on that. We have an empty room in Galen House. Perhaps your father would consider selling his stationer's shop and removing to Bampton. Should he fall ill in Oxford there is none to care for him. Though 'twould make more labor for you," I added.

"Not so much. But I fear he would not consider it. He would not wish to burden me."

"Possibly. But we will not know unless we ask. I'd like to go back to Oxford to speak again with Hamo Tanner, if he has not yet moved on to another place. I will seek your father and learn of his opinion. Bessie and John mayhap will persuade him, if I speak of them a time or two."

John took that moment to announce that he desired his own dinner, so Kate left me with Bessie and a second bowl of pottage.

I had scarce finished my meal when there came a rapping upon Galen House door. I opened it to Father Thomas.

"Mistress Kate said she expected your return this day," the priest began. "Have you learned any more of Hubert's death, or the other felonies between here and Oxford?"

"Only that the evils continue."

"Wickedness continues in the Weald, also," Father Thomas said.

"There is more mischief afoot? Come in and tell me. Does the matter involve Alain Gower and Walter Mapes?"

"Aye, it does."

I invited the priest to take his ease on the bench at the

hearthside, for the April afternoon was gloomy and cold. I lit a cresset upon the table with embers from the fire, to furnish us with some light for our conversation.

"Alain has beaten Walter, so Walter claims," Father Thomas began.

"Claims?"

"Walter was walking from Bridge Street to the Weald when men set upon him. 'Twas yesternight, near dark, but he swears he recognized Alain as one of the assailants."

"Did the attackers speak?"

"Nay. So Walter says. All three had cudgels and laid them upon his ribs and head. Eye is all blackened and ribs also, so he says. Nose is a bit awry and likely broken."

"This is a matter for you and Father Ralph and Father Simon to sort out," I said.

"But what if 'twas not Alain who attacked Walter? What if it was the felons who slew Hubert and have done much other mischief hereabouts?"

"'Twas not such men who beat Walter," I said.

"Oh – why do you say so?"

"What did the assailants take from him?"

"Uh, nothing."

"Why would thieves attack a man, leaving him broken and bloodied in the road, but take none of his possessions? This business is about revenge. Alain retaliating for the hamsoken he blames on Walter."

"But if Walter truly did no harm to Alain, as he claims, then Alain's robbers may have been of your bailiwick, or the same who did slay Hubert Shillside."

"Mayhap. When I discover if it is so I will interest myself in Walter's bruised ribs. 'Til then he and Alain are the Bishop of Exeter's men, not Lord Gilbert's. You must seek to maintain order in the Weald. I have enough to do with Bampton Manor."

Father Thomas sat quiet and thoughtful. Of the three vicars of St. Beornwald's Church he is the most energetic, but even he would allow another to do his work for him if that other man was willing. In this, he is, I suppose, like most men. And much like me, I confess it.

But I knew of no other men eager to find those who robbed and murdered Hubert Shillside. Most seemed willing to shrug their shoulders, proclaim the death a terrible villainy, and go about their business. Even Will no longer sought me daily, when I was at home, to learn if I had found the felons.

Next day was Sunday, the day for Kate's churching. She wrapped John snugly, for 'twas a chilly morning, and over his head placed the chrisom. She covered her own head with a veil, and together we walked Church View Street to the Church of St. Beornwald, where Father Thomas met us at the porch. He pronounced a blessing upon Kate and the babe, sprinkled holy water upon my wife, then gave her a candle.

Kate, in turn, gave the priest the chrisom which had covered our son, and the ceremony ending her uncleanness was done. So was her confinement. A man who has done some of his wife's work for forty days learns to appreciate her more.

I spent the next day with John Prudhomme, Bampton's reeve, inspecting flocks and herds, examining plowing and planting, surveying fences and ditches, and inquiring of John if any tenants were lax in week-work owed Lord Gilbert's demesne. As the shadows grew long I sought Arthur and told him to be ready on the morrow with two palfreys, for we must once more travel to Oxford.

Again I did not halt at Eynsham Abbey to consult Abbot Gerleys, intending to do so on the return journey, and stay the night. Although April had been dry, the winter had been wet, so the river at Swinford was deep and swift. I had found it necessary to cross the stream too many times for my liking. One slip of a beast's hoof could plunge a man into the chilly current. I was well pleased to be past the ford, safe and dry.

A hundred or so paces beyond the river I noticed my palfrey lay back her ears. A moment later the beast snorted, and after a few paces Arthur's mount did likewise, and shied to the right of the road.

I had neither seen nor heard anything to pique a horse's interest, but beasts are more perceptive of danger than men. I tightened my grip upon the reins, looked intently about, and readied myself to spur my palfrey to a gallop if need be.

Arthur saw my tension, as he had noted his own beast's heed of something of which neither he nor I was aware. "What d'you s'pose that's about?" he said, scanning the fields adjacent to the road. To the west, between road and river, lay a meadow filled with sheep. To the east was a hayfield. Stone walls separated both from the road.

"Draw your dagger," I said, and withdrew my own from its sheath as I spoke. "Hold it high so if rogues be near they will see and know we are aware of their presence."

Arthur did so, and together we rode on, appearing to any onlooker obviously alert to whatever peril might overtake us. I saw no man, nor did Arthur, so perhaps ours was but the response of men who knew of many felonies occurring near the place. But perhaps not. Mayhap there were knaves close by who intended us harm, but faded away when they saw us prepared to meet them. So I thought.

We crossed the river into Oxford on Bookbinder's Bridge and immediately sought some crowd of scholars which might point to Hamo Tanner. He and his troupe were not at the place where I had seen him two days past, so I directed my beast to the Black Boar.

I found the wrestler there before a plate of boiled eels in galantyne sauce, taking an early dinner. He looked up from his meal, saw 'twas me, and his blocky face wrinkled into a grin.

"Master Hugh… another prosperous morning," he said, glancing at his meal. The other members of his troupe were likewise filling their bellies with eels and loaves and ale.

"Come," he said. "Sit 'ere. Have you dined? No? Innkeeper!" he called out. "More eels and loaves! And ale!"

I felt guilty eating fare supplied generously from Hamo's purse, because of the questions I intended to ask him.

"Will you remain long in Oxford?" I asked.

"One more day, perhaps two, then 'tis Banbury for us. After

a week or so in any place, men lose confidence in their strength and will no longer challenge me. If none will dare me we can tempt no wagers, and our only reward comes from those who appreciate juggling, knife-throwing, and acrobats."

"Not enough income from such folk to enjoy dishes of eels in galantyne sauce, eh?" I said.

"Nay. Do you wish to see Will's arm? There is redness about the wound, but he says there is no pain. Itches, though."

"Aye. It will do so for a few days. I will have a look at it. But I have questions about the men who wounded him."

"Oh aye? Ask away."

"You said they wore black?"

"They did."

"And they ran from you when they saw that they were outnumbered? Were they fleet? Did they run as young men, or heavily, as older men might?"

"You mean did they run as you might, or as I would?" Hamo grinned. "Not as me, that's sure. They was swift. 'Course, a man will add speed to 'is heels if 'e thinks a force greater than 'is own may be after 'im."

I saw Will dining at another table and asked Hamo to call him. The wrestler brought his dish of eels with him, perhaps reasonably fearing his colleagues might help themselves while his back was turned.

The fellow sat beside me on the bench and drew up the sleeve of his cotehardie. I was pleased with the appearance of my handiwork, although Will voiced some worry.

"There is no pus, nor has been since you stitched me together two days past," he said.

Physicians declare that wounds heal best when a thick, milky pus issues from them. Laudable pus. When thin, watery pus drains from a cut there is cause for worry. But I follow de Mondeville, who taught that no pus at all is best. I was pleased to see Will's gash dry, and told him so. He seemed unconvinced. 'Tis difficult to overturn accepted error, and occasionally dangerous if 'tis a bishop's error being upended.

"When you fought the men who slashed you, were you able to see them clearly?" I asked.

Will pursed his lips. "Not so much," he said. "Too busy watchin' their daggers to take heed of faces."

"Hamo believes them to be young. Do you agree?"

"Oh, aye. I saw that much. Garbed as scholars an' the faces of young men."

"Would you say any were old enough to apply a razor to their chins?"

Will thought for a moment, then said, "One seemed as 'e might've been. Looked to 'ave a stubble upon 'is cheeks. Like 'e'd been shaved a few days past."

"Did you see any other men abroad near the time and place you were attacked?" I asked, glancing to Will and Hamo both.

I wondered if they would look to each other before replying, thinking that if they did so, such might be an indication they wished to harmonize their answers. They did not. Both men shook their heads, affirming their band was alone on the road that day, but for the brigands. Neither man glanced to the other.

The gentlemen who had sought lodging at Eynsham Abbey did not need to claim they had been attacked along the road between Abingdon and Oxford if they were not. Why do so if such an assault did not happen? Did they know such an event had taken place? How so? Did they invent a tale of being attacked to absolve themselves if interrogated regarding Will's wound? They wore gentlemen's garb when they approached the abbey, not the black gowns of scholars or monks or lay brothers.

Men may change their apparel, as Kate reminded me, but would they do so in the day, between Abingdon and Eynsham?

And why travel that road if one intended to journey to Stratford? From Abingdon to Eynsham and on to Stratford a man would be advised to travel through Cumnor and Farmoor, but there would be no need to pass through Eynsham at all, Oxford being upon better, well-traveled roads and on the way from Abingdon to Stratford. Much about this business made no sense.

Whilst I spoke to Hamo and Will, Arthur gobbled his trencher of eels, drank his ale, and belched contentedly. I had told him that, if he continued to do such, Lord Gilbert would never promote him to valet. He replied that he wished for no greater position, was too old to learn new duties, and continued the practice. Hamo seemed not to care.

I could not believe Hamo Tanner guilty of guile – although I have been wrong about such matters before – so asked no further questions of him or Will.

I went to pay the innkeeper for the eels and ale which Arthur and I had consumed, but Hamo would not allow this. I did not wish to fight the man for the honor of paying for my meal so, with Arthur, thanked him for his generosity and bid him safe travel to Banbury.

Arthur and I led our beasts through Oxford's teeming streets to Holywell Street and Robert Caxton's shop. When we arrived I was startled to see his shutters closed. There was no indication that he sought custom.

I left the palfreys with Arthur and tried the door. It was barred from within. I rapped firmly upon the door and shouted my name. This brought no reply.

Behind the shop an alley gave access to a small toft, and a little-used door opened into the building from this plot of ground. We led our beasts there and I tried the door. This entry was not so stout as the street door, and rattled against the jamb and hinges as I pounded upon it. This time when I shouted my presence I heard a reply. Shortly after, I heard the bar being lifted. Then the door swung open.

Robert Caxton's appearance was appalling. His cheeks were sunken, his thinning grey hair askew, his fingers bony and claw-like upon the bar, and the ashen cast of his face was even more pronounced than but four days past.

He did not at first recognize me. "I am unwell," he whispered, "and not taking custom... Ah, Hugh, 'tis you. Come in, come in. I bid you good day."

I followed my tottering father-in-law into the dim workroom

occupying the back of the house, thence into the shop. The only light therein came from cracks between shutters and the skins of windows, but even so I could see Caxton's store of parchment, ink, and manuscripts stood the same as I had seen a few days past. So far as I could tell he had sold nothing since my last visit. The shelves were unchanged.

"I am sorry I have no loaves or ale to offer," Caxton said.

My father-in-law was always a hospitable man, even when in years past I appeared at his shop with the obvious intention of stealing away his daughter. If he had nothing to offer guests, that likely meant that he had nothing for himself.

"Arthur and I have already dined," I said. "What was your meal this day?"

Caxton brushed my question aside with a sweep of his hand.

"Does that mean nothing?"

"My needs are met," he said.

"Your appearance says not," I replied.

The stationer was silent. He sat heavily upon a stool behind his desk, as if his legs found it burdensome to support his shriveled frame.

"I forget that I have a surgeon for a son-in-law," he said. "What else will you tell me of my health?"

"I will speak plainly. This business is too much for you and, to my eyes, is failing. You are not eating well, I think. Look – you're no more than skin and bone. You must sell this shop and come to Bampton to live with us in Galen House."

"Nay. I cannot impose myself upon my daughter."

"You think when she learns of your state, and then of your death, that will be no imposition on her?"

Caxton had no ready reply to this. He surely treasured his freedom to go and do as he would, but also knew that such days were past.

"I cannot sell this shop," he finally said.

"Why not? Surely, even though such a business as yours is in decline today, at some year in the future scholars will again be numerous in Oxford."

"'Tis already sold," Caxton said. "Last year, when I was short of funds with which to purchase more hides, I sold it to the candlemaker next door. Folk still need candles. The nights get as dark now as ever they did – although, to be sure, there are fewer folk needing to see their way."

"You now rent this house from the candlemaker?" I asked.

"Aye."

"Then you need only sell these gatherings and books and pots of ink. I will purchase the parchments, and I know a man who can assist with ink and books."

"Who?"

"Master Wycliffe. Master of Canterbury Hall. He will likely have use for your ink, and his scholars may want some of the supply. What books have you? Let me see."

Caxton had in his shop but three books: Aristotle's METAPHYSICS, Boethius's TOPICS, books one, two, and three, and ALMAGEST, by Ptolemy.

"These set books are always in demand. If no scholars need them now, there will surely be those who will, come Michaelmas Term."

"You are quick to decide my life," Caxton complained in a brave show of independence. His protest was justified. I have served as Lord Gilbert's bailiff for so many years that I have become accustomed to requiring of folk what they must do.

"You wish to remain here, then, with little custom and neither loaves nor flesh to keep you alive? When next I call upon you, I fear I will find you up the stairway in your bed, a corpse, food for worms."

Perhaps this was harsh. But it was surely also true. Truth is oft unpalatable.

"Arthur," I said, "here is my purse. Find an inn and buy there a roasted capon and as many loaves as you can carry. And here, take also the ewer upon that cupboard and fill it with ale."

"'Ow many hands you think I've got?" Arthur complained.

"Oh, aye. Well, bring fowl and bread first, then return to the inn for the ale. I will be away when you return. I intend to seek Master Wycliffe and arrange matters with him. See that my father-in-law consumes a goodly portion of the capon and half of a loaf, at least."

A short walk later I entered the gate to Canterbury Hall. The porter recognized me, tugged a forelock in greeting, and bade me enter. The central court of the hall was deserted and quiet. I assumed that Master Wycliffe led a disputation somewhere, so prowled the college until I heard voices.

I peered around the open door into an occupied chamber and saw Master Wycliffe and a dozen or so black-gowned scholars contending with an obscure remark of Boethius. Of course, most everything of Boethius is obscure. Their words brought to mind days when I also thought such matters of philosophy significant. But now I have a wife and children, my opinion of what may or may not be of consequence is somewhat modified.

Wycliffe saw me through the open door, halted in the midst of his argument, and greeted me.

"Master Hugh, good day. Come in… come in." Then, to his scholars, some nearly as old as I, he said, "A former scholar of Balliol, who some years past found my stolen books. How may Canterbury Hall serve you?"

"I will wait 'til you are finished here."

"Bah… we may as well be done. 'Tis as useless to teach Boethius to this lot as to try to pound cheese through a keyhole."

Why any man would wish to do such a thing with a cheese I did not ask, but the comparison was useful. I remembered that Master John had expressed similar thoughts of me and my fellows when I was at Balliol. I suppose that to a great scholar all other men must seem dolts.

Wycliffe closed the volume lying open before him, placed it under an arm, dismissed the scholars, and bade me follow him. A cold mist began to gather as we approached his chamber and I thought ruefully of the damp journey back to Eynsham which lay ahead of me.

An hour later, less mayhap, Robert Caxton's goods were accounted for. Master John would take the ink and books, sell for the best price he could get, and hold the funds secure in Canterbury Hall 'til I came for the coins. Six months, I suggested, and the scholar agreed that by Martinmas he should be able to dispose of ink and books.

"But when you return to Oxford you may not find me here," he said.

"Why?"

"There is much contention in Canterbury Hall. I think it likely I will be replaced."

No man could replace Master Wycliffe, I thought. Another might be found to take his position, but the fellow would not replace such a scholar.

'Twas the ninth hour before I returned to Holywell Street and my father-in-law's shop. I reported to him the scheme made with Master John, and noted that more than half the capon and three wheaten loaves lay upon his table – enough to provide for him for a few days. I gave Caxton six pence, to feed himself if I was unable to return for him when planned, and told him Arthur and I would return in two days with a cart to carry him and his meager possessions to Bampton. He sighed, but made no more objections. The prospect of seeing his daughter, and two grandchildren upon whom he had never laid eyes – and likely thought he never would – tempered the misery of losing his livelihood.

Arthur and I could not linger if we expected to reach the hospitality of Eynsham Abbey before nightfall. We prodded our beasts to a quick pace once past Bookbinder's Bridge. Beyond Osney Abbey we saw no others upon the road. This was unusual. Men are commonly about the roads near to Oxford, at their business, 'til dark. Word of the multiple felonies hereabouts had made travelers wary, I conjectured.

I had nearly forgotten my beast's odd behavior after splashing through Swinford earlier in the day, but as we came near the ford the palfrey did the same again. Her ears lay back, she snorted with displeasure, and shied to the side of the road. Arthur's beast did likewise. Something or someone had caused the animals to become agitated.

If 'twas someone who troubled our beasts it would be wise to prepare for whatever danger might lurk beyond the road. But the palfreys were accustomed to the scent of men. Why would they behave so if they detected men nearby? I again drew my dagger and lifted it before me as a sign that I sensed peril. Arthur saw and did the same.

But no hazard appeared. Within moments, as we reached the ford, the palfreys lost their fear and behaved as normal. Here was a puzzle. Had rogues lain in wait for unwary wayfarers both early in the morning and late in the day, and yet allowed Arthur and me to pass unmolested? The puzzle remained in my mind for the next mile, 'til we came to Eynsham Abbey.

"You are becoming regular guests," the hosteller remarked as we dismounted. "You will wish to speak again to Abbot Gerleys while here, I presume?"

"Aye. There are matters taking me regularly to Oxford, the felonies hereabouts among them. Perhaps the abbot has new reports which may bear on the crimes."

After a meal in the guest chamber I was invited to the ailing abbot's lodging, and we again discussed all that had passed.

"Do you know Sir Thomas Harcourt?" I asked.

The abbot nodded.

"His son was taken a few days ago. Ten pounds is demanded for his return."

"The rogues have struck again!" Abbot Gerleys exclaimed. "Ten pounds! A great sum. But if these prove to be the same felons as have done murder hereabouts they will not hesitate to slay the lad if their demands are not met."

Recalling then the skittishness of our beasts but a mile from the abbey, I warned Abbot Gerleys of it as I was about to leave his lodging.

"Was this near the place where the road is walled upon both sides?" the abbot asked.

"Aye. Meadow upon one side of the road, with sheep there, and a field of hay upon the other, as I remember."

"I will send some lay brothers to inspect the verge and see

what might have troubled your beasts. Perhaps if felons were concealed there they will have left some sign of their presence. A hundred paces beyond the ford, you say?"

"Aye."

Chapter 8

Arthur and I arrived in Bampton next day before dinner. As before I sent Arthur to the castle with our palfreys and walked from Bridge Street to Galen House. I was expected. Kate had prepared blancmange and maslin loaves with parsley butter. I told her of her father's condition, and her face fell, but when I announced that he was willing to remove to Bampton she smiled again.

"When? How will he come?"

"Tomorrow. Arthur will harness a runcie to one of Lord Gilbert's carts and we will set out again for Oxford. 'Tis a large cart. Your father's table, chair, bench, and other chattels will fit, I think."

"I will clean his chamber, and strew fresh rushes and lavender about."

"Good. We must do all we can to make him feel welcome. He'll not find it easy to set aside his living and come under our roof as a dependent. But he is old, Kate, and very ill. You must be prepared to see grave changes in your father."

"You really believe he is near to death?" Kate asked me, somber again.

"Aye, unless you feed him. I believe his purse is so thin that he does not eat."

Kate nodded. "He was always a man of healthy appetite." She paused, considering this a moment, before she moved on to ask: "You will have spent the night at Eynsham Abbey. Did you learn anything new there to lead you to those knaves who slew Hubert Shillside?"

"Nothing. But an odd thing occurred along the road. Just beyond Swinford, both going and coming, our beasts sensed something or someone which caused them unease."

"You think men lay in wait there for victims? Why did they not attack?" Kate shuddered.

"When we saw the horses troubled we drew our daggers. Perhaps the scoundrels saw us ready for them, or else saw Arthur and decided to await less formidable prey."

"I wish you were not going back that way tomorrow."

"Abbot Gerleys is sending a band of lay brothers to inspect the road. If thieves lie in wait there, they will know their hiding place is found out and will likely seek another."

"Another place along the road you may travel," Kate pointed out.

"Aye. But remember I'll be traveling it with Arthur. Come, Kate – don't look so fearful. Would you attack Arthur, a dagger in his hand withal, whatever size purse he had strapped round his waist?"

"Could you not take another though, also? Just to be extra safe. Perhaps Uctred?"

I did not fear another journey to Oxford, but thought Kate's suggestion wise. Uctred is no longer young, but he has the ropy muscled arms of a man tried by labor and strife. So I smiled at her in reassurance. "I will go to the castle and inform Uctred that he will travel with me and Arthur tomorrow."

Most men prefer not to travel, but Uctred, when I told him why I desired his company next day, grinned with pleasure. Like Arthur, he does not shirk an opportunity to crack the skulls of felons and miscreants.

Arthur had greased the cartwheels with lard, so when we crossed the Bampton Castle drawbridge next morn the only sounds were the clatter of three horses' hooves and the rumble of the cartwheels. No squeal announced our departure.

The runcie Arthur selected was capable but slow, so 'twas past the third hour when we came to Swinford. The cold river water seemed less unpleasant this day, for a south wind brought warmth to the land, a token of the summer to come.

Uctred knew to be prepared after we had passed the ford, so like Arthur and me had his hand upon his dagger as we traveled beyond the river. The stone walls either side of the road offered ideal hiding places for villains, but none appeared, nor did our beasts indicate any apprehension about their security.

Nevertheless, I kept a hand close to my dagger 'til we reached Farmoor. Perhaps a band of sturdy lay brothers, I thought, had persuaded any rogues to seek their quarry elsewhere. I would ask Abbot Gerleys upon our return.

We saw nothing of Hamo Tanner and his entertainers as we traveled the streets of Oxford. Evidently he had left for Banbury or some other place unwary young men might overestimate their strength and cleverness.

'Twas well Uctred had come along, as he proved helpful carrying Robert Caxton's goods from shop to cart. Last of all we placed pots of ink, gatherings of parchment, and books in the cart and when we'd looked round the bare shop and given Robert's key to the candlemaker, we set off for Canterbury Hall. Caxton glanced back from his perch upon the cart aside Arthur as we turned the corner from Holywell Street through the Smith Gate to Catte Street. He was leaving the home he had known for twenty years, since he had arrived from Cambridge to set himself up in the stationer's trade, but if he was troubled at this departure he hid it well. His glance to the shop was fleeting, and I saw no tear upon his cheek.

By the time we left the ink and books with Master Wycliffe my stomach was growling. We detoured past the Hind and Hounds for ale, barley loaves, and a roasted leg of mutton, then departed Oxford across Bookbinder's Bridge. I fervently hoped I need make no further journey to the city any time soon.

The runcie drawing our cart began to tire, and no wonder. It was heavy, with my father-in-law sitting by Arthur and all his possessions piled behind. Our pace slowed until I began to feel misgivings lest the beast lacked the strength to haul his load up the far bank at Swinford. Arthur could dismount to lighten the burden, but Caxton would be swept away in the current if he quit the cart.

I worried about this as we approached the ford, and because my mind was thus distracted I did not notice when my palfrey laid her ears back as before. And, I suppose, as we had passed the place in the morning with none of the beasts taking notice, I was of the opinion that whatever had caused equine concern was no longer present.

The runcie drawing the cart shied to the side of the road and would have dropped the left wheel into the ditch between road and stone wall had not Arthur yanked mightily upon the reins to hold the frightened beast on course.

Uctred immediately drew his dagger and looked wildly about, ready for an attack. But no men appeared. I had no plans to pass this way again soon but even so, the mysterious uneasiness of our beasts at that spot would cause me sleepless nights unless I discovered the cause. I reined in, determined to get to the bottom of this, and Arthur and Uctred stopped with me, looking at me askance as I sat deep in thought.

As I turned the thing over in my mind, I recalled that when we passed by in the morning the breeze was from the southwest, and warm. But now, past the ninth hour, the sky had become cloudy and the wind blew chill and from the north. Was there something beyond the stone wall to the north of the road which would not alarm beasts when the wind came from the southwest, but would frighten them when the scent came to them on a gust from the northeast?

I dismounted, giving my palfrey's reins to Uctred, for I feared the animal might dart away if she thought she was unrestrained, then unsheathed my dagger and approached the wall. I did not look back, but I heard Arthur unsheathing his dagger.

Beyond the wall lay a field sown to hay. I carefully peered over the stones, seeking some place where I could both see over the obstruction and be sure to avoid the nettles. I found such a place, stepped upon a protruding stone, looked over the wall – and then I saw the corpse. Mystery solved. 'Twas the stench of death had startled our beasts.

The dead man lay on his stomach, arms thrown up above his head. The cause of his death was apparent. His cap and shoes were gone, and the back of his head was black with blood where he had received a stroke which stove in his skull.

I remembered then that Abbot Gerleys had spoken of a prosperous tenant of Wytham who had gone missing on the road to Abingdon with a cartload of barley.

But the corpse could not be him. This man had been dead a few days only, not more than a fortnight. Who had gone missing hereabouts in the past few days?

Henry Harcourt had been taken, but he was held for ransom. Surely his abductors would not slay him and lose the expectation of ten pounds. Was the dead man young? I could not see his face, but his form was slender, as lads often are.

The dead do not decay so rapidly when the weather is cool. Perhaps it was indeed the tenant of Wytham who lay before me, shaded from the sun by the cool stone wall. And perhaps he was not slain when taken, but held captive for a week or so.

All these thoughts flashed through my mind more quickly than can be told. Arthur saw me hesitate atop the wall and cross myself. "What is there?" he called. "What have you found?"

"A dead man. Leave my father-in-law with the reins and come."

Arthur dropped from the cart and hurried to my place at the wall. 'Twas more difficult for him to see over the obstacle, being nearly a head shorter than me. But he placed a foot upon the jutting stone, hauled himself atop the wall, and looked down at the corpse. A brief glance was enough for him. He stepped back to the road and crossed himself as I had.

"We must take the fellow to the abbey," I said. "Wait here while I climb over the wall and hoist him up. Don't worry about him being scraped against the stones. He will not care."

The wall was mercifully free of nettles. I found several foot and hand holds and was soon standing beside the corpse. Before I lifted the fellow to Arthur I examined the soil about the dead man to see if anything could be learned. I found nothing incompatible with the verge of a hayfield.

I then studied the man's head and back. I found no other

injury, just the broken head. Perhaps if I turned the corpse I might find some other wound. This was odious work, but must be done. There was no other wound. The man had died of a blow to his skull.

Because he lay face down, no carrion crow had plucked at his eyes. I gave thanks for small blessings.

The dead man wore brown chauces of wool of good quality, and a cotehardie of russet wool – also of worth. This was more than a tenant farmer, even a prosperous one, robbed and slain upon the road to Abingdon. Was this indeed Henry Harcourt? Mayhap, for the dead man was youthful. But it still seemed to me unlikely that a man whose life was valued at ten pounds would be murdered.

Within a short time after death men become stiff, but after a day or two the rigor fades and their limbs are flexible again. When I lifted the corpse to the top of the wall the head and arms fell all askew. The man was not newly slain. But our beasts had told us that two days past.

Arthur reached over the stones, grasped the corpse under the arms, and hoisted him over the wall. I heard the horses snort and prance about as the dead man appeared to them, and hoped that Caxton could control the runcie.

He did so. I clambered back over the wall, skinned a knuckle in the process, then told Arthur to take the feet whilst I lifted the dead man's shoulders, and together we would place him atop my father-in-law's pallet in the cart.

The runcie was skittish and disapproved of this. Rather than mount the cart Arthur grasped the beast's bridle to restrain it, and make its labor less arduous when we reached the ford – which lay in sight now, just a hundred or so paces ahead. Beyond Swinford, above the greening branches, I could see the spires of Eynsham Abbey church and the village church of St. Leonard's.

Uctred's palfrey and my own were not pleased to follow the cart, so we went ahead, waiting beyond the ford to be certain that Arthur, the runcie, and the cart were able to climb the riverbank.

They did so, but only because Arthur hauled mightily upon the beast's bridle, thus persuading the animal to exert itself. Given the option, I think it might be still standing there in the ford.

Brother Watkin greeted us as we clattered in under the abbey gateway. "This time you are four," he said.

"Nay, we are five, but one needs no service of you," I said. "Seek Abbot Gerleys. He must be told of this corpse we found not half a mile from here."

The river was cold and Arthur, wet from waist down, stood shivering in the chill breeze. "You know where the guest house is," I told him. "Go there and dry yourself. Perhaps a fire will be lit."

Arthur needed no urging and trudged off toward the guest quarters. He was barely out of sight beyond the abbot's lodging when Abbot Gerleys appeared from the west door of the church, the guest master following close behind. The abbot had a heavy black cloak wrapped about him, yet it seemed to me he shivered, as if 'twas winter, not spring.

"Brother Watkin said you found a corpse this day," the abbot said as he came near. "Who is it? Do you know the man?"

"Nay. Is the man missing from Wytham yet absent his village?"

"Aye, he is."

"Perhaps he is found. How old was this missing tenant?"

"I'm not sure – but he had a wife and four children, and the oldest near to full grown, so folk are telling me."

"Then this is not his corpse," I said. "This man is not nearly old enough to have a son or daughter of twenty or so years."

The abbot was silent for a few moments, then turned to speak to the hosteller.

"Find Brother Bernard. Tell him of this corpse and have him fetch a bier to the church altar. Then seek Brother Oswin to assist you in washing the dead man. Save back his clothing. Mayhap 'twill be the way we can identify the fellow."

"I told you two days past of the skittish behavior of our beasts beyond Swinford," I said. "'Twas this corpse agitated them so. They scented death."

"Hmmm. The lay brothers I sent to inspect the road were lax."

"Their noses are not so keen as a beast's. I found the man lying hard against the wall opposite the road, where no man could see him unless he climbed up to peer over.

"The dead man lays in yon cart, where also sits my father-in-law."

"Ah... the stationer?"

"He has left that business and will live with us in Bampton."

"Well, you know where to find our guest house. Take him and your man there, and Brother Watkin will soon deal with your needs."

"I must leave the abbey for an hour or so. If the hosteller will provide for these, and a man I have sent on ahead to the guest house so to dry himself, I will join them shortly."

Abbot Gerleys responded with a puzzled frown. I explained.

"I may know the identity of the corpse. You remember that Henry Harcourt is taken from his manor and held for ransom?"

"Would rogues slay a man they held for a price?"

"Mayhap he tried to escape them," I said.

"But even then, why slay him?"

"If he learned the identity of his abductors they could not allow him to live."

"Ah," the abbot agreed. "Just so. They would then have slain him even if his father paid the ransom. So you ride now to Stanton Harcourt?"

"Aye. I will return with Sir Thomas as soon as may be."

When I told my need to the abbey stables a lay brother assigned there offered one of the abbey beasts.

"Your animal has traveled many miles already this day," he said. "I'll have a horse saddled and bridled for you in a trice."

From Eynsham to Stanton Harcourt is two miles, no more. Traveling there alone was of some risk, but I decided to hazard the road for the importance of the task. And Sir Thomas would accompany my return, with perhaps a groom or two.

The lay brother provided me with the abbot's ambler, so

my journey to Stanton Harcourt was swift and pleasant, with no mishap along the road. Folk in Sir Thomas's manor house were eager for news of Henry, I think, for the manor house door opened nearly instantly when I rapped upon it.

I told Walchin I must speak to his master, but the groom had no need to seek Sir Thomas. The knight was at the door immediately when he heard my voice.

"Do you bring word of my son?" he asked.

"I may. If so, 'tis an evil day." I hastened to explain. "A corpse was found a few paces to the east of Swinford. 'Tis a young man. The corpse now lies before the altar of the abbey church at Eynsham."

"When was the dead man found?" Sir Thomas asked.

"This day. I found him on our road home from Oxford. The man is unknown to any in the abbey, and the only man of any place nearby reported as missing is too old to match the corpse."

"You believe this may be my son?"

"That men would slay a captive worth ten pounds to them seems senseless, but I know of no other man missing. If you will view the man we'll know at once whether or not 'tis your lad."

"Walchin!" Sir Thomas said. "Go to the stables and saddle three horses. We travel to Eynsham. Tell Alan he is to assist and will accompany us. Make haste."

Walchin did so, and shortly we four were upon the road to Eynsham, the low sun warming our backs when it appeared between clouds. Sir Thomas spurred on his beast, and I gave thanks for the smooth gait of Abbot Gerleys' ambler.

We were expected, so the porter had not yet closed the gate when we reached the abbey.

"The dead man lies before the church altar?" Sir Thomas asked bravely as he dismounted – but I think I detected a tremor in his voice.

"Aye. Come. I will show you."

The knight squared his shoulders and followed on. The sacristan had set cressets upon stands surrounding the corpse, although these were not yet necessary for identification as enough light from the setting sun slanting through the church windows made all things visible. Two monks stood silently by the bier: one at the head, another at the feet. Sir Thomas strode up the aisle, crossed himself before the bier, then drew the shroud from the corpse.

I watched as the knight staggered back, as if the cadaver had risen and slapped him across the cheek. I knew then, without a word from Sir Thomas, that Henry lay dead before us.

"Why would they slay him?" Sir Thomas whispered. "I was near to raising the ten pounds."

He fell silent, gazing upon his son's countenance, then spoke to the corpse. "You will be avenged," he said through tight lips. "The men who did this will die. This I promise."

As Sir Thomas made this pledge Abbot Gerleys came beside me. "As you feared," he whispered.

Sir Thomas had heard the abbot approach, although 'tis not likely he knew who it was until he turned.

"I beg of the abbey a cart to take my son home," he said.

"This evening?" Abbot Gerleys asked.

"Nay. I will stay here tonight and pray for Henry's soul. Morning will be soon enough to carry him home."

The guest chamber was near full that night. Six men snored in unison. I know this because five of them kept me awake 'til midnight, and when I finally fell to sleep 'tis likely I added to the chorus. Kate has told me I do snore. In fairness, so does she – well, a little.

If there is any advantage to sharing a chamber with Arthur and Uctred and such sonorous folk it is that whilst I seek sleep my thoughts circle about puzzling events and occasionally patterns may emerge.

Henry Harcourt's death made no sense. Of course, those who slew him might continue their ransom demand, assuming Sir Thomas to believe his son to be yet amongst the living. But word of Henry's discovery would soon travel from Stanton Harcourt. When it did the ransom demand would be finished. Those who slew Henry would be disappointed his death was discovered so quickly. What need arose for the felons to meet it through murder? If Henry tried to escape them, could he not have been recaptured? If men were close enough to slay him they could surely have seized him. Was the stroke ending Henry's life unintentional, meant to incapacitate not to kill?

Whatever reason men had for doing murder, why leave Henry's corpse against a wall, only partly hidden, where men would find it when in June they mowed the hay? Why not bury the lad in some wood and strew leaves across the grave? Did those who slew Henry wish for him to be found, but not so soon? If so, why?

If I had not peered over the wall Henry Harcourt might not have been discovered 'til men entered the hayfield with scythes. What would remain of him? Enough to identify? Face and features might be marred beyond knowing, but his chauces and cotehardie would remain and Sir Thomas would surely know them.

Chapter 9

$\mathcal{S}$ir Thomas came early to the guest chamber to rouse Alan. I felt eager to return to Bampton, and as Arthur, Uctred, and my father-in-law were awakened when Sir Thomas called for his man, we four also left our beds, rubbed our eyes, splashed water upon our faces, and prepared to meet the day.

Brother Watkin had seen Sir Thomas leave the church as he entered with other monks for matins, so as soon as the service was completed he brought loaves and ale to us. An abbey cart to carry Henry Harcourt to his home was ready when we finished breaking our fast, and Sir Thomas and his grooms set out as the sun appeared and the monks entered the choir for lauds. Our beasts and cart were prepared soon after, and we followed Sir Thomas's solemn party.

As we passed through Stanton Harcourt I saw Henry's corpse carried into the church. I touched my forelock to Sir Thomas as he glanced our way, but did not interrupt our journey home. To what purpose would I have done so? Sir Thomas's bailiff must deal with this murder. I had Hubert Shillside's death to untangle, and was making little progress at the business. If the two felonies were connected, perhaps solving one would solve the other. And what of other murders and thievery to the west of Oxford? Might all this mayhem be due to the same scoundrels? Likely.

Sorrow and gladness mingled when Robert Caxton saw his daughter, his grandchildren, and his new home. Galen House, named for the great physician of antiquity, is but a few years old, built in the new fashion, bricked between posts and beams on the ground floor, and with glass windows upon the lower story, with a roof of tiles. Sir Simon Trillowe, now deceased, burned the previous Galen House when he tossed a brand to the thatched roof. Such arson will not happen again.

Caxton was pleased to see Kate, Bessie, and John, but I could see in his eyes that in Galen House he saw the structure in which he would die. Such knowledge will create a somber mood within the most jocular men, which Robert Caxton never was.

Arthur and Uctred helped me unload the cart of my father-in-law's possessions. We placed bed, table, bench, chair, and chest in a ground-floor room used sparingly until now – only to house some injured person who required treatment for several days.

Kate had been busy at the hearth, and so when Arthur and Uctred departed for the castle with beasts and cart we sat to a dinner of stockfish in balloc broth and maslin loaves.

"Oh," Kate exclaimed. "I forgot to tell you – Lord Gilbert has returned. Yesterday."

"Then I must go to the castle and tell him of Hubert Shillside."

I would have preferred a more leisurely meal, but it is not wise to keep a great lord waiting when one possesses news he will want to hear.

I found Lord Gilbert, his son Richard, his guests, grooms, and valets at dinner in the hall. Lord Gilbert did not wait for me, but I for him. As this was a fast day there were fewer removes, so the wait was not long.

John Chamberlain showed me into Lord Gilbert's presence in the solar, where he prefers to spend his time, many hours alone, or with a small assemblage of friends. Since Lady Petronilla's death Lord Gilbert seems more pleased with keeping his own company than to be a part of some noisy society. Only one other was present in the solar. Lord Gilbert introduced me to a knight of his fee, Sir Reginald de Broc. The name seemed familiar, but I couldn't place it – and then I remembered. I wondered if the knight was a descendant of one of those who had rid King Henry II of his "meddlesome priest" some two hundred years past; but this seemed no time nor place to ask.

It took an hour to relate the felonies, both real and suspected, which had occurred in the past weeks between Bampton and

Oxford. As I spoke, Lord Gilbert occasionally raised an eyebrow. This was a mannerism I had tried to emulate in years past, but could never master. One eyebrow only. Try it.

"Does Sir Thomas seek the felons?" Lord Gilbert asked, speaking of Thomas de la Mare, Sheriff of Oxford.

"I assume so," I replied.

"You have traveled to Oxford many times in the last fortnight or so but not told the sheriff of the evils in the county?"

"To what point? He will surely know of the felonies."

"Oh, aye, I suppose so. Sir Thomas is not the most energetic of men, unless he's approaching his dinner," Lord Gilbert chuckled. "Well, next time you travel to Oxford speak to Sir Thomas, even if he is unlikely to exert himself overmuch in pursuing the rogues responsible."

From the castle I walked to Father Thomas's vicarage, where his clerk answered my knock upon his door. I wished to know from the priest if strife continued in the Weald. Not that I felt responsible to end it if it did, but trouble amongst the bishop's tenants and villeins could spread readily enough to Lord Gilbert's lands. Father Thomas assured me peace prevailed in the Weald, although Alain Gower's stolen possessions had not been recovered, nor had evidence been found to implicate any man in the theft, not even Walter Mapes, whom all men apparently thought responsible.

Matters of manor business occupied me through Saturday. Two of Lord Gilbert's tenants, according to John Prudhomme, were shirking week-work. I had spoken to these same fellows in past years about the same transgression, and fined both of them. Words and fines have done little good. Since the plague, men know the value of their labor – inferior though it may be. Most lords and nobles possess much fallow land, need more workers than they have, and try to attract tenants from other estates, although the Statute of Laborers forbids such practice. So the effectiveness of my attempts to keep discipline with such malefactors is limited. I speak harsh words and threaten new penalties, and when I leave them the fellows smile and continue their ways. The only hold I have over such men is that Lord Gilbert is a fair master, the soil of Bampton is fertile, and tenants and villeins know I deal justly with them. Not all bailiffs do so. And where else might they find a bailiff who can set their child's broken arm when he topples from an apple tree where he has been stealing his lord's fruit?

Tenants of Bampton Manor have chosen John Prudhomme to be reeve for many years, his prosperity earning respect amongst his peers. His house upon Catte Street is large and well kept, which is surely why when he and his wife and children returned home Sunday after mass, they found hamsoken done and many valuable possessions taken. Among these were a glazed bowl from Italy, a set of pewter spoons, a small chest wherein John kept his wealth – nearly fourteen shillings, he said – and his dagger, which he had not worn to church.

"Why would thieves want my wife's bowl?" John asked as I surveyed his damaged door.

"They do not, I think. It will be sold in Oxford or Abingdon or Witney before the week is out. What was its value?"

"Paid a shilling and four pence for it."

The intruders had used a chisel to carve away the wood of the door from its hinges. This could be done silently, or nearly so, ensuring that no man would hear them about their mischief. There would be few folk about at that time anyway, as all are expected to be at mass, or if servants, busy about preparing their masters' dinner. Men who would steal another man's chattels care little for their souls, so do not concern themselves if they forsake God's house.

"Come with me," I said. "Perhaps we may find your stolen goods before the thief has had opportunity to hide them away. Little reason to raise the hue and cry. The felons have had time to make their escape."

"You have some man in mind? You know who did this?"

"A man of the Weald has been accused of a similar felony."

"Ah! Walter Mapes. I've heard of the charge made against him."

John had come for me straightway when he discovered his loss after returning home from St. Beornwald's Church. I had not even had opportunity to sit down to Kate's dinner when he pounded upon Galen House door. So the miscreants – I suspected that more than one man had been involved in the hamsoken – might not have had time to conceal the stolen items.

John and I hastened to the Weald and Walter Mapes' hovel. I pounded upon the fellow's insubstantial door and it immediately swung open. Apparently Mapes, his wife, and their brood were not long home after mass. Or that is what other folk were to think.

Mapes tends always to peer out at the world from under a scowl, so I cannot be sure that he was especially offended to see me at his door. But likely he was, considering our past encounters.

I bid the man "Good day" and smiled. He did not return either the sentiment or the expression.

"What d'you want?" Mapes growled.

"Valuable goods were stolen this morning whilst honest men were at church," I said. "Did you and your sons attend mass?"

"Of course. Against the law not to, unless a man be ill."

"Who would have seen you there?" I said.

Mapes ignored my question and went straight to the point. "I haven't taken no other man's goods."

"Who can attest that you attended mass this day?" I repeated. "I was there and do not remember seeing you or your lads."

"Richard Mersh seen us. Was right behind me. An' Roger Thursby."

I knew of these men by their reputation, which was little better than Mapes'. They were of the Weald, and it occurred to me that, for a share of the spoils, such men might cheerfully forsake the truth.

"Fetch Father Thomas," I said to John. "I will remain here. Make haste."

If I demanded of Walter Mapes that he open his hovel to a search for stolen goods, 'twould be best to have at my side a representative of his lord, the Bishop of Exeter. He might protest, but would not deny entry to Father Thomas as he possibly would to me. My authority did not extend to the Weald, and Mapes knew it.

"What d'you want with Father Thomas?" Mapes said.

"He is needed to assist in the search for John Prudhomme's stolen goods."

"What? 'Ere? I've no man's possessions."

"Then you'll not be troubled if we search your house and barn."

Mapes folded his arms. "Search where you will. An' you don't need to wait for John to return wi' Father Thomas."

The man stood aside from his door and invited me to enter. I knew as I did so that I would find no stolen property here. Either because he had not done hamsoken, or because he was confident that the goods were well hidden elsewhere.

I entered the dark, shabby dwelling and waited a moment 'til my eyes became accustomed to the gloom. A fire glowed upon the hearth stone, its smoke contributing to the tenebrous atmosphere. The man's wife looked up from the pot she tended, then went back to stirring her dinner. The older children, who with their mother had heard my conversation with their father, glared at me. No doubt they learned this from their father. If I discovered that Walter Mapes had stolen from Alain Gower and John Prudhomme, he would hang, and his sons would have another reason to hate me. Evil men always find ways to justify their sins and place guilt upon those who find them out.

The hovel was of two rooms, one quite small, and the larger no more than four or five paces in length and breadth. I poked through bedclothes and a chest before John returned with Father Thomas. The priest was not pleased to have his dinner interrupted, I think. But whether or not Walter Mapes was the target of his ire I could not tell. He growled at all of us.

Together the priest, John, and I investigated the smaller room, which was barely large enough for the pallets of Mapes' children. We prodded the matted rushes upon the floor, then left the house to examine the toft for any recently disturbed earth. We saw none, and the small barn and decaying henhouse held no valuable items belonging to either Walter Mapes or anyone else. If Walter Mapes was a thief he had concealed his gains well. It occurred to me that if Roger Thursby or Richard Mersh would vouch for Walter's presence at mass, whilst he was in truth elsewhere, they might also harbor the ill-gotten gains. Did Mapes have other friends who might do the same for a share of the loot?

Neither I nor Father Thomas could search every household in Bampton or the Weald whose tenant might know Walter Mapes. And, for all his unappealing reputation, Mapes might indeed be innocent of the felony, if not of many others.

Mapes had stood silently, arms folded, a slight smirk occasionally decorating his face, whilst we searched. Did his grin mean that he had outsmarted us, or did his confidence arise from a clear conscience? There is no window through which we may see into a man's soul. This is just as well. Although I might desire to see truly another man's nature, I prefer no man peer too deeply into my own. That prerogative belongs only to the Lord Christ.

We gave up the search, bade Mapes "Good day," and set off for Mill Street. I glanced back as we neared the mill and saw Walter yet standing before his door, the mocking smile still on his face, along with the purple bruises from the blows he had received a few days past.

The king has commanded all men of the realm to practice with bow and arrows. The French and their friends in Scotland make such proficiency necessary if the kingdom is to endure. Lord Gilbert, as with most of his station, requires his tenants and villeins to hone their skills at the butts upon warm Sunday afternoons, and encourages participation by awarding a penny each to the six most skillful archers. 'Tis my duty as bailiff to oversee the practice and award the prizes.

So I hurried from the Weald to Galen House, devoured my dinner of leach Lombard, and hastened to the castle forecourt where Arthur and three other grooms had erected the butts.

Although not of Lord Gilbert's manor, nor of my bailiwick, men of the Weald generally appeared upon these Sunday afternoons to fling arrows at the targets. Among these was Walter Mapes. When he took his place at the line he lowered his bow and cast in my direction the same grin with which he had favored me an hour earlier.

Arthur had measured only a hundred paces from line to butts, because I told him that this being the first session of the season we must not challenge the archers overmuch. Come August we can increase the distance to two hundred paces or so, as decreed in the king's ordinance.

Participants notched six arrows at each try, and by the third or fourth volley most were placing two or three arrows into the target, which was the width of my arm from chin to fingertips. Not Walter Mapes. The man hit the butt with four arrows at his first attempt, and at the fourth round placed all six within a circle the size of a pig's bladder.

He had snagged one of Lord Gilbert's silver pennies fairly, but it pained me to present him with the coin. 'Twould have been more bearable had he not approached me for his prize with that intolerable smirk yet spread across his face.

Partway through the contest Lord Gilbert appeared, accompanied by his guests Sir Reginald and – new to the castle – Sir John Lynum and his lady Alyce. There ensued much doffing of caps and tugging of forelocks when they appeared. Lady Alyce applauded daintily when an archer hit his mark, and her appreciation of skill was much valued, I think, for blushes colored the cheeks of these robust archers.

My father-in-law attended the archery practice and, as we strolled back to Church View Street afterwards, he spoke of what he had observed.

"One of the men who won coins, the shaggy fellow, smiled as though he had gained more than a penny."

"Walter Mapes," I said. "And perhaps he has. You heard me tell Kate that John Prudhomme was robbed this morning whilst all good men were at mass."

"Aye. And you think this Mapes is not a good man?"

"He claims witnesses who will place him at the church whilst the theft was happening."

"Will you question the witnesses?"

"To what purpose? He would not name them unless he was sure of their testimony – and perhaps he tells the truth. Perhaps he is innocent of the felony, for all of his past misdeeds."

"He looks guilty," Caxton said.

"Aye, I give you his looks. He has been guilty of so much wickedness for so long that the appearance comes naturally to him. But Father Thomas and I searched Walter's house and barn and found nothing."

"So perhaps," Caxton observed drily, "he grins in triumph."

Chapter 10

I acknowledge that I had hoped Walter Mapes to be guilty of slaying Hubert Shillside, and hoped also that I might discover evidence of his complicity in the robberies of Alain Gower and John Prudhomme. This would send a vile and repulsive man to the scaffold and conveniently clear the mysteries troubling Bampton and the Weald. Mapes might call on the testimony of friends to place him at St. Beornwald's Church when John Prudhomme's house was looted, but could he be sure such fellows would be willing to risk placing their own necks in a noose to exonerate him of a murder?

The trail of Hubert Shillside's slayers had, after twenty-eight days, gone very cold. I could question Wealdsmen about Walter Mapes' activities during Holy Week, but I doubted any would remember. Unless Mapes had done something quite out of the ordinary – or a man I might question had assisted Mapes in slaying and robbing Shillside, in which case he wouldn't be regaling Lord Gilbert's bailiff with the tale. But if the man had slain Bampton's coroner, he had not spent any of the stolen coins. Mapes seemed as poverty-stricken now as he ever was.

A man as poor as he, now in possession of ten shillings, would be tempted – even forced by life circumstances – to spend some of his new wealth. I resolved to pay close attention to Walter and his home. The thatching of his roof was rotten and no doubt leaked in a hard rain. Would he soon replace it? His wife cooked on a hearth stone in the middle of his house, the smoke – some of it – passing out through vents at the gable. Would he have a fireplace built to rid his house of the reeking fumes? Like most cotters Mapes rented oxen from more prosperous men to plow his fields. Ten shillings would purchase an ox. Would he soon expand his barn to accommodate such a beast? Or would he hire an even poorer man than himself to assist when the time came to cut hay or harvest oats and barley? I am a patient man, willing to wait and watch. I resolved to avoid the man so much as possible, that he would not suspect my eye was still upon him.

But what if he did not slay Hubert Shillside? What if the haberdasher's death was at the hands of felons nearer Oxford? Men who wore black robes, or sometimes a green cotehardie or particolored chauces and a blue cap with long liripipe. Mapes may have known Shillside was to travel to Oxford, but other men might have come upon him by chance.

Through that Monday morning I pondered deep on such puzzles until Kate returned from the baker with warm maslin loaves with which we broke our fast. During her confinement this was one of my duties when in Bampton. Kate did not seem displeased that the task was now once again hers. Resting for forty days in a darkened room, unable to leave Galen House, was, she claimed, the most objectionable part of bearing a child. A week, or perhaps a fortnight, to recover from the experience, she said, would be welcome. But forty days?

Since joining us at Galen House my father-in-law had recovered his appetite. But his stomach would not bankrupt me, and I rejoiced to see color return to his cheeks. If he continued to consume Kate's cookery with the ardor of these recent days, he would soon show a paunch under his long cotehardie.

We sat at the table consuming the warm loaves with last week's ale which was beginning to go stale. Kate has oft volunteered to brew our own, but the baker's wife brews well, and the village taster has never required of me that I fine her for watering her ale.

Robert Caxton enjoyed talking of his days as a prosperous burgher of Oxford. Good days of years past are pleasant to remember. More recent times filled with affliction not so much, and so his conversation generally visited the past. There were, to be sure, unpleasant topics of days gone by upon which he touched from time to time – the death of Kate's mother being one of these – but such a subject was uncommon for him. Caxton is not a morose man.

"Business was poor enough," he said between chewing his loaf and downing ale, "but being robbed thrice was more than I could deal with."

"Robbed?" I said. "You never mentioned such. Did you seek a constable?"

"Oh, aye. Went to the castle to make complaint. Did no good. If a man of Oxford wishes to be secure in his possessions, 'tis his own strength and wit must make him so. Seeking justice of the sheriff will do him little good."

"What happened? Did men break down your door in the night?"

"Nay. Happened in the day."

"All three times?"

"Aye. The first time young scholars came to the shop, enquired of parchment and ink, and when I produced what they sought they seized it from me and ran. I followed them out with no delay, shouting the hue and cry, but they were lost amongst the black-clad scholars always thick upon Holywell Street."

"Have other shops also been plundered?"

"Aye."

"Were the proprietors young men or old?"

"Hmmm. Most I know of were aged fellows, like me."

"The candlemaker who purchased your shop. Had he been robbed?"

"Nay, I think not. He never spoke of it."

"Is he young or old?"

"Your age nearabouts, I think."

"Young enough to chase and apprehend a fleet-footed scholar, you think?"

"Aye, mayhap."

"Three times this happened? When was the first?"

"Last autumn, a few days after Martinmas. After the theft I had little coin to purchase more skins, and the rogues took nearly all of my gatherings. That's when I sold the shop. Custom had been poor for some years."

"You did not seek a loan?"

"I did, but the fees were ruinous. I'd not enough custom to pay the interest, much less the debt."

"You would have lost the shop, either way?"

"Aye," Caxton replied softly.

"When the thieves made off with the parchment, how many took part in the theft?"

"Four the first time. Next time, just before Candlemas, there were three. Then, a fortnight before Easter, four did the felony."

"You could not recognize any as those who had robbed you before?"

"Nay. They came late in the day, when 'twas near dark. I'd lit neither candle nor cresset, to save the expense."

"Yet the streets were busy so they could lose themselves in the throng," I said.

"Aye, and the dark."

"What would scholars do with so many stolen gatherings? How many were taken?"

Caxton rubbed his whitened whiskers, did some mental calculations, then answered. "Eight gatherings first time. Not so many when the second and third thefts happened. Five then, but two of the last were of finest calf. And the first time I had two rolled skins, also."

"They were taken as well?"

"Aye, and five books taken before Easter. I tried to stop the fellows when they seized the books, but they knocked me down and were off before I could rise to my feet."

"Five books? What titles?"

"Set books. I dealt in such because I could be sure of selling them. Two of Aristotle, RHETORIC and CATEGORIES. One of Lombard, called SENTENCES. And Euclid's ELEMENTS. Also Boethius's TOPICS, the fourth volume."

"Were the books new?"

"Not RHETORIC. Others were."

"Was RHETORIC blemished or marked in any way that it might so be known? Had some scholar written his thoughts in the margins?"

"Aye, so 'twas. Some careless fellow had stained several pages with spilled ale, or some such drink."

"Careless, or drunken," I said.

"Aye, perhaps."

I did some calculations of my own. "Your loss was more than ten pounds, then."

"Aye. I had not enough custom to acquire more skins and hire more scribes to replace my lost books and recover the loss."

Would scholars who risked a noose find use for so much parchment, or would they seek to sell it to monks and friars and other scholars of the university? And did they indeed risk a noose, or could they plead benefit of clergy if caught? I thought such fellows would prefer coins, to exchange at an alehouse, over having their own vellum for copying rented manuscripts.

"Why did you not tell me of these thefts when I first came to you a month past? Your loss was great. I might have used my position to enquire."

"Aye. Mayhap. I hadn't thought your arm would reach as far as Oxford."

My obligations increased. I needed to discover who had slain Hubert Shillside. I must find who had done hamsoken against John Prudhomme. And now I felt a duty to see justice done for my father-in-law. I resolved to visit Master Wycliffe, to learn from him of any recently offering to sell parchment or books to him or his scholars at Canterbury Hall.

I sought out Arthur later in the day, instructing him to ready two palfreys for the morn, when we would once again set out on the Oxford road. He seemed less than overjoyed at the prospect. One journey to Oxford might be a diversion. More than that in six months was wearisome.

Nor did Kate look pleased, even though I explained my purpose was to seek justice for her father.

"If you find the felons, what then? Will their discovery mean my father can regain his stolen goods?"

"Nay. The rogues will have sold their loot and spent the coins."

"So they will hang, and that will serve as justice for my father?"

"Justice cannot be made perfect," I replied. "If we fail to seek it because it will be blemished when we find it, nothing remains but to quit the search and give villains free rein to do whatever evils take their fancy."

"I suppose," Kate sighed. "But when you seek justice you seem to put yourself in the way of men who work injustice."

She reached out her hand and touched the scar upon my cheek, engraved there by those who assaulted me two years ago in my search for whoever had slain a man and left him to burn in Bampton's St. John's Day blaze.

I could not fault her logic. Evil men cannot be discovered and apprehended from a distance.

Arthur and Uctred appeared before Galen House Tuesday morn shortly after dawn, riding two of Lord Gilbert's palfreys and leading a third.

"Too much wickedness about," Arthur explained, seeing my surprise at Uctred's addition to our party. "I thought a third dagger might persuade peevish folk to seek easier prey. Lord Gilbert agreed."

My escorts had already broken their fast at the castle kitchen, so I drank a cup of ale, took from Kate a fresh barley loaf, and mounted to the saddle of my beast.

In little more than an hour we reached Stanton Harcourt, where I sought Sir Thomas and information of his son's death, if any was to be had.

When I rapped on the manor house door, a servant directed me to a stable behind the house where, he said, Sir Thomas was attending a mare which was ready to foal.

"Oswald has scratched his head and belly but neither of these exercises has found who slew Henry," he said when I enquired after any new knowledge in the matter.

He patted the mare's head as he spoke, then turned and spoke to another man behind him in the dim recesses of the stable.

"Edmund, here is Master Hugh, bailiff to Lord Gilbert Talbot in Bampton – the surgeon who drew my rotten tooth."

The youth stepped forward, bowed, and greeted me politely; a handsome lad of perhaps eighteen years. This, then, was the scholar who had brought friends from Oxford to feed at his father's table. The Trinity Term had begun, but Stanton Harcourt being so near Oxford I did not wonder at his presence at his father's manor. Sir Thomas explained anyway.

"Henry, my oldest, is slain, so Edmund will inherit. He has enjoyed small success as a scholar, so he has given up his studies to return here and assist me in manor business."

Light from the open door was obscured, and we three turned to see who had entered, blocking the sun. 'Twas the village priest.

"Has Rohese given you a foal yet?" the priest asked.

"Nay... but 'twill be soon. Tonight or tomorrow, I think. We'll leave her to peace an' quiet 'til then," Sir Thomas said, and motioned us to the stable door.

I had learned what I wished to know. Henry's slayers had not been discovered. I bid Sir Thomas "Good day," and left him to deal with his sorrow and his pregnant mare.

At Oxford we once again made our way to the Black Boar to take our dinner. The inn this day served capons in gaucelye, a pleasing dish, and we ate our fill before leading our beasts on to Canterbury Hall.

Master Wycliffe, the porter said, would likely be found in his chamber. I left the palfreys in his care and sought the master, Arthur and Uctred following. I found him concluding his own dinner, a simple pottage and a loaf. He rarely dined with his scholars, proclaiming that a morsel in silence was worth a banquet in the hall of a king. I might have felt guilty for enjoying my own tasty meal, but remembered that Master Wycliffe cares little for the pleasures other folk enjoy. So long as he has his books and a simple meal he is content.

Wycliffe had left his door open, the better to enjoy the warm spring day. Elsewise the stones of the chamber would retain the cold of the previous night.

I rapped my knuckles on the doorpost and the scholar looked up from his book, spoon halfway from bowl to lips. My shape was black in the doorway, sunlight behind me, so Master John did not at first recognize me. But when I spoke a greeting he rose from his bench.

"Ah... Hugh. 'Tis you. Come in. You are here to learn if I have sold your father-in-law's books?"

"Aye, and to learn if any man has approached you or any of Canterbury Hall's scholars seeking to sell parchment or books."

"Hmmm. I was about to tell you that the three books you left with me have not found buyers, and now you ask if some other has offered to sell books to me. Why so?"

I explained the thefts my father-in-law had suffered which contributed to driving him from Oxford and his business. Master John listened quietly, then when I had finished the account turned from me, walked to a cupboard, and from a shelf lifted two gatherings of parchment.

"These," he said, "I purchased from a ragged scholar near a fortnight past. He asked but fourteen pence for two gatherings. A bargain, so I thought at the time."

"But no man has presented books he would sell? Have you heard of others being offered books?"

"How long past? This is Oxford. Scholars are always buying and selling or trading books."

"The five set books were stolen near to Easter."

"What titles?"

I told Master Wycliffe the titles of the stolen books, and he promised to watch for any of the five being offered, especially if the price was lower than might be expected.

"Books a man might have paid twenty shillings for in years past now bring little more than half that," Wycliffe said. "The plague has taken so many scholars, there are fewer to seek books and the knowledge they contain. But books do not perish of plague. There are as many now as ever there were, and scribes make more, so we who love books find our expenditure much reduced."

"Books may be transported with ease," I said. "Mayhap my father-in-law's books have been sold in Cambridge."

"Aye, it could be. 'Twould help identify the stolen books if there was some mark by which one might be known – some man's name inscribed, or notes written in margins."

"There is. Aristotle's RHETORIC is stained. Ale spilled upon some pages. The other books were new, unmarred, so no man had misused them or written his thoughts in the margins."

"Hah. I forget that you have seen my books. Men who come after me will know my mind, even though I will have returned to dust, for the scribbles I have written, my opinions of the author's thoughts. No doubt whoso inherits my books when I am in my grave will rue my scratching. Pristine books, unsullied by my notions, would be of greater worth."

"Perhaps not. There are scholars today who would give much to know your thoughts. Surely there will be like men in future years."

"Perhaps, when I feel death near, I will burn my books, or ask some friend to do so. Then my thoughts will go with me to the grave."

"Never! What if Boethius or Aristotle had done such a thing? Think of the loss to scholars, to all of mankind."

"You place me with Boethius and Aristotle? I had thought you a wise man, but I see now you lack judgment."

"I am wise enough to know a sage when I meet one."

"Did you think so when you sat under my tutelage at Balliol College?"

"Probably not. You seem to have grown wiser as I have grown older. Or mayhap 'tis the other way round."

"Aye, it may be. Well, I shall be alert for an ale-stained RHETORIC."

I visited seven stationers and booksellers that day. In their shops I found two new copies of SENTENCES and ELEMENTS, which I suppose might have been once shelved in my father-in-law's shop. Of this there was no way to know. The proprietors both claimed the works to have been commissioned by them from copyists who earn a living in Oxford bent over their desks, reproducing such volumes. All of the shopkeepers promised to keep a sharp eye for an ale-stained copy of RHETORIC. I held out little hope they would do so.

Chapter 11

The Eynsham Abbey hosteller was not surprised when the porter's novice called for him to wait upon us. I had become a regular visitor to the abbey, spending nearly as many nights there as in my own bed at Galen House. This did not please me, but duty is often onerous, which is why, I suppose, men so regularly seek to evade their obligations. This is not merely my own conjecture – it is laid down in Holy Writ – for does not the apostle warn us, "Have no fellowship with the unfruitful deeds of darkness"? And he goes further than that. It is not enough that we merely abstain. To turn away will not suffice. "Rather, expose them." So says St. Paul. And what he wrote to the Ephesians speaks also to my conscience. I cannot escape it. So, to expose deeds of darkness to the light I must find myself all too often upon the roads, sleeping away from my Kate, risking felons and knaves, seeing to it that the deeds of darkness do stay unfruitful.

Still, it's not all penance. The abbey's ale was fresh and its pottage of peas and beans flavored with ample portions of pork. I suspect a Cistercian monastery might not have been so liberal. Such monks, forbidden to partake of flesh themselves, are not disposed to allow their guests such pleasures as are Benedictines. Which is why, I suppose, Cistercians look upon their Benedictine predecessors as a feeble remnant of what they once were.

I had finished my pottage and was considering a bed when the hosteller entered, announcing that Abbot Gerleys, informed of my arrival, wished for me to visit his lodging. I was eager to do so. If he or some other of the abbey had discovered the felons who so vexed the shire, the guilty men might be the same who had slain Hubert Shillside, and a part of my obligation would be met.

Not so. No felons had been apprehended between Eynsham and Oxford, and, indeed, hamsoken had been done again but three days past on an abbey manor, whilst husband, wife, and children were at work in a field. I was pleased to see that Abbot Gerleys seemed well, free of the ague and its debilitating influence. I asked of his health, and he proclaimed his recovery from the fever.

"So – what brings you this way again?" the abbot asked. "It's always good to see you, but I don't flatter myself you're that enamored of us. Have you some new clue regarding the murder of your man from Bampton?"

"Nay. I know nothing more of that felony than when we last met, and am unlikely to learn more of the rogues unless they commit more crimes and in doing so leave behind some clue."

"Such men may become careless in their wickedness," the abbot said. "Success brings imprudence. But if you do not seek felons, why are you again upon the road?"

I explained to Abbot Gerleys that I sought more than murderers. I told him of my father-in-law's loss, and my fruitless search for stolen set books. The abbot seemed thoughtful as I completed the tale.

"RHETORIC was one of the stolen books, you say?"

"Aye, and the only one identifiable."

"Oh? How so?"

I explained that some previous owner had carelessly spilled ale upon some pages, thereby reducing the value of the book.

Abbot Gerleys' brow furrowed at this report. He turned to the monk who attended him and told the lad to seek a Brother Matthew. The youth hurried away, and the abbot turned to me to explain.

"Shortly before Easter a ragged scholar appeared at our gate. He sought lodging and a meal. He could no longer afford his studies, he said, and so was leaving Oxford to return home – near Bristol, I believe he said. He carried his possessions in a sack slung over his shoulder, and a small sack it was. He possessed but one book, which he told Brother Matthew was of no further use to him, as his days as a student must end. The lad asked if the abbey would purchase this book, as the weight of it would hinder his journey and the coins he might acquire for it would speed him upon his way."

"The book was RHETORIC?"

"Aye. We already have a copy, but such a work is valuable enough that an extra is useful."

"Was the book stained?"

"I've not seen it, but Brother Matthew said we paid only sixteen shillings for it, which is a bargain for sure. I felt guilty we did not offer the poor scholar more, and that he was so reduced that he accepted the sum with considerable eagerness."

"If he was genuinely a poor scholar," I said. "What do you remember of him? Was his apparel worn and tattered?"

"Aye. 'Twould not warm him upon his journey, threadbare as it was."

"He stayed in your guest house one night, and then was away?"

"Just so. Brother Watkin sent him on his way with two loaves fresh from the oven."

"Was the lad scrawny and ill-fed?" I asked.

"Odd you should ask. He seemed fleshy enough. Didn't appear to have lived on bread and water for many terms."

A figure darkened the abbot's door as he spoke. "Ah, here is Brother Matthew, who keeps the key to our book cupboard."

The newcomer bowed and Abbot Gerleys addressed him.

"A fortnight before Easter we purchased a copy of Aristotle's RHETORIC."

"Aye, from a poor scholar."

"What was the book's condition? Had it been ill-used?"

"Seemed of some age, but I'd not say 'twas damaged."

"No pages stained?"

"Not as I remember, but I didn't turn over every leaf."

"Is it in the book cupboard?"

"Nay. Brother Walter has it."

"Fetch it, please."

Brother Matthew seemed surprised by the request, but monks carry out their abbot's orders without question. He turned without a word and disappeared toward the monks' dormitory.

"You believe the abbey may have acquired one of my father-in-law's stolen books?"

"I hope 'tis not so, but I would not have this abbey profit from another man's loss."

"My father-in-law said several lads were involved in the thefts. Mayhap they divided the spoils. Odd, though, that he said nothing about the thieves being meanly clothed, as the youth who sold you RHETORIC was. Perhaps 'twas too dark to notice. He said the thefts occurred as he was about to shutter the shop for the night."

"Aye," the abbot agreed. "And when a man is being robbed his mind may be so unsettled that he will not recall the details of the incident."

We fell into a companionable silence, each turning over his own thoughts regarding the abbey's recent purchase. A few moments later I heard footsteps in the passage beyond the abbot's chamber and Brother Matthew appeared, carrying a book.

Night was near, and the abbot's lodging growing dark. Abbot Gerleys took the book from the librarian, laid it carefully upon his table, then lit four candles and a cresset so we could inspect the pages with more light than his windows could supply.

We found the stained pages nearly halfway through the book. Some scholar had indeed been careless, for the ale, if such it was which produced the blemish, had discolored four leaves of parchment and made the ink of one page dissolve to the extent that the letters swam and lost clarity, although the leaf was yet readable.

"I never noticed that," Brother Matthew said as Abbot Gerleys examined the stained pages. "No wonder the fellow was willing to part with the book for such a price."

"You believe this is your father-in-law's stolen book?" Abbot Gerleys asked.

"I cannot be sure," I admitted. "But 'twould be an astonishing coincidence if two different men had spilled ale upon two different copies of RHETORIC."

"It would indeed," the abbot agreed. "So tomorrow, when you return to Bampton, you must take the volume with you. If your father-in-law recognizes the work as one taken from him, he must keep it or sell it, as he wishes. If 'tis not his stolen book, you may return it when next you pass this way – which is likely to be soon, as the number of felons seems to be multiplying and you seem to be in pursuit of them all."

"I and my father-in-law are in your debt," I said. "Not all abbeys would endure such a loss.

"What else can you tell me of the youth who sold this book?" I asked Brother Matthew. "You have already said he did not seem to be starved and he wore threadbare clothing. Was it a gown such as scholars wear?"

"Aye," Brother Matthew affirmed.

"What of his shoes? Or did he go bare of foot, as a poor man might now that the days are warmer?"

"He wasn't barefoot. I didn't really pay attention to his shoes, but I'm sure he wore a pair."

"What of his face and features?"

The librarian shrugged, nonplussed. "I can bring to mind nothing very memorable about him. He had brown hair."

"Long and shaggy," I asked, "as if he'd not visited a barber for many weeks?"

"Nay, not long. And he was newly shaved."

"He was old enough to shave his whiskers?" I said.

"He was. The stubble upon his chin was two or three days grown. Odd that he'd been shaved and barbered but a few days before he had to plead such poverty he must sell us his only book."

"Pride can be expensive," Abbot Gerleys said. "Some men will spend their last farthing to maintain appearance."

"If appearance was his care, he should've purchased a newer gown," Brother Matthew said wryly. "Few would notice his trimmed hair or shaven cheeks with that shabby gown before them."

"Brown hair, you said," I persisted. "Brown eyes also?"

"Aye, think so. It's been six weeks."

"Anything memorable at all about the lad's countenance? Warts? Moles – that sort of thing?" I asked.

"Nay, he was too young for warts. But now I think on it, the scholar had a mole upon his left temple, betwixt eyebrow and ear."

"If the lad passes this way again, seeking lodging, we will ask him where he came by the book," Abbot Gerleys interjected. "And if his answer is not credible we will hold him and send for you."

I left the abbot's chamber with that understanding between us and RHETORIC under my arm. Neither Arthur nor Uctred could read, but nothing would do when they heard my tale but to inspect the stained pages.

"Waste of good ale," Uctred declared as he peered at the leaves.

"Just as well it wasn't wine," was Arthur's opinion, "else them pages'd be purpled an' worse than they are." Arthur is a man who can see the good in even a bad situation.

He is also able to dismiss all care and worry when his head is upon a pillow and so falls readily to sleep, snoring vigorously to announce to others his somnolent condition. This seemed not to trouble Uctred, who soon joined him in a rasping chorus.

Perhaps I am becoming accustomed to Arthur's noisy nocturnal resonance. I lay abed considering how a book could pass from Caxton's shop, through the hands of thieves, to a poor scholar and thence to Eynsham Abbey. The obvious conclusion was that the poor scholar was one of the thieves who had robbed my father-in-law. Moments after this thought I awoke to the morning sun illuminating the guest chamber's single window.

After a loaf and a pint of the abbey's ale we continued our homeward journey through Stanton Harcourt. I had two questions for the Harcourts, father and son. For the father I wished to know of progress in discovering who had slain Henry. Of the son I would ask if he knew of, whilst he had been a student at Oxford, any poor scholar who had a mole upon his left temple, and who had quit the university and his studies some six weeks past.

The answer to both questions was "no."

"I don't know many from other halls and colleges," Edmund said. "But as for Queen's I remember nobody with such a blemish on his face."

Edmund had been a student of Queen's Hall, Sir Thomas explained, and this did not surprise me. Queen's regards as its duty the training of priests and such as will take holy orders. Its fellows are lads like Edmund, younger sons who will not inherit, so must seek another living, although most, like those at Balliol, hail from the north, Lancashire and Yorkshire.

Sir Thomas was in the middle of telling me he had dismissed his portly bailiff for the fellow's incompetence in discovering who had slain his heir, when a thought came to me. "The wisp of green wool I plucked from the tree – does Oswald yet have it?" I asked him.

"I suppose so. I've given the fellow 'til Whitsuntide to leave his house. He's not departed yet to seek new employment. You want the strands?"

"The threads will be of use if ever a suspected murderer is found who wears a green cotehardie."

"Match the wisp with the rogue's clothing, eh? Well, the bailiff's house is just there, beyond the church and across the road. Come with me and we'll fetch the bit of wool; you can keep it safe until it may be needed."

Sir Thomas, Edmund, and I left Arthur and Uctred with the beasts at the manor house and walked the short way to the bailiff's residence. Oswald came to the door only after Sir Thomas had pounded vigorously upon it for some time. I believe the man had been yet abed.

"Here is Master Hugh," Sir Thomas said. Oswald nodded

sleepily at me. "He will have that wisp of green wool he found and left with you."

"He's found a match?" the bailiff asked. I saw his eyes widen and the somnolent expression disappear from his face. Perhaps this change in the man was brought about because he thought I had succeeded at finding the men who had slain Henry whilst he had not. So I thought.

"Nay, but I have confidence he will do so before you ever would. Fetch the wool."

Oswald glanced from Sir Thomas to Edmund to me, shrugged, and turned from his door to enter the dim recesses of his house. Sir Thomas followed close behind, then Edmund, and I entered the house last. Modesty would not permit me to precede Sir Thomas or his son. This was wise, as well as mannerly, although I did not realize it would be at the time.

Oswald went to a small chest set upon a sideboard, opened it, and rummaged about within it. He seemed perplexed, lifted the chest, and walked with it to the open door where the morning sun illuminated the opening. As he passed Edmund he stumbled and fell headlong into the rushes covering his floor. Edmund, being nearest, sprang to assist the fellow to his feet, which task, due to the bailiff's girth, took some effort. The lad took Oswald's hand and elbow so as to raise him to his feet, then bent to retrieve the fallen chest. And its contents.

Two silver spoons had fallen from the chest, and a pouch of coins. There were also several buckles and a small dagger. And there was a badge of St. Thomas, indicating that Oswald had gone on pilgrimage to Canterbury to worship at the saint's shrine.

Oswald was sufficiently padded that the tumble harmed little but his pride. He took the chest from Edmund and continued to the open door and sunlight. At the doorway Oswald pawed through the chest again, then eventually lifted his eyes to Sir Thomas and spoke.

"It ain't 'ere."

"What? The green wisp of wool I entrusted to you is missing?"

"Aye. It was 'ere in this chest last time I looked."

"When was that?"

"Two days past. I remember because I saw a gentleman an' his grooms ride past an' one of the grooms wore a cotehardie of green. I went to me chest to fetch the fragment an' see was the fellow's garb the same."

"And was it?" Sir Thomas barked.

"Nay. Forest green 'is cotehardie was. Not like the scrap I 'ad."

As he spoke I saw Oswald lift the chest to Sir Thomas, as if inviting him to inspect its contents for a scrap of yellow-tinted green wool.

"Two days past you say the wool fragment was there, and it's now gone?" Sir Thomas said.

"Aye."

"And you've not opened the chest since the green-garbed man rode past?"

"Nay."

"Perhaps," I said, "the wool fell from the chest when you dropped it just now."

At this thought my three companions turned as one to gaze at the disordered rushes where Oswald had fallen.

Edmund stood closest to the place, and so was first to drop to his knees and paw through the rushes for the missing bit of wool. I joined him, whilst Sir Thomas and the bailiff stood aside so as not to block the light from the open door. We found no wool, green or otherwise.

Oswald yet held the small chest before him, as if offering the box as evidence of his guileless state. That the green woolen filaments were not in the chest was clear. Where the threads might now be was another mystery to add to the conundrums already vexing my life. And I'd thought I had enough.

Did Oswald destroy the wool in anger at Sir Thomas for removing him from his position? Or was the bailiff simply careless? Or did Oswald intentionally spirit the wool away? But if so, why?

"Whitsuntide, remember. You must be away by then," Sir Thomas said, through gritted teeth, as we abandoned the search.

Oswald bowed unctuously and promised that he would be.

"There will be another to have your place and this house the Monday after," Sir Thomas said.

Oswald bowed again, then turned and replaced the chest upon the sideboard. I put the matter from me. I had enough to puzzle me already. I needed no new riddles to bewilder me this day. I determined to put green woolen wisps out of my mind.

It is easy to resolve a thing, less easy to carry it out. The more I was determined not to think on green wool and what it might have to do with felonies, the more difficult I found it to put the missing fragment from my mind. So as Arthur, Uctred, and I traveled on from Stanton Harcourt to Bampton I thought of little else but the absent wisp of green wool.

Chapter 12

Caxton knew his stolen book the moment he laid eyes upon it and saw the stained pages. "What will you do with it?" I asked. "Bampton has no scholars eager to buy it."

"I suppose you could return to Oxford with it and sell it to some other stationer or bookseller," he replied. "But I'd realize small profit from it. You should keep it, as payment for my board here at Galen House."

I had read and studied Aristotle when at Balliol College, but had always rented the books I used. I had never thought to own a copy of RHETORIC, much as I might admire the philosopher. I was perhaps overeager to accept the offer.

Kate set to work preparing our dinner of stockfish in balloc broth whilst Caxton and I played with Bessie and John. I tossed Bessie into the air, a sport she dearly loves, until the little lass cackled with delight. My father-in-law had crafted a doll for Bessie from scraps of linen and wool and a bit of a broken beech tree branch come down beyond Bushey Row in a storm. Next, he said, he would make a cradle for the doll.

With the fish Kate also prepared sops in douce. The sun was well down toward Lord Gilbert's forest to the west of the castle when we finished our meal. Bessie was delighted to discover sops in douce and would have consumed the entire platter had her parents and grandfather not devoured their share before she could do so.

During the meal I told Kate how the green wool fragment had gone missing. I shared with her my thoughts about its origin and loss, wondering if the wisp might have aught to do with the death of Hubert Shillside. I will not share these speculations here, as most were far from the mark. One, however, was not. 'Tis a pity I considered that conjecture least likely of the possibilities before me, so did not act upon it until all other likely explanations were found unsatisfactory.

It is our custom, Kate and I, to move a bench to the toft as the sun is setting, there to enjoy the last of its warmth as we converse upon sundry matters. When my father-in-law joined the household we continued the practice, including him. The bench is long enough for three.

Caxton and I sat placidly upon the bench whilst Kate put Bessie to bed and fed John. She joined us as the western sky was turning from a golden hue to pale pink.

"Is the Stanton Harcourt bailiff so inept that he would misplace evidence that might help untangle a felony?" Kate asked.

"Sir Thomas said he had threatened to dismiss the man many times for his incompetence."

"Think you the wool might have fallen from the chest when the bailiff fell and the chest flew from his hand?"

"We searched the rushes carefully and found nothing. Surprisingly, they had been recently renewed and were quite clean. We would have seen anything uncommon to a floor, I think."

"What of the lad?"

"Edmund? What of him?"

"You said he helped the bailiff to his feet," Kate said. "Might he have seen the wool and gathered it up before anyone knew 'twas gone from the chest?"

"Why would he do so? Besides, Oswald could not find the wool when he first opened the chest. It seems likely that the wisp was already missing."

"But if 'twas not, and his stumble was but a pretext – what then?"

"'Twould mean that Edmund and the bailiff are conspiring together to keep me from having the wool."

"But why would they do so?" Caxton said.

"Because," Kate said with a tone of resolution in her voice, "they do not wish the older brother's murderers to be found, and will put any obstacle they may in the path of the man who seems most likely to find the felons."

I had considered many reasons why Henry Harcourt might have been slain, but an envious younger brother had not been part of my conjecture.

"Has Sir Thomas any other sons?" Kate asked.

"Nay. Two daughters, I believe. One already wed, the other but a lass."

"But if Edmund was involved with men who took and slew his brother, why would the bailiff be party to his felony?"

"Bailiffs can be bribed," Kate said. "You have said so, many times."

"Any man may be bribed," Caxton said, "if he cares more for this world than the next, and many do, I think."

I could not argue the point. Bailiffs do have an unsavory reputation, and if Oswald was as grasping as most, then he might participate in, or ignore, a murder if 'twas in his interest to do so.

But the man had lost his position, or was soon to do so, for failing to discover the felons who had taken and slain Henry Harcourt. How, then, could he be involved in this murder and the disappearance of a woolen fragment if the business would cost him his post? Might a current loss become a future gain? If so, I could see no way to prove it.

Henry Harcourt's death was distracting me from seeking those who slew Hubert Shillside, and I must not allow this. Sir Thomas must govern his own manor, and if Oswald was unable or unwilling to serve Sir Thomas as the knight required, he could seek another, more competent bailiff. No doubt he was already doing so.

The sky faded from pink and yellow to grey and black. Our conversation faded with the sunlight as we considered the sinful nature of man. Such contemplations are not, for me, conducive to slumber but apparently the thought of evil does not affect my father-in-law as it does me. Or perhaps he had begun to consider more pleasant matters. He snorted, twitched, and nearly fell from his end of the bench as sleep overcame him.

"I am for bed," Kate said in response to her father's awakening start.

Caxton and I stood, stretched in agreement with Kate, and followed her through the door. I carried the bench to its accustomed place in the kitchen, then bolted the door before following my Kate up the stairs.

I tried to make ready for bed in silence but John must have the ears of an elephant. He awoke, evidently decided to turn his wakefulness to some useful purpose, and demanded to be fed. 'Twas too dark to see Kate roll her eyes, but I am sure she did so. I know my wife nearly as well as she knows me.

John awoke again some time well past midnight and when the lad awakens desiring nourishment, we all do. Not only does the babe possess a pair of sensitive ears, but he also can make himself heard from one end of Church View Street to the other when he wishes.

While John nursed I thought on our evening conversation. In the few times I had met Edmund Harcourt I had discerned no guile in him. The bailiff, on the other hand, I would not trust with a farthing. No doubt I am as predisposed to mistrust bailiffs as other folk, even though I am one.

When a man commits a felony its purpose is naturally to bring him some benefit. Why else would he do it? Unless to benefit a close friend or kinsman. Who will gain from Henry Harcourt's death? Edmund, surely. But what if Henry's death was inadvertent? Then the felons who seized him would have had the same purpose as those who slew Hubert Shillside and did hamsoken in so many places hereabouts. The love of money is the root of all evil, as the apostle teaches. Of course, not all who love money will resort to felony to obtain more of it. I, for one, do not disdain a few more shillings in my purse, but would not rob or slay another to get them.

Yet what if my fortunes turned and I saw Kate and Bessie and John facing want and starvation? Would I then hold fast to the Lord Christ's teachings? I pray that I will never be brought to such a pass, but if I am, that I will hold fast, be found true.

Kate arose early next morn, the first day of May. For two days she had gathered spring flowers, yellow broom and bluebell and meadow buttercup, which she now wove into garlands to dress the doors and lower windows of Galen House.

By the time I deserted our bed men were busy erecting the maypole where Broad Street and Bridge Street meet at the center of the village. Neither I nor my father-in-law was quick to devour our loaf and ale so as to observe the festivities. Pretty maids with blossoms woven through their tresses, dancing about the maypole, did not interest us as such an exhibition might have in years past. Why should it? I am wed to the most beauteous wife in the shire, and Caxton is at an age where he is become more interested in the next life than the charms of the present.

So by the time Kate, Bessie, John, I, and Kate's father made our way to the maypole a piper had already begun a tune and maids were dancing about, attracting the attention of young men – and some not so young. Courting season had begun.

Every resident of Bampton and the Weald joined the Mayday throng to encourage the dancers and welcome in the summer. Who, on such a morning, concerns himself with thoughts of thieves and murderers? I did not, but watched Bessie's eyes flash with delight as she sat upon my shoulders and observed the maidens swirl about the maypole in ever decreasing spirals.

Kate had once joined in the maypole dancing, but had now more mature responsibilities. Our dinner this day was one of these. So whilst I and her father remained with Bessie as the spellbound child watched the last of the dancers complete their circles, Kate took John and set out for Galen House. She had prepared a capon for roasting for our dinner, and wished to set the fowl to the flames.

Folk began to drift away to their dinners when the last dance was done, Robert Caxton and I among them. We had just turned from Rosemary Lane to Church View Street when I saw Kate, John cradled in her arms, running toward us. She would be unlikely to do so if she had glad tidings for me. I was, therefore, somewhat prepared for her report.

"Hamsoken," Kate gasped when she was but a few paces from us.

"Where?" I said. "Who?"

"Galen House – whilst we were watching the May dancers! My silver spoons are gone!" She looked distraught. "I don't know what else is taken. I came for you just as soon as I saw what had happened."

Galen House is of two stories, with glass windows upon the ground floor and walls there of bricks between posts and beams. The upper story walls are of wattle and daub, and the windows there of oiled skins. It is the house of a prosperous man, and its construction would proclaim it so, even to a passing stranger. If felons wished to rob a house while the village gave attention to the maypole, a glance would show any man Galen House offered greater gain than most in Bampton.

I hurried my pace in response to the unwelcome news, Bessie bouncing upon my shoulders and giggling as if my haste was great sport.

Kate had hurried to seek me without thinking to close our front door behind her. It stood open as I approached, Kate and her father hurrying in my wake. I lifted Bessie from my shoulders, gave her over to Kate, and plunged into my house.

I saw nothing amiss in the hall, but the kitchen was another matter. Broken glass littered the flags below the window, and the door to the toft was open. Some man had broken the window, climbed through, ransacked my home, then departed through the rear door, unseen. Or men. The breaking glass had not been heard, for the adjacent houses were empty, their occupants watching the dancers, and the laughter and shouts of those who encouraged the maids would have covered the sound.

Kate, standing in her kitchen and peering about at our loss, began to weep. I came near to doing so as well. I asked Caxton to comfort his daughter, then ran from Galen House to raise the hue and cry. I knocked on every door between Galen House and John Prudhomme's home, bidding those I roused to meet at Galen House. When they had assembled I divided those present into four groups to follow roads leading from Bampton. I held out little hope the thieves could be found, but if we made no effort it was sure they would not be.

Why I thought several felons were involved in my loss I could not at the time have said. But later, after taking inventory of what was missing, I became sure the theft had been the work of more than one man.

Six silver spoons were taken, two pots of bronze, a brass basin and ewer, and five pewter plates. Three knives were missing, and the chest in which I keep my instruments and physics. This is not a large chest, but one man could not carry it away and all the other goods as well. A ham which Kate had hanging from an overhead beam was gone also. The thieves would eat well this day.

And Aristotle's RHETORIC was nowhere to be found.

I hurried to the stairs to learn what might have gone from the upper floor. Perhaps the felons had been frightened away before they could seek more booty, for I could discover nothing missing there. Even my fur coat, and my Bible, kept in an unlocked chest, were unmolested.

I tallied our loss; it would cost thirty-three shillings and four pence to replace all that was taken. The scalpels in my instruments chest were of finest steel, from Milan. Where I could find new to replace the stolen blades, I knew not. Likely not in Oxford. Perhaps in London the scalpels might be replaced. 'Twould be easier to find the felons and recover the loot.

What would thieves do with scalpels and needles and silken thread, a trephine, and a book? Probably sell them, after smashing open the locked chest to discover what within it might be so valuable that the goods were secured in such a box. Felons may attack their victims with blades of various sorts, but my scalpels would not suit for such villainy. No help for it, I must go back, yet again, to Oxford, there to search out as many surgeons as I could find. Should my instruments be offered for their purchase, they would be alerted to identify the seller and send word to me. Not only that, but I needed to seek out the stationers and booksellers as well.

I must go immediately, forestalling the danger of my instruments finding buyers before the surgeons of Oxford heard of the stolen goods. I wondered if they would care, even if they knew. Would a surgeon rather see justice done, or bag the chance of a fine Milanese scalpel for but a few pence?

"What are we to do, husband?" Kate sobbed when I came in from raising the alarm.

"We will do as other folk, until I find the felons and see our goods returned. We will eat from wooden trenchers and you will cook our pottage in a clay pot. For now, you must set the capon to roasting whilst I visit the castle."

"The castle?" Kate said. "Why so?"

I explained that my instruments, and the herbs and physics which were also in the chest, would be of but small value to felons of themselves, but the money they could raise selling the implements would interest them mightily.

"Ah," she said. "And Oxford is where the villains will find surgeons and physicians to purchase your scalpels and such."

"Just so. And I cannot tarry. Arthur and Uctred must make ready to travel with me tomorrow. The rogues may already be on the way to Oxford to sell their wares."

How many times had I traveled to Oxford since spring dried the roads? I had no desire to count. Too many hours spent on a palfrey's back, and to no useful purpose. Would this new journey to Oxford prove any more profitable than the others? Only if I made haste, for the thieves would not tarry over their unlawful trade, but would exchange their loot for coins with all dispatch.

While the capon roasted upon the spit I set off for the castle. There I found Arthur in the hall at his dinner, licking his fingers in appreciation of roasted pork and maslin loaves. Lord Gilbert at the head table glanced my way, but paid me no more attention; his guest, Sir Bogo Loring, was speaking in his ear.

"We are robbed," I said to Arthur.

"Who?" He looked up at me in astonished indignation.

"Kate and I – Galen House. This morn, while we all attended the maypole, men broke in."

Arthur kicked back the bench, upsetting Uctred and Kendrick, his companions at dinner. The racket caused Lord Gilbert to break off his conversation and glare at the cause of the uproar.

"Are the villains flown?" Arthur asked. "We must saddle some beasts and be after them. What has been taken?"

"Sit you down and finish your dinner," I said. "I have raised the hue and cry, but no man has seen strangers about Bampton, or men carrying away loot. The felons have got away, but tomorrow we will seek them in Oxford."

"Oxford? You think the rogues hail from there? What of Walter Mapes? Folk do say he stole from Alain Gower."

"Besides our platters and spoons and such, the thieves made off with my instruments chest and a book. They will have little use for the instruments but to sell them, and where might they sell a book but Oxford?"

"Oh, aye. They won't find buyers of stuff like that hereabouts."

"Have two palfreys ready tomorrow at first light. We may catch the felons if we can get to Oxford's physicians and surgeons and stationers before they can dispose of their loot."

"Three palfreys," Arthur said. "Uctred will want to see this business concluded, an' if there be three or four culprits about, an extra dagger will be useful." He looked at me thoughtfully. "You think the villains who robbed Galen House might be the same who stole from Alain Gower an' slew Hubert Shillside an' Henry Harcourt? Otherwise there's an awful lot of wickedness about all of a sudden. Seems odd to me that, out of a clear blue sky, folk between here an' Oxford would find the shire swarming with thieves an' murderers."

"I take your point. As for Walter Mapes, I will enquire among the folk from the Weald if he was seen this morning watching at the maypole."

He was, and with his sons.

The kitchen window, its glass panes mostly smashed, lay open to any who might wish to crawl through. I would not leave my Kate alone in such a circumstance for fear the felons might decide to return and resume their plunder of Galen House. For some reason they had neglected to pillage the upper story. If, when they broke open my locked chest, they understood the worth of what I owned, they might reappear to complete their thievery, hoping for yet more goods of value to glean.

I went first to Simon Carpenter and procured from him three sawn boards, each long enough to attach across the window frame. Then from Edmund, Bampton's malodorous smith, I purchased twelve iron nails and borrowed a hammer. I nailed the boards across the broken panes, each a hand's width from another so that some light could enter through the boarded window, but yet close enough that no man, nor even a child, could pass between them and gain entry.

A man with an iron bar could pry the nails loose, of course, but not silently. I made plain to Kate that, while I was away in Oxford, if she heard anything amiss in the night she should push open an upper window and shriek out a cry for help. Neighbors would hear and come to her aid. Even if they did not, any rogues trying to prize the oaken boards from the window would surely be frightened away by the screeching.

The capon was roasted and our meal ready when I finished securing the window. We ate in silence, apart from the occasional forlorn sniff from Kate. Even Bessie, who is usually voluble at table, was mute. The boarded window brooded over us, extinguishing conversation.

When nothing remained on our table but capon bones and the crumbs of the maslin loaves we had used as trenchers, my father-in-law rose from his bench and left the kitchen. I heard him stirring about in his chamber and a few moments later he reappeared dragging his straw pallet, wrested from his bed.

Caxton hauled the pallet to the boarded window and laid it out beneath the opening. He then turned to the hearth and took from its place our iron poker. This he laid beside the pallet.

"If any man comes through that window in the night he must pass by me," Caxton said. "My ears be not so good as in past days, nor my arm so strong, but if any man awakens me in the night he will find me yet stout enough to deliver him a blow."

I believed him. My father-in-law was no longer the frail creature we brought home from Oxford. Kate's cookery was adding to his flesh and color daily, and the man I had thought ready for St. Beornwald's churchyard now seemed likely to pass through the lych gate on his feet for many more years before he needed a bier to bear him.

Chapter 13

Arthur is a reliable assistant. He and Uctred appeared before Galen House as the morning sun first illuminated the spire of St. Beornwald's Church and the saints adorning its buttresses.

We hurried the castle palfreys, which they likely did not appreciate, and entered Oxford shortly after the third hour of the day. I knew the location of several of Oxford's surgeons, and from them learned of two surgeons new to the city.

In passing from one surgeon's establishment to another we passed the Black Boar, where we took our dinner, a stew of pilchards, the day being a fast day.

By the ninth hour we had visited all the surgeons of Oxford. None had yet been offered my instruments, but I was confident some of them soon would be. I promised each two shillings if they would send a lad to Bampton with news if scalpels and forceps and cannulae and such were offered to them at bargain prices. All agreed to do so. Some may have meant it.

The last surgeon we visited was found on Fish Street near St. Michael at the Southgate, so 'twas but a short way to Canterbury Hall and Master Wycliffe. He had not yet sold any of my father-in-law's set books, and was incensed to learn that RHETORIC had been stolen again.

"'Tis as evil to steal a man's book as to steal his wife," the scholar said. This was a sentiment I had heard him express on a previous occasion. As Wycliffe had no wife he can be forgiven his error.

"A book can comfort a man as well as any wife," he explained.

"Not upon a cold winter eve," I said.

Wycliffe was silent for a moment. "Well, you would know more of that than I," he said softly.

"From Kate I learned the comfort of a loving wife. From you I learned the pleasure and comfort which a book may provide. I have discovered the best of two worlds.

"When I last visited you, you told me you had purchased two gatherings from a poor scholar," I said.

"Aye. Wore a ragged gown."

"Was the lad scrawny from lack of food? Do you remember any features to identify him? Had he a mole upon his face?"

"Hmmm. For all his tatters he seemed healthy enough. Had a mole above his cheek, as I remember."

"The same lad sold RHETORIC to the monks of Eynsham Abbey some weeks past," I said. "The mole confirms it!"

On our way to Bookbinder's Bridge, and the road to Osney Abbey and home, we passed two stationers and a bookseller whose shops I had not previously visited. I halted briefly at each establishment, begging the proprietors to be on the lookout for any man trying to sell a copy of RHETORIC with ale-stained pages. These burghers all knew Robert Caxton and, although they had been competitors, frowned to learn of his loss and mine, agreeing to send word to Bampton if the book was offered to them. I believed they would do so.

I had done all that I could in Oxford this day to recover my stolen goods. As so many times in the past weeks, we three hastened to Eynsham to once again seek shelter and a meal at the abbey guest house.

Fifty paces or so beyond the Swinford river crossing, with the spire of the abbey church in view, I happened to glance toward the verge and caught from the corner of my eye a gleam, as of the rays of the setting sun reflecting from some polished thing. A flash only, then the glint was gone.

I was eager to reach the abbey, but curious as to what might have caught my eye. I drew my palfrey to a halt, dismounted, and passed the reins to Uctred. He and Arthur looked on as I approached the place where I had seen the brief gleam.

This discovery was fortunate. Had I turned my head another way, or had we passed the place a few minutes earlier or later so that the sun reflected differently, I would never have seen the object which now lay at my feet. Was this coincidence, or did the Lord Christ direct my gaze? Who can know? I will put the puzzle in my mystery bag, and ask the Savior when I meet Him in the next life.

The polished blade of a scalpel lay in the grass. Was this one of my stolen instruments? If it was not, why else would such a blade be discarded along a road?

The scalpel was of excellent quality, possibly Milanese, as were mine. I held the blade before me, the better to examine it in the fading light.

"That yours?" Arthur asked when he saw what I held.

"I can't be entirely sure. 'Tis much like one of mine. I had four in my chest: one small, one large, and two of middling sort. This is the right size to be one of my middle blades."

Arthur dismounted, handing the reins of his beast to Uctred, and strode across for a closer look. After examining the blade he glanced to the grassy verge where it had lain.

"Ho... what is there?" he said, and bent to pick up an object which had caught his eye. I did not at first see the thing, as Arthur's broad back was between me and the item which had drawn his attention.

Arthur turned and held before me a splinter of dark-stained oak. This fragment was slightly longer than my hand, and at one end was broken. At this fracture there were indications of two holes bored through the wood, at which place the oak had snapped due to the weakness there.

"What d'you suppose this is?" Arthur said.

I knew what it was. "'Tis a piece of my instruments chest. And this," I said, lifting the scalpel, "has fallen from the broken chest. See there, where rivets once pierced the oak and fastened hinges to the top."

Arthur examined the find, then spoke. "If them rogues smashed your chest 'ere, where's the rest of it?"

The answer to that came quickly enough. We found what remained of my chest in a tangle of primroses growing wild beside the road, their flowers now nearly gone as spring was well begun.

A rock, the size of both Arthur's fists placed together, lay near the shattered remains of my instruments chest. Here was the tool used to smash open the box. Were the felons disappointed when they learned its contents?

We found no more of my instruments, but scattered about the verge and the patch of primroses were my pouches of herbs and physics. None of these remedies were missing, although Arthur and I searched diligently through the primroses before we found all.

"Why d'you think them knaves chose this place to smash open your chest?" Arthur asked.

I looked to the river, high and flowing fast from spring rains, and replied.

"The men who did this felony were on foot, and did not wish to carry a chest across the ford, so they broke it open here to learn what of value they had. Had they been mounted, the river would have presented no great obstacle, I think."

The hinges, hasp, and lock had suffered only small damage. I collected them and placed them in the bag I had attached to my saddle that morning in hope of this day retrieving my instruments. Simon Carpenter could use the metal to construct a new chest.

When our searching produced nothing more, we mounted the beasts Uctred had been patiently minding, and proceeded the half-mile to Eynsham Abbey.

We had approached the abbey gatehouse so often in the past fortnight that the porter seemed to expect us, and bid us enter with a wave of his hand. His assistant glanced our way and set off for the guest master and some lay brothers to care for our beasts. All this happened with scarcely a word spoken.

I took the bag from my palfrey's saddle before the animal was led to the abbey stables. As I did so Brother Watkin appeared, and he spoke when he drew near.

"Ah, Master Hugh. Abbot Gerleys will be glad to know that you are back with us again. He has news."

I wondered what this news could be. It did not take long to learn.

Now the days were longer as the year drew near its height, the monks of Eynsham Abbey were permitted a second meal before darkness drew them to their beds after Compline. I heard the prior strike the tabula, calling the monks to the refectory for what would likely be a light supper of barley loaves, with perhaps some cheese, and ale.

Abbot Gerleys appeared at the door of the guest house as the thumping upon the tabula ceased. Behind him two lay brothers appeared with our supper: a basket of smoked herring, wheaten loaves, and a ewer of ale.

We stood when the abbot entered, but he gestured us to resume our seats and bade us begin our meal. "You will remember that I spoke of a man gone missing from Wytham a fortnight and more past?" he began, sitting down at the table with us as we broke the bread.

"Aye. Taking a cartload of barley to Abingdon, was he not?"

"He was. Did so often. He supplied some of the ale wives of the town, so I'm told. He has been found."

The abbot's tone caused me to think the worst. "Dead?" I asked.

"Aye. Corpse found along the road near to Botley."

"The cart and horse and barley?" I said.

"Nothing found but the corpse. He was set upon, slain, and his chattels taken."

"How was he found?"

"A traveler saw carrion crows rise from the brushy verge of the road as he approached and thought to seek the reason for their interest."

"No doubt others, less inquisitive, had passed by and seen the same birds," I said, "but were not curious enough as to the cause to investigate. Is it sure the corpse was the man from Wytham?"

"It is. His wife knew his garb."

"His garb? Not his face?"

"The man had lain there dead for some weeks. Crows and worms had left little but his bones."

"And no man saw the felons at this evil deed?"

"Nay. The corpse was found half a mile north of the town, where the road passes through a copse."

"No men tending their fields near to such a place," I said, "and the felons could lie in wait for a prosperous traveler, unseen by their victim until they were upon him."

"Just so. Will you have more herrings and ale?"

Arthur took that moment to belch approval of the meal and I took this to mean we had eaten our fill. Perhaps I was mistaken. Arthur glanced reprovingly at me as I told Abbot Gerleys we were sated.

"But what brings you to Eynsham Abbey this time?" the abbot asked. "Do you yet seek those who slew your coroner?"

"I do, but this journey is because of my own loss."

I explained the Mayday thefts at Galen House, my search through Oxford for surgeons who might be approached to purchase my instruments, and the discovery an hour earlier of my shattered chest and overlooked scalpel. When I concluded the account – during which the abbot had assumed a thoughtful expression – he spoke.

"Did you have within your chest a trephine?"

"Aye, I did." The question puzzled me.

"Yesterday, shortly before vespers, a man appeared at the gate and showed the porter an instrument which he wished to sell to our infirmarer."

"This was a trephine?"

"It was. Brother Guibert declined. Said he had no skill to use such a thing, and the fellow went on his way. Odd that the abbey would be offered a stolen book and later a stolen surgical tool... if stolen it was."

"Did the fellow say why he had a trephine he wished to sell?"

"We must ask Brother Guibert. Maurice!" Abbot Gerleys called for the monk attending him who had remained outside the door to the guest chamber. The man's head immediately appeared.

"Fetch Brother Guibert. Quickly now."

The face disappeared and the sound of hurrying footsteps followed, then faded.

I asked if there were more reports of hamsoken in the neighboring villages.

"Nay. None have been reported to us. If any abbey possessions had been plundered I would surely have heard of it, although of course other holdings might suffer attack and we here at the abbey not know of it."

Brother Guibert must have been found at his supper. As he entered the guest chamber I saw his cheeks flex as his tongue sought fragments of his meal caught betwixt cheeks and jaw.

"Ah," Abbot Gerleys said, speaking to his infirmarer. "You will remember Master Hugh."

Brother Guibert surely would, as our last encounter was not altogether pleasant. The infirmarer nodded agreement and bowed to me.

"Yesterday a man appeared just before vespers with an instrument he wished to sell," the abbot said. "What can you tell Master Hugh of the man and the tool?"

"The man? Young, he was. And did not know what he possessed."

"The instrument he wished to sell? He did not know what it was?" Abbot Gerleys said.

"Knew it was for surgery of some sort, and as it was circular, the fellow had a notion of what he had, but didn't know of a certainty."

"What did he wear?" I asked. "Was he garbed in a scholar's gown, or did he wear layman's clothes?"

"Wore a green cotehardie, a blue cap with long liripipe, and particolored chauces. He was no pauper, nor scholar either."

"Did the fellow say how he came by the trephine, and why he offered it for a price?"

"Said as how he found it along the road near to Eynsham, had no use for such a thing, and thought the abbey infirmarer – meaning me – might wish to have it. So he said.

"But I have no skill in surgery, and told the man I had no use for the instrument. I am an infirmarer and herbalist. I am no surgeon. I have no desire to open a man's head, nor any other part of his anatomy."

"Did the fellow seem disappointed that you refused his offer?" I asked.

"Nay. Shrugged his shoulders and went his way."

"Which way was that? Toward Oxford, or to the west?"

"To Oxford. I watched him go. Traveled alone, and I thought as he set off that he'd best step lively or he'd be caught on the road when darkness came and be well short of his destination, if Oxford was his goal. Of course, he could seek lodging at Osney Abbey. Might get there before nightfall."

A man from someplace far from Oxford might not know of the felonies done upon the roads hereabouts, and so travel alone without understanding his peril. But even without the recent attacks near to Oxford most men prefer to travel with others for mutual protection. Did this traveler know that he had no need to fear villains upon the road? Did companions in treachery wait for him a few hundred paces from the abbey gate?

"What of the green cotehardie? Did it have a yellowish tint, or was it of forest green?" I asked Brother Guibert.

The infirmarer rubbed his chin, then answered. "Yellowish green, it was. Much weld with the woad."

Was this the same cotehardie which had left wisps of wool upon the rough bark of an oak at Stanton Harcourt? Or was it coincidence that a man wearing such a garment had found my trephine, if mine it was? Did the thieves who made off with my chest, then smashed it along the road, overlook two of my instruments after they broke apart the chest? A trephine is larger than a scalpel, but if my instruments were scattered when the chest burst open, men, especially were they hurried, might not see the tool.

Conversely, a traveler along the road might easily overlook a scalpel, small as it is. But for the reflection of the setting sun I would likely not have noticed the blade. A trephine is larger, more easily seen if abandoned along a road.

These thoughts echoed through my mind as my head rested upon a guest chamber pillow that night. I must seek the lost wisp of green wool which the Stanton Harcourt bailiff had mislaid. If I could find it, and if Brother Guibert could identify the strands as similar in tint to the garment worn by the man who had offered the trephine, such congruence might mean the same man was involved in the death of Henry Harcourt and the theft from Galen House. Did he also slay Hubert Shillside?

Chapter 14

Tiny bits of green wool suffused my dreams that night. And also my thoughts next morning as we broke our fast with loaves from the abbey oven. Kate's suggestion that Henry Harcourt's death would profit his younger brother, and that Oswald's tumble might have allowed the transfer of the green woolen fragment from the bailiff's chest to Edmund, seemed less far-fetched the more I considered it. But how might I discover if such an exchange had occurred?

If this did happen before my eyes, and before Sir Thomas's, it would mean Edmund and Oswald were both determined no one could identify him who had leaned against an oak and sent a ransom demand to Sir Thomas.

I shared these thoughts with Arthur and Uctred as our beasts carried us from Eynsham toward Stanton Harcourt.

"How badly does Sir Thomas want to discover them as slew 'is lad?" Arthur asked pensively. "Bad enough to maybe see 'is younger son hang for doin' away with the older? He'd have no heir remainin' but for daughters."

Here was a new thought. If Edmund had to do with Henry's seizure and death, would Sir Thomas prefer not to know? Ignorance might sometimes be a comfort to those who must act upon knowledge.

Plowing and planting was nearly concluded, so men found other occupations this day. We passed folk at work repairing fences, cleaning ditches, and mending houses and barns from winter's ravages. Some of these took the opportunity of our passage to rest from their labor and lean on mattocks and spades to examine us as we passed.

An hour after departing the abbey we came to Stanton Harcourt. At the edge of the village five men were at work trimming back an overgrown hedge enclosing a field newly sown to oats. Edmund was one of the five, supervising the labor of others, as if these men needed a beardless lad to teach them how to cut back a hedge.

As we entered the village I saw Oswald leave his house. He seemed at first on his way to the manor house, or perhaps the church. But he glanced in our direction, hesitated, then turned to us. I thought he intended to hail us. Perhaps he had found the missing wool.

Not so. The rotund fellow hastened past. He nodded a greeting as if his haste was too great to dally in our company.

Arthur, Uctred, and I halted our palfreys at Sir Thomas's residence, and when his servant answered my rapping upon the door I asked for the lord of the manor.

"Ah, Master Hugh," Sir Thomas greeted me. "My aching jaw is well healed. Much thanks to you."

"I am pleased, but 'tis not your health which brings me here this day."

"You wish to know if Oswald has discovered the felons who slew Henry, then? Alas, he has not, and I expected no better."

"It is of that I wish to speak to you."

"You have learned who the villains are?" Sir Thomas said, his features brightening.

"Nay, but I have a request to make of you in that regard."

"Then come in, for you are most welcome. Walchin, take Master Hugh's men to the kitchen and fetch them ale. And two cups for us, in the hall."

Sir Thomas led me to his hall, the ale arrived, and I told him of the theft at Galen House as we refreshed ourselves.

"And now you are homeward bound from Oxford, with scalpel, hinges, hasp, and herbs," Sir Thomas said when I concluded my tale.

"I have been fortunate to recover some of what was taken. Perhaps my luck will continue, or improve, if the rogues try to sell instruments to some honest Oxford surgeon or stationer who will then seek me and point to the thieves."

"And so you visit Stanton Harcourt, seeking my aid? How can I be of service to you in such a loss?"

"Nay. My purpose here is of another matter. I am puzzled about the disappearance of the green wisp of wool which I plucked from the oak. Your bailiff claims he last saw it in a chest which lay upon a cupboard table, and has no notion of where it now may be, or why it is missing."

"Your tone speaks beyond your words," Sir Thomas said. "I saw the chest. He spoke true. The threads were not there."

"Aye. I saw this also. This was after he fell and the chest emptied its contents into the rushes."

"You think the wool may yet be hidden in the rushes of Oswald's house?"

"Mayhap, but I doubt it so. We do not know if the wool was in the chest before he tripped."

"He said not."

"So he did. But you have said that he failed in the past to discharge his duties as you wished. Can you believe all that he says?"

Sir Thomas was silent for a moment. When he spoke it was slowly, his words chosen carefully.

"If the green wisps were in his chest before he tumbled and dropped it to the rushes, but were no longer there when he offered the chest to me to examine, someone must have plucked the threads from the rushes, or they are yet there. Only you and Edmund searched through the rushes for the contents of the box, to replace them within. We will go to the bailiff's house and search the rushes again. I pray we will discover the wool."

Arthur and Uctred appeared from the kitchen as Sir Thomas stood and I motioned them to follow. We passed the village well in silence, Arthur and Uctred surely curious as to our destination but confident that patience would reveal all.

Sir Thomas rapped vigorously upon the bailiff's door. More vigorously than need be to rouse the man. There was choler in the blows, and I thought as his fist struck the door that his knuckles would be tender on the morrow.

"I saw Oswald leave the house as we came to the village not an hour past," I said. "Mayhap he has not returned."

Sir Thomas turned from the door to me, seemed to consider some matter, then lifted the latch and pushed open the door.

"'Tis my house," he explained. "I'll visit it when I will."

He left the door open the better to see the place where Oswald's chest had emptied its contents into the rushes. The place was less than two paces from the threshold, so sunlight bathed the rushes with light. If some trace of green wool had been overlooked three days past and yet remained we would surely find it.

We did not. The four of us, upon hands and knees, sought some greenish tint, our noses a hand's breadth from the rushes as we sorted through the stems. Sir Thomas sighed and stood, signaling the end of the search and its failure.

"Which way did Oswald travel when you saw him last?" Sir Thomas asked.

I pointed to the north edge of the village, where the road curved beyond the last house and disappeared from our view. "He seemed hurried," I said.

"Oswald? Hurried? Some calamity must be upon him. The man does nothing more swiftly than need be."

"He must have felt some need," I said. "Perhaps he had some message for Edmund."

Sir Thomas gazed at the place where the road to Eynsham disappeared beyond a house. The hedges being trimmed were no more than two hundred paces farther.

"We shall see," Sir Thomas said, and strode off in the direction his bailiff had taken.

As we passed the last house and the road straightened before us we saw Oswald returning to the village. His pace was slower than when he had departed the place. Whatever urgent matter had propelled his rotund form away from the village it seemed no longer pressing. In the distance Edmund and his companions were yet at work at the hedges, moving farther from the village as they neared the end of their toil. The tenants were at work, I should say. Edmund stood near the road staring in our direction, hands on hips. He was too far distant to read his expression, but his posture indicated displeasure. I was feeling a bit petulant myself. Few things in my life had gone well in the past weeks, and many had gone awry.

Oswald evidently felt a need to explain his departure from and return to the village.

"Seein' to the hedgin'," he said when he drew near.

"What? You think Edmund incapable of the task?" Sir Thomas said.

"Nay. Just seein' to my duty."

"Your duty 'til Whitsuntide," Sir Thomas growled. He fixed the bailiff firmly with his fierce eye. "I don't suppose you've found the green woolen threads you mislaid?"

"Nay. Completely disappeared. I kept an eye out, too."

"Continue to do so – until Whitsuntide."

"Whitsuntide, aye." And with that reply Oswald scurried off toward the village, if a man weighing twenty stone or near so can be said to scurry anyplace.

Sir Thomas cast one last glance to his son and tenants, and I saw the lad turn from his father's gaze and interest himself in the hedging. There was a message in the brief meeting of their eyes, but I could not discern what it might be. Likely something to do with the incompetent bailiff and his coming departure from Stanton Harcourt.

Sir Thomas turned and stalked after Oswald. Arthur, Uctred, and I followed. Sir Thomas seemed not in a conversational mood, so I held my tongue. I had little to say, anyway. Whether or not the man would challenge his son on his part in the evaporation of the green woolen threads was for Sir Thomas to decide, not me.

And what if the youth denied any involvement? Would Sir Thomas believe him? Likely. I had seen no reason to mistrust Edmund on the few occasions I had met him. Oswald knew more of the missing threads than he would admit. Of this I felt entirely sure. What, then? Demand of the man that he permit a search of his house? I could not insist upon such an inquiry, but Sir Thomas could.

Oswald cast us a passing glance as he ducked into his house. Was his expression that of a man soon to lose his position, or of a man worried that what he wished to hide might be made known?

I increased my pace and drew even with Sir Thomas. "Have you considered an examination of Oswald's lodgings?" I asked. "There is some reason we do not have that wisp of wool, and Oswald, for all his protests otherwise, may know what it is."

"Oswald's been incompetent, but I've not known him to lie to me."

"Is that because he has not, or because he is proficient at it?"

Sir Thomas was silent, then stopped in the street, studied first me, then the bailiff's house, and said, "Have you time to assist in a search?"

"Aye. 'Tis not a great house."

We found nothing. Sir Thomas assigned us each a chamber, and Oswald stood red-faced, arms crossed, whilst we examined his cupboard, his pots and pans, the chest in his sleeping chamber, and sought loose boards and fissures where a bit of fabric might be hidden. Perhaps, I thought, the bailiff had simply discarded it, or set it to blaze upon his hearth fire.

Whatever the reason for the missing wool Oswald now knew we mistrusted his explanation for its disappearance, which was really no explanation at all. Did he expect us to believe some miscreant had learned the fragment was in his possession, crept into the house, and made off with it? Could that have happened? How would such a knave know the bailiff's chest held the incriminating object?

Edmund and Sir Thomas's tenants returned to the village for their dinner as we left the bailiff's house. We joined them, and Sir Thomas invited me to take the meal with him in his modest hall. His chamberlain frowned briefly when told of the additional guests, but quickly made a place for me with Sir Thomas, his wife, Edmund, and a daughter at the high table, setting places for Arthur and Uctred among the grooms and pages.

'Twas a fast day, so no flesh nor fowl was served. The first remove was stewed herrings, the second a pottage of peas and beans, and the third remove was a dish of eels in bruit with manchets. For the void we were served apples and pears with honey and ginger and wafers with hippocras.

From the corner of my eye I observed my companions at the high table. None seemed to have much appetite, although the various removes seemed to me well prepared and savory.

I was seated beside Edmund, and the lad seemed to lack conversation as well as appetite. My efforts to begin discourse met with little success. He answered my questions as shortly as courtesy allowed, and of opinions he offered none.

I thanked Sir Thomas for the meal, bid him and Edmund "Good day," and with Arthur and Uctred mounted our beasts and set off for Bampton. I turned to look back some way from the village and saw two men afoot following upon the road, but thought no more of them as our beasts soon outdistanced the walkers.

Where Church View Street meets Bridge Street I dismounted and sent my palfrey to the castle with Arthur and Uctred whilst I walked north to Galen House. An hour after I passed through my door there came a knocking upon the doorpost. The two men I had seen leaving Stanton Harcourt stood before me. I recognized them by their garb, for when I saw them leaving Sir Thomas's manor they were too distant to identify faces.

"You are Master Hugh de Singleton?" one asked.

"Aye. How may I serve you?"

"'Tis we who do you service. We come from Master Wycliffe at Queen's Hall."

"Queen's? He is master at Canterbury Hall."

"No longer. He is replaced. A monk now serves in his position."

I knew something of the controversy raging in Canterbury Hall. The hall was founded ten years before as a place where monks and secular scholars might mingle, test, and learn from one another. This blending had not been successful. Monks protested when the master of the hall was a secular, and secular scholars objected when a monk was placed over them.

"What brings you to Bampton?"

"Master Wycliffe has seen your book."

"RHETORIC?"

"Aye, the book stolen from you."

"Master John is sure 'tis mine?"

"Aye. It bears the ale-stained pages you spoke of."

"Did a scholar attempt to sell him the book?"

"Not him. A monk of Canterbury Hall has bought it. He bragged to Master Wycliffe of his bargain. Cost but twelve shillings, the monk boasted, because a few pages were stained.

"Master Wycliffe told him that the book was stolen but a day before, but the monk will not give it up."

"When does Master John take a room at Queen's?"

"He has done so this day. We moved his chattels this morning, then set off at his command to tell you of your book."

All this time I had forgotten hospitality with hearing of the discovery of my stolen book. I remembered my obligation and invited the fellows to take refreshment. Kate had prepared a pease pottage in a new pot, which, I discovered, my father-in-law had purchased in Witney. This we served our guests along with maslin loaves and ale. After dining at Stanton Harcourt I had little appetite. That Caxton had walked all the way to Witney and returned with a heavy pot indicated the speed of his recovery from the frailty of his former self.

"Did the monk who purchased my book speak of the man who sold it to him?"

"Master Wycliffe asked. A poor scholar, the monk said, meanly garbed, his gown tattered and threadbare, his cheeks in need of shaving and his locks unkempt."

"Had the scholar any other features which might aid in discovering him? What color was his hair?"

One of the men shrugged and grimaced in indication of his ignorance. But the other said: "Master Wycliffe asked the same of the monk, who remembered the lad who sold him RHETORIC had a mole upon his temple, betwixt eye and ear."

The same man had stolen RHETORIC twice! Once from

Robert Caxton and once from me. It must be so. How many young scholars will have a mole upon their temple? Did the fellow know he had stolen and sold the same book twice? Had he turned over the pages and seen the stain?

It was sure also that the supposedly impoverished scholar did not leave Oxford, as he had told Brother Matthew he must, but had returned. Should I do so also, and prowl the lanes and streets of Oxford seeking a scholar with a mole upon his left temple? I dismissed the thought. There must be a way to find the lad if he had returned to the town.

And the miscreant had not entered Galen House alone, of this I was sure. I might discover the thief who had twice stolen RHETORIC but fail to find his felonious companions.

Master Wycliffe's servants had walked far this day. I would not send them back to Oxford without rest. I went to Father Thomas to borrow two straw pallets for the night, and shortly after my request his clerks arrived at Galen House with them.

Kate had purchased a pint of honey from Gerard, Lord Gilbert's verderer, so our supper that evening was maslin loaves with honey butter. Such a repast nearly made a fast day pleasurable.

Next morn at dawn Master John's servants set off for Oxford. I sent them off with maslin loaves and three pence each for their trouble. Kate, her father, and I did not break our fast before mass, as is the custom on Sunday, but men who must walk sixteen miles should not do so on an empty stomach.

Father Simon's words failed to hold my attention that day – though, I have to confess, even with no pressing matters to distract me, I do sometimes find my mind wandering in Father Simon's homilies. I caught Will Shillside's glance as we departed the church porch and thought I discerned reproach. I had not discovered who had slain his father and he likely despaired of my ever doing so. When dark thoughts overcame me in the night I felt the same.

Kate had prepared capon in kyrtyn for our dinner that day. The meal drove all gloom and despondency far from me. At the ninth hour Arthur and others of Lord Gilbert's grooms had the butts in place beside Bampton Castle moat, and 'til nearly sunset men of Bampton and the Weald loosed arrows in practice and competition. Will Shillside took part as, of course, the king required him to do, and I noted the fellow was waxing adept with a bow. I tried to avoid his gaze, for failing to do so caused self-reproach to start up again.

Lord Gilbert and his guests were present for the competition, so it was his privilege to award the six pence prize money to Bampton's most skillful archers. He did so with a grin upon his broad, ruddy face, which it pleased me to see. Since Lady Petronilla's death his smiles have been rare. Perhaps it was less worthy of me to also feel glad Walter Mapes won no penny from Lord Gilbert this day.

As the archery competition drew to a close ominous clouds appeared in the western sky, and folk hastened home from the castle forecourt to avoid the threatening downpour. The village streets filled with scurrying householders intent on reaching shelter before the rain fell. The throng included Walter Mapes – I saw him dash across the bridge over Shill Brook before leaving Bridge Street for the Weald. But he came from the village rather than the castle. This did not arouse my curiosity at the time, so many were hurrying hither and thither. I should have paid closer attention.

I had raised the hue and cry when I discovered hamsoken done to Galen House, so all folk of Bampton and the Weald knew of my loss. I suppose most must likewise have heard how the thieves gained entry. Few, however, knew of the precaution I had taken to secure the shattered window so that no others might use the same aperture to enter my house. But some did.

I had told my father-in-law that he need sleep under the boarded window no longer after I returned home, but could return his pallet to his chamber off our entrance hall. He refused, claiming my presence might not be enough to deter felons bent on mischief.

I countered his argument by pointing out that few homes in Bampton, and none in the Weald, had glass windows. Oiled skins sufficed, and could be sliced silently in the night to allow rogues entry into a sleeping house. Whereas the glass in those of our windows remaining intact would break with a crash, and the boards I'd nailed across our kitchen window could only be removed to the accompanying squeal of drawn nails. Such a racket in either case would surely arouse both him and me. Still, he would have none of it, and obstinately bedded down upon his straw mattress beneath the window as Kate and I, with Bessie and John, climbed the stairs to our chamber.

I am accustomed to being awakened in the night, as is the father of any infant – excepting those nobles and wealthy burghers who may employ nurses to care for their progeny in a distant wing of the house. But the din which roused me that night was not the result of John's squalling, nor was it a matter for Kate's attention rather than my own.

Imprecations I could not distinguish arose from the ground floor of Galen House, shouted loudly enough to awaken the quick and the dead of all Oxfordshire. It can only have been my somnolent state made the shouts and howls from below indecipherable to me.

Although I could make no sense of the uproar, I had wits enough to understand the noise could mean no good thing. I fumbled in the dark for my dagger, withdrew it from its sheath, and ran to the stairs in but kirtle and braes, as Kate shouted a question and Bessie and John woke up to add their own frightened howls to the din.

I stumbled down the stairs. 'Tis a wonder I did not impale myself upon my dagger, for I carried the weapon before me as if I expected to meet some assailant coming up as I descended.

Pausing momentarily in the darkness at the foot of the stairs, to ascertain whence originated all the uproar, I heard next a dull thud, as if a man had swung a staff against a sack of barley. A scream of torment followed this straightway. Then silence for perhaps the space of two heartbeats, then I heard another thump, followed by yet another howl.

All this din came from the kitchen, which space was as dark as a heretic's heart, or should have been, the single window to the room being boarded over and so allowing little moonlight or starlight to enter the room.

I hurried there as best I could with no candle lit, and saw the dim glow of a new moon where the darkened window should have been. Then, suddenly, the square of faint light was darkened. As I peered at the place I heard the sound of some man exerting himself, then the opaque rectangle of the window reappeared.

All this time I had been silent, attempting to discover what mayhem had come upon Galen House by what I could hear, which was loud but baffling, and what I could see, which was near to nothing. I finally found my voice.

"What man is here?" I shouted – to give warning as much as seek information.

"'Tis me," I heard my father-in-law say. "The rogue has fled."

"Rogue? What rogue?"

"Came through yon window, as you said could not be done."

"And fled? You are sure?"

"Aye, but not before I delivered two strokes with me poker. Caught the knave with both blows. He'll not soon return, I think."

Kate's cookery had indeed been marvelously restorative. Two weeks past Robert Caxton could hardly have lifted the fire-iron, much less laid it across another man's ribs or skull with enough vigor to compel a thief to abandon his nefarious scheme.

A few coals yet glowed dimly upon the hearth. I used one to light two cressets and in their flames examined first my father-in-law and then the window. Caxton was breathing heavily, but seemed otherwise sound. He assured me he had taken no blows, but to the contrary had delivered a few. He seemed exceedingly proud of the encounter, as might a man who thought his days of combat were well past, then discovers he has yet the strength to defend his own against a scoundrel.

In the light of the cressets I could see the boards I had nailed to the window frame were missing. I leaned through the opening and saw them on the ground below the window in the moonlight.

"Were you awakened when the nails were drawn from the boards?" I asked.

"Nay. My ears are not so good, but I'd still have heard that."

"As would I," Kate said. She appeared in her kitchen clutching John, Bessie trailing alongside fearfully, holding tight to the skirt of her mother's shift. "What has happened?"

"Some man tried to enter Galen House in the night, but your father has driven him away."

"I was awake in the night," Kate said, "awaiting John's wish to be fed, as is oft my custom, when I heard the clamor begin. I heard no squeak of nails drawn from wood, which I would have done, even over your snores."

I opened the door to the toft, took a cresset with me, and kneeled to inspect the boards. Each nail had been drawn so that but a tiny portion of the point remained visible. Just enough to hold the slats in place, but so little that with his hands a man might draw them from their position. Quietly.

Two paces from the scattered boards I saw what appeared to be the coppiced shoot of a beech or similar tree. This limb was longer than my arm and as thick, straight and smooth. It had not been there in the toft the previous day.

"How did you learn of the intruder?" I said to my father-in-law, "if the miscreant made no sound when he came through the window?"

"Stepped on me, didn't he. It was too dark to see me on my pallet 'neath the window, so when he put his foot against what he thought was the flags he trod upon my ribs. Gave us both a start."

"That's when the shouting began?"

"Indeed. Couldn't find my poker at first, dark as it was an' the poker black. And when I did get it in hand I wasn't sure where the fellow was. I just gave a good swing and must have caught him square. He let out a screech, and next I saw was the form of some man scrambling to the window. So I gave the fellow another stroke to hurry him on his way. That's when you came. You know the rest."

'Twas early morning, but not yet dawn, when this altercation occurred. The sliver of the moon gave enough light so I could see to replace the boards, and with a mallet drive the nails back into place, or nearly so. What good that might do I could not say, but I felt comforted knowing the boards were in place again. When had the nails been drawn so that the removal of the obstacle to felonious entry could be made silently? Perhaps, I thought, with all of the evil about the shire, I should invest in shutters for my windows.

We of Galen House, along with most residents of Church View Street, had attended the archery practice on Sunday. A man could easily linger anywhere along the streets between Galen House and the castle, watching to see if we all had passed by. He would know then that he might draw the nails without alarming me or Kate or my father-in-law.

But why not complete the deed and enter the house then? Was the felon unsure of our return? Would he rather enter a house knowing its inhabitants slept, or hoping so, than enter a place being uncertain of the owner's return? None of these conjectures discovered the truth, as I was to learn.

I could not contemplate taking my rest again, as my blood was up and a return to sleep would surely elude me. I urged Kate, however, to return to bed. She could accomplish nothing by keeping vigil for the remainder of the night, and she would sleep easy knowing I stayed on guard 'til the morning. A new mother must rest when she can, to renew her strength and provide for her babe.

Caxton and I sat together on a bench as Kate took our little ones back up. Our ewer caught my eye. Kate had filled it on Saturday with ale fresh-brewed by the baker's wife. I poured two cups full of the ale, and Caxton and I drank together in silence. A few moments later we consumed two more cups. The ale was well brewed, and Bampton's ale taster was honest and would not accept a bribe, so the brew was not watered. Kate would need to purchase more when came the new day.

Perhaps 'twas the ale, or the silence of the night, but I and my father-in-law began to drowse as dawn neared. The frenzy of conflict had faded. But had I returned to my bed I am certain I would have lain there awake, alert, staring at the ceiling beams. Somnolence at such times will only overtake me when I would remain awake. When I would sleep, I cannot.

So it was that I was swaying upon the bench when my father-in-law said, "Ho! What is there?"

The two cressets, along with the first light of dawn penetrating the crevices between the boards replaced over the window, had illuminated something on the flags which caught Caxton's eye. I watched sleepily as he rose from the bench, stepped toward his pallet, and bent to lift some object from the floor. His back was to me as he held the thing close to his eyes, then answered his own question.

"A tooth, by the saints! See here…" And he held the tooth before me. "I must've smitten the fellow across his mouth."

"Aye," I agreed. "If he lost a tooth to your blow he'll likely have torn and bloody lips, and perhaps other teeth loosened."

"I gave the fellow another blow as he darted for the window. Caught the rogue in the ribs I think. Too dark to know for certain."

"You did well. A man who has suffered bruised or broken ribs and a smashed mouth will not likely attempt hamsoken again at the place where he was wounded."

I heard John demanding his breakfast and moments later I heard Bessie's childish speech. Her words were indistinct, but no doubt she felt ready for her sops of bread and milk. My own stomach began to growl in response to these incentives.

How to discover the man who had entered Galen House in the night occupied my mind as I consumed a loaf to break my fast and drank my meager portion of the remaining ale in Kate's ewer. I need not have been so troubled about the matter. The culprit was soon identified.

Chapter 15

There came a rapping upon Galen House door as I consumed the last of my loaf and ale. I opened the door to see Father Thomas. I greeted the priest and invited him in. I could offer no ale. I hope he was not much disappointed.

"How may I serve you?" I said when Father Thomas had seated himself upon a bench.

"'Tis not me who needs your service," he said. "I am come from the Weald. Walter Mapes' lad summoned me an hour past. His father, he said, was injured and wished my attendance upon him."

"Injured? How so? What did Walter wish of you?"

"Before you came to Bampton I was often summoned when folk wounded themselves, or needed herbs to deal with some affliction. I have not your skills, so I am no longer called to minister to the injured or ailing."

"But you were asked to treat Walter Mapes this morn?"

"Aye. Too much ale last night, he said. Tried to cross Shill Brook near to his house, slipped, and fell headlong upon rocks. His face is bruised and bloody and his teeth askew. Complains of his ribs, as well."

"Why did he not cross the stream upon the bridge?"

"Who knows what a drunken man will do?" The priest shrugged. "I told Walter his injuries are beyond my competence. I told him I would send you to deal with his hurts."

"Was he pleased to hear you say so?"

"Nay. He did his best to dissuade me. Said you'd demand more coin than he could pay."

"You've treated men's injuries freely in the past?" I asked.

"Aye. Walter knows this, so sent for me. He is a poor man, and for all his faults and villainies is worthy of our care as one of God's creation."

"Aye, he is. But my instruments have been stolen and I have

not replaced them yet. I fear that I can do little to aid the man. Describe to me his wounds and I will see what I may find to deal with the hurts."

"He has lost a tooth, perhaps several, but I cannot be sure. His lips are so torn and bloody and swollen that an examination of his teeth is difficult. And he complains of his ribs. Says he cannot bend and that it pains him even to lay abed."

"Did you inspect his ribs? Could you see a bruise?"

"Aye. There is a place behind his right arm beginning to purple."

"Odd, don't you think, that he fell face-first upon a rock, but when he tumbled into the stream 'twas his back which also received an injury?"

"Hmmm," Father Thomas muttered and tugged at his beard. "Didn't consider that. Mayhap he fell twice, once damaging his ribs, another time doing injury to his face."

"Perhaps," I agreed. But I knew this explanation was not true.

From Kate's sewing chest I took her finest needle and a spool of flaxen thread. The needle was larger than I would have wished for the delicate work of stitching a man's lip, and flax is a poor substitute for silk in such a situation, but I had at the time little concern for Walter Mapes' comfort or future appearance. I was certain 'twas his tooth Caxton had found beside his pallet. As for the scoundrel's ribs, even if one or more was cracked, there was nothing to be done but allow time to mend the fracture.

I had no wine with which to bathe Mapes' torn lips, but as my pouches of herbs had been discarded and found, I could give Walter a thimble full of crushed hemp seeds to soften the pricks of the needle when I patched his face. He must provide the ale, for I had none.

For a moment I considered withholding the hemp seeds to let Mapes receive the full measure of pain for his misdeed. I do know the Lord Christ commanded us to do good to those who use us badly and not return evil for evil. But what man could swallow such medicine without a bellyache? The Lord Christ

164

would never have needed to be so firm in His commandment if it was going to come naturally. I managed to put down this upwelling resentment with a moment's struggle.

So I placed a rather large needle and the flaxen thread in a small box, which I carried in a leather pouch with the crushed hemp seeds, and set off for the Weald and Walter Mapes' hovel.

Father Thomas had told the man he would send me, so I was expected. The door stood open to the warm spring morning, and I saw the face of one of the sons peering through it. He saw me approach and turned away – to tell his father of my arrival, no doubt. The lad reappeared before I reached the door, tugged a forelock, and greeted me. His words and tone were pleasant, as well they might be to greet a man who could repair his father's mangled face.

And mangled it was. 'Twas too dark within the house to see well, but light enough to see how severe an injury my father-in-law's blow had done to Walter's face. His nose was askew and likely broken again, his upper lip torn in two places, swollen and hanging from a flap of skin. His beard was stiff with caked blood. Only one tooth was found on our kitchen floor, but it seemed to me that three or four at least were missing. Mapes' lower jaw hung open. I thought perhaps it might be broken. My father-in-law had delivered a cruel blow for a man so frail he looked near death but a fortnight ago.

Walter lay on a straw pallet and watched me as I examined his injuries. He did not speak, and I wondered if he could. Perhaps his tongue was also damaged. His lips were so swollen, and so much blood caked his mouth, that I could not tell if it was so. I wondered how a cup of ale with hemp seeds could pass those ruined lips.

I would need better light to see the work I must do to repair the man's wounds, so I told Mapes' two oldest lads to take their table out to the toft and then help their father out to lie upon it. They did so, but had to go slowly, Walter creeping along painfully, unable to suppress a groan as his ribs protested the move.

"You fell upon rocks in Shill Brook, Father Thomas said."

Mapes nodded, then grimaced. Pain is nature's way of telling a man he should desist from whatever is causing his discomfort. But speech, given the condition of the man's mouth, could hardly have brought him less torment than nodding.

"You lie," I said. "Last night you entered Galen House intent upon some felony. My father-in-law was alert to your entry and did this wounding with a poker from our hearth."

I thought Mapes about to shake his head, so continued, "Nay, do not deny it! We found one of your teeth upon the floor near the window you used for entry.

"What did you expect to gain from this felony? Do you not know that Galen House was plundered five days past? Much of value I owned has been already taken."

I waited for an answer, thought I would receive none, but then through mangled lips Mapes spoke. I could scarcely make out his words.

"Din't 'ant yer goods," he mumbled.

"If you do not wish to pass what remains of your life with a ruined face you will tell me why you came in the night to my house. I can patch you together, but I will not do so unless I find truth in you."

Mapes looked away, as if considering the bargain I had offered. He apparently found it acceptable.

"'In't inten' 'heft," he said.

"Theft? You didn't intend theft?"

"Aye."

"What, then? Why make preparation in the day, loosening the nails from the boards I placed over the broken window, if you did not intend to steal from me?"

"'Ad a clum wi' 'e. 'As gonna 'eat you 'ith it."

"Clum? Eat? Ah, the staff I found in my toft... a club. You came to Galen House with a club to... beat – to beat *me*?"

"Aye."

"Whatever for? What cause did I give you?"

"'Old 'olk I s'ole Alain's goo's. 'In't."

"You would enter my house and lay a club aside my skull

because you believe I told others that you are guilty of hamsoken? Not so. 'Tis others who have said so to me. Will you take a club to all those who think ill of you?"

I did not expect an answer to this question and received none. I wished to stitch up the man's wounds and see no more of him. If he had done hamsoken at Alain Gower's house I would leave the proof to the vicars of St. Beornwald's Church, whose business it was.

To the man's wife I said, "Bring me a cup of ale."

The woman disappeared into her hovel and returned with a wooden cup. One sniff told me that the ale had gone off, but freshness was not its purpose. I produced the crushed hemp seeds, poured them into the cup, stirred the mixture, then explained to Walter, his wife, and eldest son what I was about. The cup I gave to the woman, told the son to lift Walter upright, and watched as Walter groaned his way to a sitting position.

Much of the ale dribbled down Walter's chin and dropped from his bloody, unkempt whiskers. Perhaps half of the liquid passed his lips. That must suffice. I had no more crushed hemp seeds with me.

My experience with such palliatives is that they take effect about an hour after being consumed. I told this to Walter and said that I would return in good time to deal with his injury. Whilst he waited I wished to have words with Father Thomas and return to Galen House for my razor. I could not mend the tears in Walter Mapes' lips with his matted whiskers interfering with the work. I told the wife to set a kettle of water upon her hearth to warm it for use upon my return.

Father Thomas's clerk answered my rapping upon the vicarage door, and invited me to take a seat in the modest hall whilst he fetched his superior. The vicarage was a comfortable and well-supplied abode. Draperies, well-stitched, hung against an exterior wall of the hall, and a sideboard displayed a collection of cups, bowls, plates, and utensils. Most of these were pewter, but a few were of silver. I remember hearing Master Wycliffe say that a poor man should not be required to tithe if his village priest owned more of this world's goods than he. Most priests would consider such talk heretical, I'm sure. Master Wycliffe spoke these words to poor scholars, who likely agreed with him. Now, a decade and more later, when some are priests and subdeacons, their opinions are likely modified.

"Ah, Hugh, have you dealt with Walter Mapes' hurts? He did terrible injury to himself, did he not? 'Twill teach him to indulge so."

"Nay on both counts," I replied.

Father Thomas peered at me beneath furrowed brows, then said, "Both counts?"

"Aye. Both. I have not yet repaired his mangled lips. I gave him crushed hemp seeds in a cup of ale, to lessen his pain when I stitch him together, and am waiting for the herb to do its work. And Walter did not do injury to himself falling upon rocks in Shill Brook."

"Then what caused his wounds?"

"Do you know of rocks in Shill Brook, anyplace, large enough that if a drunken man fell against them he would give himself such lacerations as Walter now has?"

The priest pursed his lips, lowered his brows in thought, then spoke. "Few stones of any size in the brook. Most are but pebbles."

"Aye. His wounds came in the night. He spoke truly there, but 'twas my father-in-law who caused them."

I explained the source of Walter Mapes' injury, and why the man had sought to enter Galen House.

"Intended to beat you?"

"He said so."

"Why would he accuse himself? I've never known that fellow to speak the truth if a lie would serve him better."

"A falsehood would not serve better today. I told him I would not mend his lips unless I first had the truth from him."

"Ah... and there is no other surgeon hereabouts to deal with his hurts if you will not."

"Just so."

"I wonder," the priest said, pulling at his beard, "why Walter was so incensed that he would seek to do you harm? You are not the only man of Bampton and the Weald who thinks ill of him."

"Perhaps he intended to deal with other men at some later time. Or thought me an instigator of the most recent tales told of his felonies."

"Surely that would be Alain Gower."

"Aye, most likely. But Gower's house has been entered in the night recently enough that he will be alert to such a thing occurring again. And Gower is a brawny fellow. If he discovered Mapes in his house in the night he could do the miscreant great harm, whereas I am a slender man. Mapes likely assessed I'd be easier to tackle."

Father Thomas was silent for a moment, then spoke. "What do you wish me to do about this?"

"Walter is the bishop's tenant, and you and Father Simon and Father Ralph are the bishop's agents in the Weald. I wish you to make it clear to Mapes that he is not to be seen about Church View Street or near Galen House. I have not yet discovered who slew Hubert Shillside, nor who has taken goods from Galen House, and seeking the brigands will likely take me from Bampton again. If the fellow thinks I am away, he might seek to avenge himself and his reputation by attacking Kate or her father."

"Surely not," the priest said. "Not after you mend his wounds."

"You have seen the best and worst of men," I replied. "Would you trust a man like Walter to think himself obliged to me for my service to him?"

The priest was again silent for some time. "Men like Walter," he finally said, "see grievance over gratitude."

"Aye, as do many men, I think. And so I ask of you to make him understand that he must keep himself well away from Galen House."

"I will do so."

I hurried from the vicarage to Galen House, where I collected my razor and Kate's cake of castile soap.

"What are you about?" she said when she saw me on my way out with her soap.

"I must shave Walter Mapes' whiskers before I can stitch his mangled lips," I replied.

"Did he truly fall against rocks in Shill Brook?" Kate asked.

"Nay. 'Twas he your father smote when he tried to enter Galen House in the night."

"Why did he do so? Did he not know we have already been robbed?"

"He did, but did not seek our goods. Rather, he wished to punish me because he believes me responsible for telling folk that he did hamsoken against Alain Gower."

"Punish you? How would he do so?"

I led Kate to our rear door, opened it, and pointed to the cudgel which lay yet in our toft where Walter had dropped it as he fled.

"That was the weapon he intended to use against me, and perhaps you also."

Kate shuddered. "And now you will use my best soap to treat the villain?"

"We are to do good to those who use us badly. The Lord Christ requires it of us."

Kate did not reply, but pursed her lips. This was reply enough. 'Tis not always convenient to do as the Lord Christ commands.

Kate's castile soap would not burn, as would the soap of ashes and lard his wife would make, when I washed Walter's wounds and softened his whiskers. Why did I wish to spare the man from greater affliction? He would not have spared me.

I was yet considering this thought when I arrived at Walter's house. He was upon his table, as I had left him, and did not turn his head when his wife greeted me. I took this as a sign that the hemp seeds had done their work.

Mapes' wife disappeared into the house, and a moment later, without my asking, reappeared with a battered kettle. The water within was not hot, but warm, and would suffice.

With water and soap I made a lather with which I cleansed caked blood from Mapes' beard and softened the bristles. I then applied my razor to his upper and lower lips. All this time Walter lay unmoving, but when he saw me produce the razor his eyes widened. Perhaps he feared that my hand might prove unsteady so near to his neck. The thought did occur to me.

Shaving the fellow was as arduous a task as stitching his lacerated lips, and took nearly as long. The hemp seeds had done their work, or the man was inured to pain, for he winced but twice as I pierced his torn lips with Kate's needle and drew the flesh together with the flaxen thread. One of the tears took four stitches, the other needed five.

The man's nose was also askew, and must be dealt with or 'twould point to his sinister side for what remained of his life, which might be but few days if he continued to creep into other men's houses in the dark of night. I told Walter that his lips were mended, and that he must brace himself for even greater pain whilst I straightened his crooked nose.

His nose had only just begun to heal from the beating men had delivered him. Perhaps this is why it so easily bent when the poker won the battle of flesh against iron.

"Blink your eyes," I said, "if you understand what I am about to do. This will cause you much pain, but 'twill be brief. Blink once if you wish me to proceed, blink twice if you prefer to escape pain and go to your grave with a crooked nose."

Walter blinked his eyes. Once. I watched carefully to see did he blink again. He did not.

Straightening a broken nose is much like drawing a rotten tooth. The business is best done quickly. Slow and gentle will not alleviate suffering. I took Walter's rather bulbous and purpled nose gently between the thumb and forefinger of my right hand, then with one movement I pulled hard and twisted the nose straight. I was finished before Mapes could cry out in pain. Which he did, and then swooned. I felt no remorse for being the cause of this torment.

Walter's senses returned to him, and I said, "Before I depart I will see what damage was done to your ribs. If one or two are cracked there is little I or any man can do to heal the breaks. Only time will do so."

The man's kirtle was threadbare and bloodstained. I drew it up to his shoulders and saw a welt extending round from his dexter side to disappear under him as he lay upon the pallet. The mark was fiery red, but would soon be purple. I pushed a finger against the bruise where the discoloration crossed a rib. Mapes responded with a gasp.

"'Tis sure one rib at least is broken," I said. "There is nothing to be done for such a fracture but give the break time to mend. Six weeks will pass before it will be knit together. You must do no strenuous labor in that time, nor twist your body. If you do, pain will tell you to desist. Such pain is your friend. When it strikes it will deliver a message that, whatever it was you did, you must avoid doing it again. If broken ribs are moved and twisted overmuch they will not mend properly. Heed the pain when it tells you to halt whatever you were doing to make it hurt.

"I am done here. I will return in a fortnight to remove the stitches from your lips."

I replaced needle, flaxen thread, razor, and soap in my pouch, then said, "You may bring four pence to Galen House in four days. I will examine you then, to see how the injury heals."

I left the toft followed only by silence. Neither wife nor sons spoke thanks for my effort on Walter's behalf. And Walter also was mute, although he might be forgiven, as his sewn lips and stupefied brain likely worked together to render him heedless of good manners.

At Galen House I found Kate and my father-in-law hard at work making ink. Last autumn Kate and I had prowled forests seeking oak apples. These we had collected in a basket and allowed to dry and harden. This day Kate and her father were at work crushing the galls to powder, then to mix it with copperas and gum arabic. I was pleased to see them at the business, as my supply of ink was depleted and I could foresee the account of Hubert Shillside's death extending over many gatherings of parchment.

Chapter 16

In seeking thieves and murderers I had neglected manor business. After a dinner of capon mawmene and apple moyle I sought John Prudhomme and together we inspected work on Lord Gilbert's demesne lands. All was well. Ditches were cleared of winter debris, fences were in good repair, plowing was completed and crops sown but for a field of peas to plant for a later harvest.

Tenants were busy at their gardens, planting cabbages, onions, and leeks, and some, who possessed larger tofts, included crops they might sell: flax and hemp, woad and weld. My supply of crushed hemp seeds was low. When the hemp was mature I would find a ready supply.

Late that Monday, past the ninth hour, I left the reeve to his own work and returned to Galen House. A surprise awaited me as I passed the path to the Weald. Walter Mapes' oldest son was waiting where the path joined Mill Street, hidden behind some low foliage. He stepped from his concealed place when I was no more than five paces from him.

The lad is a strapping youth, and his sudden appearance startled me. My first thought was of self-preservation. I feared he might be intent upon delivering the drubbing my father-in-law had prevented a few hours past. I am not so fleet of foot as before I was wed. Kate's cookery has reduced my speed, but I was prepared to take to my heels and seek the castle forecourt and safety when the lad spoke.

"I'm obliged to you for mending me father's wounds. He'd not say so, but me mum sent me to tell you she's beholden to you."

I relaxed at this announcement and thanked the lad for his kindness. I wondered why he had hid himself until I drew near to him. A glance into the Weald explained. His home was visible from where we stood, and from a window or open door his father could see us, should he rouse himself from his pallet and look to Mill Street.

The youth saw me look toward the house and divined my thoughts. "Aye... hid myself so's 'e'd not see me waitin' 'ere for you. Saw you goin' about with John an' knew you'd pass by when you returned."

"You do not want your father to know of your gratitude?"

In answer the lad stepped back toward the shrubbery so he was again hidden to anyone peering in our direction from his house.

"Why do you conceal this conversation?" I asked.

"He don't beat me as 'e once did, 'cause last year I struck 'im when he did so. Bigger'n 'im now. But 'e'll take it out on Mum does 'e see me speakin' to you."

"How will he know what it is you have said?"

"He won't, 'cause I wish to say more'n 'e'd think."

"What is it that your father does not know that you are about to tell me?"

The youth cast a wary eye toward the path to the Weald, then, satisfied that no man was near, spoke softly.

"Father don't like for folk to tell what they know of thievin'."

"Why so? Not even to deflect Alain Gower's wrath?" I asked.

"Poor folk got to live, 'e says, an' so takin' from the rich be no sin – but tellin' a bailiff or constable or sheriff of a felony so the poor thief gets hung, that be a sin. So 'e says."

"Do you agree with your father?"

The youth shrugged. "Sometimes, when me belly's empty I think mayhap 'e speaks true."

"Alain Gower has plenty. Does your father believe that he was robbed justly?"

"Aye. That's why 'e'd not speak of them as did hamsoken."

"Your father did not break in and steal from Alain, but knows who did?"

"Nay, 'e don't know who did, but 'e won't tell you or Father Thomas what 'e does know."

"Because he dislikes Alain for charging him at the bishop's hallmote for stealing his furrow?"

"Aye. Said if a man stole from Alain 'twould serve Alain right, him havin' more'n we."

"If your father doesn't know who entered Alain's house in the night, what is it that he does know but will not speak of?"

"We seen the men who did so."

"In the dark of night you and your father saw men enter Alain Gower's house?"

"Aye. Seen 'em leave, too."

"How many?"

"Four."

"Why were you not abed at such an hour?"

The lad did not reply, but rather looked about him as if seeking some hidden listener. He saw none, and spoke.

"Now that cows is put to grass we goes out on moonless nights to milk them as may be left in pasture an' not brought to barn. To make butter an' cheese."

"You were about in the night, past curfew?"

"Aye. Waited 'til Janyn was done with 'is rounds." (Janyn was chosen beadle at hallmote last year.)

"Four men, you say, entered Alain's house?"

"Nay. But three did so. One stayed out in the toft."

"A lookout, then, to warn others if men approached?"

"Aye. S'pose so."

"'Twas dark, but what did you see of these men? Did you draw close to them? Did you hear them speak?"

"Aye. When we saw them approach we knew they was likely about thievin'. Who else goes about in the night past curfew?"

"Who, indeed?" I agreed.

"Father put 'is finger to 'is lips an' we followed, quiet like, to see where it was they was goin'. Went straight to Alain's house."

"But 'twas too dark to see who it was you followed?"

"Aye."

"Were the villains young or old? Could you see well enough to know?"

"They walked like young men, easy like, not stiff. They didn't wear beards. We could see that. When they stopped at Alain's house we was no more'n ten paces from 'em."

"Close enough to hear them speak?" I asked.

"Aye. They didn't say much an' whispered when they did. One of 'em, leader, I s'pose, told another to stay put in the toft an' keep watch."

"What were his words? Were you close enough to hear all?"

"He said, 'Edmund, remain 'ere an' watch the path. If you see or hear anything amiss call out a warnin'.'"

"You are sure he said 'Edmund'? Not Edward?"

"Aye. Edmund. For sure. I 'eard 'im plain."

"How did the man speak? As you – or as a scholar might?"

"A scholar, 'e was, by my judgment. Not of the commons, I think."

"I know 'twas dark, but could you see if the rogues wore scholars' gowns of black, or did they garb themselves as we?"

"Like you, I'd say. Too dark to see of a certain, but they wore no gowns. I could see that."

I thanked the lad for this information and bid him seek me if he remembered anything else of that night which might later occur to him. He agreed to do so. From my pouch I took a halfpenny and pressed it into his hand.

I left the youth standing behind the foliage and was across the Shill Brook before I saw him peer warily toward his home, then set out on the path to the Weald, feigning nonchalance. In this he seemed to me convincing. Perhaps he had experience in prevarication so as to shield himself from his father's blows.

Edmund is a common enough name. Not so common as Thomas or John, but there are surely many Edmunds about Oxford. Nevertheless, the only Edmund of whom I had knowledge residing between Bampton and Oxford, where felonies were become common of late, was Edmund Harcourt. He is young. Would the master of a band of thieves choose him to stand guard whilst the others did their villainy – perhaps because of his callow years?

'Twas surely too dark on that moonless night men entered Alain Gower's house for him to see if one of them wore a green cotehardie. And the malefactors would not think their felony had been observed by stealth – they'd expect discovery to give rise to loud indignation. Here was an advantage I must devise some way to exploit.

But Alain Gower's loss was not of my bailiwick. I must seek the men who slew Hubert Shillside. Did the felons who entered Alain's house not content themselves with thievery, but also slay those from whom they stole goods? If apprehended, the punishment is the same. A man will find himself at the end of a hempen noose doing the sheriff's dance for either crime. Why not, then, slay your victim, as the penalty will be no greater than if the man be allowed his life? And a dead man can say nothing of his assailants to lead to their apprehension. Hubert Shillside told me only that his murderers had a blade to slash free his purse, and had broken it in his ribs. Since every man owns a dagger, Shillside's corpse proclaimed little of material value.

A wisp of green wool, however, of yellowish tint – that might tell much, if only it could be found.

I pondered upon these things as I trudged home to Galen House. Kate thought my business that afternoon only that of Bampton Manor, so when I told her of meeting Walter Mapes' son she stopped her work and desired of me to tell all that the lad said, only turning her attention from me to stir a pot of pease pottage which simmered upon the embers and would soon be our supper.

"The lad is not much like his father, then," she commented, "if he appreciates all your toil for his father – and that despite the injury the old scoundrel meant to work on your person."

"Perhaps he follows his mother's character," I said, "or his thrashings when he was younger have driven from him all admiration he may ever have held for his father. He's been used ill. Mayhap if he can do his father a bad turn it brings some satisfaction – recompense for what he's suffered at Walter's hands."

"A man may create a son like himself, or unlike," my father-in-law chipped in. "But few men know how to do so. I have lived long enough to see good men set an example of probity for their sons, yet watch as some sons abandon the path they were taught. And sometimes, rarely, I have seen scoundrels whose sons have grown to useful manhood."

"Walter Mapes' lad must be such a one," Kate said. "The youth has seen how despised his father is and wishes not to be considered the same."

"Yet," Caxton said, "'tis more likely that a good man will have sons of whom he can be proud than the other way round."

"The men who injured Alain Gower and stole from him – do you think," Kate asked, "these may be the same who have done other felonies hereabouts, and may have slain Hubert Shillside?"

"This would be a convenience was it so," I replied. "Solve one villainy and solve them all. I wish my work could be so simple."

"Perhaps it is," Kate said thoughtfully. "Mayhap you have but one mystery to uncover, rather than many."

"This may be the truth of it," I agreed. "There are matters in common to the felonies which have happened betwixt here and Oxford. Four men, occasionally three, are seen to be involved. But sometimes they wear scholars' gowns and sometimes they wear the dress of young gentlemen."

"Which may mean only that they have wit enough to seek to brush dust over their tracks," Caxton pointed out. "Which, then, is truth? Are the felons scholars who adopt the clothing of young gentlemen, or are they young gentlemen who don the garb of scholars?"

"Mayhap they are both," Kate said. "Scholars are most often young gentlemen."

"And both scholars and young gentlemen are oft in need of funds," Caxton added.

"All men need money," I said. "I have never known a man, no matter how wealthy, who did not desire a few more shillings."

"Or pounds," Kate said. "Even the king has need of greater wealth."

"Indeed," Caxton agreed. "How can he regain lost lands in France, or protect that which he has, without more coin?"

How, indeed?

John took that moment to let out a lusty wail. I take his volume at such times as a good omen. It seems to me unlikely that an infant who can make known his demands for a meal with such a racket could be unhealthy.

A soft rain began as we consumed our supper. There would be no sitting upon a bench in the toft, observing the sun dropping beyond Lord Gilbert's forest, this evening.

So for a while we played at Nine Man Morris, taking turns. One must sit idly by, for only two can play. We tired of the game and chatted of this and that, then my father-in-law asked would I read to them. "From what?" said I, for now the prized copy of RHETORIC was a second time stolen, I had no books in the house except my herbals and Henri de Mondeville's treatise on surgery. Interesting to me, but hardly made to enthrall a party on a summer's evening.

"Read us from the Bible then," said Kate's father. "The 'pistles are a comfort, and the doings of St. Paul sometimes exciting – the man who fell out of the window while the apostle was preaching, or the time the great man himself escaped his captors bundled in a laundry basket, or the time an angel let the Christians out of prison, or –"

I interrupted to suggest he might like to pick a passage himself, but he shook his head, "Nay. You know I have no Latin. Well, enough to pick out some of the meaning from a saying painted on the wall in church, but not to read it out. Kate neither. Find one of your favorite bits and let's hear that."

So I opened the book on the table under the window, to catch the last of the light, picking out a passage I knew well enough to run my finger along the words and render them in our mother tongue as I went.

"Let it be from the beginning of Paul's epistle to the Romans, then," I said. I cannot boast that it flowed so smooth as I'd have liked, but well enough to take the meaning of it. And when the chamber grew too dark to see the words, I lighted the cressets and read the second and third chapters as well. Caxton seemed discomfited when I had done.

"Who, then, will see heaven, if it be as the apostle has written?" he said. "I have not the wealth to free myself from purgatory for a thousand years or more." Glancing to Kate, he observed, "Nor have you, no matter how you might grieve to think of me a prisoner in that awful place."

He sat looking crestfallen, his shoulders sagging. Give him a hearty dinner or a vile intruder, a patch to dig or a wall to mend, and Robert Caxton will rise to the challenge. But this? Try what you might and still be so mired in sin that death opened a gate to purgatory – it defeated him, I could see that.

"Well," I ventured cautiously, "I think there may be more to it. A little hope, a little grace, a chink of light for such as we."

"How so?" he asked, his voice still dull and sad. "What's to help us? Sooner or later death comes, and then the reckoning."

I cleared my throat. I had to tread carefully here. Heresy is a serious thing. "We *are* all sinful," I ventured cautiously. "Every one. But, look you, the Lord Christ has made a way to escape the penalty of our wickedness. It is written, it's set down. He died for the sins for which we deserved the punishment. We have but to put our trust in Him, and we are freed – so long as we seek to sin no more, of course – from the penalty due us."

"Aye." Caxton shifted restlessly, waving his hand in dismissal of my proffered hope. "This I know. So holy mother church teaches. Yet what of the pain of purgatory? It makes me sick to think of it. And there can be no men so holy they will escape its torments."

"Surely." I did not wish to say more. It could be dangerous if the wrong men got wind of it. I know this because I once spoke too freely upon the subject. The bishops frown upon any discussion of purgatory. Unless such a place exists, why pay the church for prayers? Why buy indulgences and pardons? The clergy would be thinner men without our fear of purgatory.

I glanced toward Kate from the corner of my eye, at her

face so thoughtful and serious as she considered these things. My Kate. How could such a virtuous wife be yet sinful in the Lord Christ's eyes? Yet it must be so, else the Scriptures lie. I do not know how this can be. I admit I do not understand the ways of God. His thoughts and the words of Holy Writ are too deep for me. But how should I wonder at this, I who have trouble understanding the ways of other men, made like me? If I can't understand why Walter Mapes would black his wife's eye when he's in his cups and a sour mood falls on him, how can I expect to measure the mind of God?

My father-in-law yet held fast to his course of making his bed on the pallet beneath the boarded window. I could see the only way I would convince him to return to his chamber was to visit the glazier in Witney and engage the man to repair the shattered panes and twisted lead. And apprehend the rascals that threatened our household peace. I resolved at least to see the glazier the very next day, having no path toward the discovery of Hubert Shillside's slayers emerging clear before me. Although, to be sure, I must investigate Walter's lad's report that one of Alain Gower's assailants was named Edmund. With delicacy, mind. Nothing ham-fisted or over-hasty. I needed to think carefully on the matter.

Because of the expense, I had installed but two glass windows in Galen House when the home was constructed: one in the kitchen and one in the hall. The others were of oiled skins, as were those in most homes. Even Lord Gilbert has glass windows in only his solar and one wall of the hall. Light may enter a chamber through oiled parchment or linen, but Kate loves the light we get from a glass window and to be able to see into the toft, even if the view is somewhat distorted. So I determined to bear the expense and see the glass restored.

I'd heard of no attacks upon the road to Witney so I did not seek Arthur or Uctred to accompany me when, bright and early next morn, I sought a palfrey at the castle marshalsea and set off for Witney. The town is but five or so miles north of Bampton. I expected to seek the glazier, complete my business, and return to Galen House in time for a late dinner by the sixth hour.

The journey to Witney proved uneventful, which any traveler would find agreeable. I believe few folk in Witney can afford the glazier's work, for he promised he could attend to my shattered window the next day. Six diamond-shaped panes were cracked and broken. The man assured me he had glass enough on hand to repair the breach, and lead also. A shilling and three pence the repair would cost me. A small price for a happy wife who would once again be able to gaze at the world beyond her henhouse from her kitchen window.

The road between Bampton and Witney wends for the most part through fertile fields and meadows where contented sheep crop the new grass, and oats and barley and peas are planted. Only occasionally does the way enter a wood.

It was at one such place on my return where, from the corner of my eye, some motion uncommon to a forest caught my attention. I thought at first I had surprised a hart or hind. Not so.

Two men suddenly appeared in the road before me, brandishing daggers. I drew my palfrey's reins sharply to spin the beast about, and as I did so two other armed men appeared upon the road whence I had come.

Then an odd thing occurred. One of the men who had appeared in the road before me took flight and disappeared into the wood from whence he came. As there were now two men blocking a retreat to Witney, but only one obstructing my path to Bampton, I spurred my palfrey and guided the beast directly toward the remaining brigand. I had no intention of halting to ask the fellow what it was he wanted of me. He was not waving a dagger before my nose to stop me and inquire after my health.

The palfrey reacted to my spurs with a satisfying leap. The single thief before me took notice of this bound, hesitated but for a moment, then dove for the verge to avoid the charging horse. It occurred to me as we – man and beast – swept past the fellow that he wore a green cotehardie with perhaps more weld than woad. I was not about to stop my galloping beast to learn if somewhere the garment had a frayed place where a wisp of wool had been torn away. I doubted not that it was so.

None of the men who wished to waylay me were mounted, or if they had been they had concealed their beasts in the wood, so even a slow-footed palfrey could easily outpace these pursuers on foot.

After a mile or so I slowed the laboring animal and, as the immediate danger had passed, began to consider the event. Most puzzling was the disappearance of one of the two felons who had sought to block my way forward. Had he not retreated back into the wood I might not have been able to make good an escape. Whilst I directed my beast at one man the other might have slashed my leg, or the flank of the palfrey, as I passed.

Was the fellow a coward? Did he recognize me and fear that I might know him also? If so, he and his companions had only to slay me to protect his identity, which, if they were the same felons who had waylaid Hubert Shillside, they seemed willing to do. Mayhap murder was a measure that the thief was unwilling to countenance. But whom did I know who might be a brigand, and where would I have associated with such a man? Walter Mapes, perhaps? More likely he was home abed, nursing his wounds. Would the son of a landed knight do felonies in his father's shire? I began to believe it so.

Such thoughts wandered through my mind as the palfrey carried me to Bampton. Kate worries too much. 'Tis, I believe, a feature of her gender. So I resolved that I would not speak to her or her father of this escape.

Chapter 17

Kate had prepared leach Lombard for our dinner. I did not need to pretend delight in the meal, for such fare is a favorite of mine. I have many favorite meals. Indeed, whatever Kate prepares seems to become another favorite. Mayhap I have an unsophisticated palate. Or perhaps Kate is skilled at cookery. What difference does it make?

After my dinner I sought Will Shillside. Alice told me he was hoeing weeds from a field of peas, and where I might find him.

The sun was warm this day and Will had doffed his cotehardie, working in kirtle only, sweat beading his lip and forehead. He seemed pleased to briefly rest from his labor when he saw me approach.

"I give you good day, Master Hugh," the youth said. But there was no warmth in his words. He resented, I knew, my lack of progress in discovering who had slain his father. I could not blame him. I was a disappointment to myself.

"Do you travel soon to Oxford to restore your supply of pins and buckles and such, or will you abandon your father's business?"

"Aye. I must do so soon, but Alice is fretful lest what befell my father might also come to me."

"Tell me of your plans before you undertake the journey."

"You believe it will be dangerous? You agree with Alice?"

"If you travel alone, aye, 'twill be perilous. But you need not make the journey alone."

"Who would accompany me?"

"I, Arthur, Uctred."

"Just to see that no harm comes to me you would do so?"

"Not for that reason only. I am considering laying a trap, if you are willing. Such a ruse will be dangerous, true enough, but I can see no way to seize the men who attacked your father but to take them in the act of a felony."

"Must Alice know of this?"

"Nay. Only that you travel to Oxford to renew your merchandise and that you will journey with three others. But she must tell no one else that you will have companions. You must impress on her that she is to speak of only your traveling, not we who will travel with you. No man knows whether or not the men who slew your father knew beforehand of his plans. If the men who attacked your father are of Bampton or the Weald, or some man of Bampton told others of your father's travel, then Alice's words may help bait the trap."

"She will wonder why she may not speak of you who will accompany me. If I tell her 'tis a trap being set she will worry even though there will be four of us upon the road."

"Calm her fear in whatever way you think best. But do not permit her to speak of we who journey with you. Now, on another, but related, matter, when your father did business in Oxford did he often go there by way of Stanton Harcourt?"

"Always. There is no haberdasher in that village, so Sir Thomas and his tenants would place orders for goods when father passed through on his way to Oxford. He would deliver the stuff upon his return. 'Twas profitable business for him, and I will continue it."

So Hubert Shillside was well known in Stanton Harcourt. If he had recognized one or more of his assailants as from the village, the rogues might have realized that they could be identified and chose then to add murder to robbery.

One of the felons who did hamsoken to Alain Gower was named Edmund. Edmund Harcourt would profit from the death of his older brother. He would know and be known by Hubert Shillside because of the haberdasher's regular visits to Stanton Harcourt. And he would know me, and know that I would recognize him, if some band of thieves with which he associated should attempt to rob me upon the road. He was the son of a knight. Did other men know that it was the son of a landowning knight of a nearby village who robbed them? Were these victims then silenced so that Edmund could not be identified?

No band of thieves could have discovered I would travel to Witney this day. I had only decided to do so in the night. They hid in the wood, ready to pounce upon any man who appeared. Is this why sometimes only three men attacked their victim? Did Edmund know whom it was the miscreants were about to confront on some occasions, and absent himself to avoid recognition by the victim?

Here were many questions but few answers. Suppositions, aye; answers, nay. My mind was centering upon Edmund Harcourt as the key to unlocking these mysteries. I must guard against this. I have been bailiff of Bampton Manor long enough to know that, when seeking felons, things are not always as they first appear. Then again, sometimes they are.

"When do you wish to visit Oxford?" I asked Will, who stood patiently waiting while I ruminated on these knotty matters.

"Soon. My supply of pins is exhausted, and I have but three buckles and a few yards of various ribbons."

"Thursday, then? That will give you and Alice two days to speak of your travel. Do not make an issue of the business, else you might arouse suspicion where we want none. But if a housewife asks for pins, tell her you have none, but will visit Oxford on Thursday to renew your supply."

From Will's pea field I went to the castle and told Arthur and Uctred we would journey with Will Shillside to Oxford on Thursday, hoping to be attacked. Or hoping Will would be attacked. My plan was that Arthur, Uctred, and I would travel mounted a hundred or so paces behind Will as he walked the road. If he saw or heard anything amiss he would be told to turn, cry out for aid, and run to us, leading the felons to their capture. If they scattered when they saw us galloping toward them we, being mounted, would surely take one or two of the rogues, and from them the Sheriff of Oxford would have methods of discovering the names of the others.

Will performed the first part of the scheme well. Wednesday eve at supper Kate mentioned that John Prudhomme's wife had complained that Will had no pins. But, she had said, he hoped soon to renew his supply, being off Thursday to seek goods in Oxford. She said every woman in the village agreed Will Shillside was foolhardy, not brave, traveling alone to Oxford for a packet of pins with so much theft and violence in the offing and the ruffians still at large. But what can a man do? He must make his living. I nodded sagely at this, and bade her ask God to watch over Will when she offered her bedtime prayers.

Arthur, Uctred, and I set off upon our palfreys from the castle at dawn on Thursday. We joined Will at his house, and waited there as he walked from the village. Alice watched and chewed upon a knuckle, afraid the babe she was about to bring into the world would have no father, I suspect. I had explained the plan, and its dangers, to Will the day before. There was nothing very sophisticated about my strategy. A simple scheme has less chance of going awry. Will was ready to accept the risk if doing so might bring his father's murderers to justice.

"What if I reach Stanton Harcourt and no thieves attack me?" Will asked when I reviewed the plan. "Men of the village will see you as you pass through behind me, and the trap may be exposed. Mayhap the felons reside there."

"When we see you enter the village we will leave the road and circle the place through fields and forest 'til we come to the road to Eynsham. We will wait then for you to pass, as your business in the village will take some time, then resume our place behind you. It is unlikely the felons will accost you close to the village where your shouts might be heard. You should be safe for that short distance entering and leaving the place."

So I hoped.

"If no men have attacked before you come to Eynsham we will do the same."

"What if men see you follow me from Bampton?"

"Even if they do, they'd find it difficult to forge ahead of you to warn thieves of a trap. 'Tis possible, I suppose, but such men will need to be fleet of foot to pass us by and warn of our intentions, even if they guess what we are about."

'Twas a practical, cautious scheme in my estimation, but it failed. Perhaps, had I given the plan more thought, I would have devised a better one.

Will was not attacked upon the road to Stanton Harcourt, nor between that place and Eynsham. Nor did any brigands appear between Eynsham and Oxford. Will sought Martyn Hendy, purchased the goods he would sell at Stanton Harcourt and Bampton, and together we four departed Oxford and set off for Eynsham Abbey, Will mounted behind Uctred for the return journey. I was much cast down for the failure of my plot.

While in Oxford I visited two of the surgeons and three of the physicians I had asked to watch for my stolen instruments. None had been offered such tools at any price, bargain or not. So they claimed. Perhaps they spoke true. My profession has made of me a suspicious man. I wish it was not so, but mayhap 'tis best, as my dealings tend often to be with men worthy of suspicion.

There was no reason to continue the ruse as we returned next day to Bampton. Men would not likely rob another who carried pins and buckles and ribbons and such rather than silver pennies and groats. Unless, perhaps, the villains wished to impress a lass with a gift of pins and silken ribbons. Lads will do many things to attract a maid. All men know this well, for all men were once lads.

Abbot Gerleys was told of our arrival at the guest house and sent his servant to request my presence in his lodging. I thought he desired news of my search for felons, and he did, but he wished more than that.

"Ah, Hugh, you are well met. I had considered sending for you."

"Why so? Have you information of recent felonies hereabouts?"

"Nay, more's the pity. 'Tis this," he said, removing his cowl and bending toward me so that his scalp was visible. I saw him touch a place upon the side of his tonsured head with a finger, and saw there through the parted hair a sore that was red and oozing pus.

"I cannot see what afflicts the top of my head," Abbot Gerleys said. "Brother Guibert says 'tis a contusion resulting from some injury. But I do not recall striking my head recently."

I drew close and inspected the sore. 'Twas reddened, raised, and swollen. A small opening appeared in the center of the lesion and, as I watched, a small burst of yellow fluid issued from it.

"When did this sore first appear?"

"A fortnight past, perhaps a few days less."

"Do you sleep with the window open?"

The abbot furrowed his brow in puzzlement. "Aye. But what has my sleeping practice to do with this affliction?"

"'Tis a cow fly larva has made its home in your scalp, I believe."

"Cow fly? Ah, I remember last year a few of the abbey cattle had a similar affliction. Did some insect make its way through my open window in the night?"

"Likely. What of the cows? How did the abbey deal with their lesions?"

Abbot Gerleys shrugged. "We didn't. After a few months the swellings on the beasts declined and the discharge dried."

"And a hole was found in the beasts' hide where the sore had been," I said.

"Aye. The hides were near to worthless."

"'Twas likely cow flies, and one is now growing in your scalp, an egg having been deposited there in the night."

"What is to be done? Must I wait until the insect hatches and takes flight?"

"Nay. This you must not do. The maggot will travel through your body and reappear elsewhere. It must be removed immediately. Send for Brother Guibert. Tell him to bring his smallest pincers, such as he might use to remove a splinter from a man's thumb."

The monk who served Abbot Gerleys was dispatched to the infirmary and shortly Brother Guibert appeared. In his hand he carried a delicate instrument, and his face wore a puzzled expression.

"It would be helpful," I said, "to have wine with which to cleanse the sore after the larva is extracted."

"Fetch wine for Master Hugh," the abbot instructed Brother Guibert. The monk hastened off to do his superior's bidding.

I told the abbot to move his chair to the window, where I could better see what I must do. The afternoon was quickly becoming evening and did I not make haste the business might best be delayed 'til morning.

The sore was nearly as large as a penny, and raised to a height of two pennies stacked one atop another. With my thumbs I pressed upon the sides of the swelling and watched as thick fluid issued from the small orifice at the center of the sore.

The flow of pus ceased, and in its place I saw, as the tiny hole expanded, a white, glistening shape appear. But when I reached for the pincers the larva receded, no longer visible. I called the abbot's servant to aid me, and showed him how he must press his thumbs against opposite sides of the lesion. His visage reflected distaste for the work, but he did as instructed and the larva immediately reappeared. I employed the pincers to grasp the visible end of the maggot and began a slow, steady pull. The creature was reluctant to leave its home, and did not come free of the abbot's scalp readily. But I persevered, and after a time of constant but gentle pressure the larva popped free of Abbot Gerleys' head.

I held the creature before the abbot. It wriggled, and was nearly the thickness of my littlest finger and half as long.

"Hah… so that thing has been growing in my head! What say you, Master Hugh? Must I close my window before I seek my bed at night?"

"Nay. I think not. Such insects are rare in England. Whilst I studied in Paris I learned that they are more commonly found in warmer climes: Italy and Spain and Africa. It is not likely that you will be so afflicted again."

"And if I should be, I shall call upon you to deal with it again," the abbot said with a grin. "And should one of our cattle be afflicted again, we will know the cause and deal with it better than before."

Brother Guibert arrived with a cup of wine as the abbot spoke, and I bathed the sore so as to speed its closure and healing.

"You have traveled to Oxford again?" Abbot Gerleys said, changing the subject. "Are you yet seeking stolen instruments, and your book? Or have you found them?"

"Aye, and nay. I seek, but do not find. But we rode to Oxford this day on another matter. We thought to lay a trap for the felons who have done theft and murder hereabouts."

"From your words and expression I think your snare failed."

"Aye, it did."

"Have you suspicions who the men might be that you intended to entangle?"

"One of them, perhaps."

"Has the fellow behaved in such a way as to give you cause?"

"He has, but his behavior, so much of it as I can be sure of, is not enough for the King's Eyre to convict him. And it may be that I see guilt where none is."

"Because you see what you wish to see?"

"Aye."

"Explain to me your trap."

I told the abbot how Will Shillside was to walk alone, tempting brigands on the wooded stretch of the road, and how we noised his journey abroad in Bampton and Stanton Harcourt.

"Either word of the lad's travel did not reach the felons' ears," the abbot said, "or they suspected the snare you laid for them."

"I believe that they must have smelled a rat. There has been so much banditry on the roads hereabouts that men rarely travel alone."

"Unless they be fools," the abbot said.

I did not mention that two days past I had journeyed to Witney alone.

"So a solitary man walking the roads might not be seen as an easy victim," Abbot Gerleys continued, "but rather the brigands might view such a fellow as too convenient. How far behind the lure did you travel?"

"A hundred paces. Perhaps a little less."

"That might be well enough where the road bends and climbs, but where the path is straight men lying in wait for a victim might see you in the distance."

"'Twas a risk. But to separate farther from Will would have been a greater risk. We might not have heard him call for aid or come up to the rogues in time to prevent harm to the lad."

"Ah, just so. Tricky business, attempting to lure a wicked man to his doom. What will you do now?"

I had thought much upon this very subject but had no ready answer.

"Tomorrow we will return to Bampton. Will has purchased goods in Oxford for Sir Thomas and other folk of Stanton Harcourt. We will halt there long enough for him to conclude his business."

"I wish you Godspeed," the abbot said, "and much thanks for ridding me of my uninvited visitor." Abbot Gerleys looked down to his table, now dim in the shadows of his chamber, where the white maggot was yet visible, writhing in an attempt to regain its host.

He picked up the larva, dropped it into the empty wine cup, and said to the servant, "Take this to the fish pond and toss it in. Feed the pike."

Brother Watkin brought loaves and ale to the guest house early next morning. We reclaimed our beasts and entered Stanton Harcourt before the third hour. There was nothing for Arthur, Uctred, and me to do while Will visited houses where folk had requested goods of him. I did greet Sir Thomas and inquire of him if Oswald had discovered any information regarding the murder of his son. I was not surprised when he answered "Nay."

While we spoke, Edmund entered the manor house in the company of a youth perhaps a year or two older and a stone heavier. A friend from Oxford, I assumed.

I departed the manor house and returned to Arthur and Uctred, whom I had left waiting patiently with our beasts whilst Will did business and I greeted Sir Thomas. The two men had been at ease when I left them, but Arthur no longer was. He was much agitated. This is unusual, for the man is of a phlegmatic nature.

"Did you see 'im?" Arthur said in an excited whisper as I approached.

"See who?"

"The lad with Edmund! 'Ad a mole upon 'is left temple, just 'ere," he said, and raised his index finger to point out the place. "Could see it from 'ere, twenty paces distant."

Edmund's friend had passed me so that the dexter side of his face was visible. I saw nothing of a mole upon the opposite side of his face.

"Never seen a man with a mole like that, and in the exact same place as on that ragged scholar what we was told tried to sell your book."

"Remember," I said, "that we were told the ragged scholar had been recently shaved and his locks trimmed. And he seemed fleshy enough, 'twas said."

"Aye, so we was. Well, that fellow with Edmund is old enough to shave 'is whiskers, an' has done so not long past. You suppose he's the man what 'ad your book? What would Sir Thomas's lad be doin' in company with an evil fellow like that?"

I did not immediately reply. Arthur saw my hesitation and said, "Oh," as the answer occurred to him. "But 'is own brother? 'Ow could a lad do such a thing?"

"Mayhap he did not. There are yet too many suppositions and too few facts."

"If there be evidence, 'ow we gonna get it?" *We*, he had said. He was beginning to believe himself a vital part of keeping Bampton Manor safe. And he was.

I thought back to the moment Edmund and his friend passed whilst I spoke to his father. Did his eyes dart from me to Sir Thomas? Did he seem anxious about some matter? I did not know the youth well, so had no way to compare his usual comportment to what I had observed when he appeared moments earlier. I had thought, when I first met him, that Edmund seemed without guile. But if a man is enough of a knave he might be duplicitous enough to cover his deceit.

Walter Mapes' son had heard one of those who did hamsoken addressed as "Edmund." Did another also possess a mole upon his left temple? In the dark of night who would know? Did another of Alain Gower's assailants wear a green cotehardie? Such a color would appear black, or nearly so, in the dark of night.

The green woolen wisp would tell me much if it could be found. Was this why the fragment had disappeared? It must not be permitted to speak? I had wondered at this, and now I began to believe it so.

There was a chain here. Perhaps Edmund was a link – he and his friend with the mole. Another link may be he of the green cotehardie. Four men, usually, had been involved in the felonies plaguing the shire. There must be a fourth link, unidentified.

Stanton Harcourt's bailiff had possessed the green woolen wisp before it vanished. Was he the fourth link to the chain? Nay, he could not be. The man was too fat to prowl roads and fields seeking to plunder the unwary. A fifth link, then? Four who robbed and murdered and one who did not?

If Oswald was a party to the wickedness, but not one who stole and murdered, what role did he play in this drama?

I thought on these things as we departed Stanton Harcourt. Will again rode behind Uctred. To spare the beast some weight his sack of goods was fastened behind my saddle. I heard the occasional jingle and clink as buckles of various sizes and quality smote against each other.

Any chain is likely to have a weak link. If I had correctly identified five links in the chain of wickedness encompassing the shire between Bampton and Oxford, which link would be most readily snapped? Oswald, I thought. But what tool might be used to break him?

Kate provided the answer.

She had prepared a dinner of stewed herrings, for it was a fast day. As we ate, I spoke to her and my father-in-law of the failed plot to entrap felons, and described the partial identities I had learned, the links in my chain of connections.

"This Edmund was a student at Queen's Hall?" Kate asked.

"Aye, he was."

"Is that not a school for the training of priests?"

"It is."

"If Edmund Harcourt joined with others to plunder and slay honest folk, it seems most likely that he would combine with friends, and most of his friends would likely be other scholars of Queen's Hall."

"Edmund is no longer at Queen's Hall," I said. "He assists his father on his manor. Wise words, nonetheless. His friends were more than likely made at Queen's, and may yet be associated with the school."

"Suppose this is true, and you find some way to prove it so. What will happen to Edmund and his companions?"

"They are likely all clerks, and tonsured, so will plead benefit of clergy."

"And the church hangs no man," Caxton said. "They will go free."

"The bishop would demand penance of them, which might be severe... but they will not hang for their felonies."

"But that bailiff, if he is a party to their evil deeds, he would surely hang," Kate said.

"Aye," I agreed. "Surely. Unless some mitigating circumstance persuaded a sheriff and judge to leniency."

"Such as providing king's evidence against his felonious companions?" Kate smiled.

"Just so. Oswald may be the weak link of this criminal chain. A few solid blows and he might shatter."

"How will you deliver the blows?" Caxton asked.

"The man must believe that I know all. Or more than I do, at least. If he realizes the weakness of my position his lips will shut tighter than a mussel.

"Monday early, I am off again to Oxford, to Queen's Hall. The provost will know of Edmund Harcourt's friends."

Chapter 18

He did. Early Monday morning Arthur, Uctred, and I set out again for Oxford. I had hope that, depending upon the outcome of a discussion with the Queen's Hall provost, this might be the last journey I would make to Oxford for many months. Unless news should come to Bampton of my stolen instruments.

We did not pass through Stanton Harcourt, but chose a different road, through Standlake and Cumnor. I did not wish for Oswald or Edmund to see me too often, for fear it would arouse their suspicion that I was close to uncovering the evil they had done. Mayhap those suspicions were already aroused, which might account for the failure of the trap I had laid. If they had done evil, that is. If I was not misguidedly seeking to implicate innocent men with the terrible deeds of others.

Eager to learn what I could from the master of Queen's Hall, like a hound on the scent I felt reluctant to interrupt the pursuit of felons. But my rumbling stomach would not be silenced until we three had consumed a roasted capon, maslin loaves, and ale at an inn near to Queen's Hall.

The provost of Queen's Hall was Henry Whitfield. Likely I would have had difficulty being admitted to his presence, but John Wycliffe was now resident and tutor there while he studied for the degree of bachelor of theology. This hall furnished a logical place for Wycliffe to teach and study, as it had been founded thirty years earlier by Queen Philippa's chaplain – whence the school's name – as a hall for lads from Cumberland and Yorkshire. Wycliffe came to Oxford from Yorkshire. I sought Master John first, and asked of him an introduction to the provost. This he was pleased to provide, as I had in years past discovered who had stolen his books and seen them restored to him.

"No man has tried to sell me any of the set books stolen from your father-in-law," Wycliffe said when he saw me approach.

"As I am no longer master at Canterbury Hall, men with books to sell no longer seek me out. As for RHETORIC, the monk who purchased it will not yield it without a suit. I have enquired."

"'Tis not my stolen book brings me to you. I need to have audience with the provost of Queen's Hall."

Master John raised his eyebrows at this request. I hurried to explain.

"You will remember when I was in Oxford several weeks past, I spoke of felonies and murders in the shire to the west of Oxford?"

"I do. Have you discovered the men?"

"I think I may have done, though I am not certain. I suspect a youth hailing from a village 'twixt here and Bampton may be involved."

"Suspect?"

"Aye. I cannot prove it. Not yet."

"And Henry Whitfield may help find the proof?" Wycliffe said incredulously. "How could a scholar who closets himself away be useful to you?"

"The youth in question was a scholar at Queen's Hall. A younger son. His older brother has been slain, so he will now inherit his father's estate."

"And the younger need spend no more dreary hours studying to provide for himself as a cleric," Wycliffe completed the thought.

"Aye. I am wondering who the lad's friends were while he was at Queen's Hall."

"Well, you are right to try Master Henry. Come, we will seek him."

As Master John had intimated, we found Henry Whitfield bent over a large tome, in a chamber so small it gave hardly enough room for desk, bench, bed, and scholar. And Whitfield is not a large man. He is scrawny enough that I conjecture the fellow is often so absorbed with a book that he forgets his dinner. I like books, and fancy myself a scholar. But I am not so enamored of study that I'd overlook suppertime passing. Perhaps that is why I am a bailiff and surgeon, and not a doctor of theology. And, of course, I have Kate. Even with my nose in a book I'd catch the savory aroma of her cooking spreading through the house. It would call to me.

"Edmund Harcourt? Aye. Amiable lad. Not very sensible. No scholar, either," Whitfield said when I asked of the youth. "His friends? Had Edmund many? Yes. Likeable fellow. He often took friends to his father's manor, he being from close by and most others of Queen's Hall from the north. And his closest friends? Hmmm. Roger Chirk, I'd say. And John Bast. And Ivo Bellers. Those three I'd often see with Edmund. Poor lads, all three. Aye, he was thickest with them."

I listened intently, committing the names to memory and enquiring: "Are the three you named yet enrolled in Queen's Hall, or have they, like Edmund, withdrawn?"

"Odd you should ask that. Since Edmund left the hall the other three have dropped off in their studies, often absent from lectures and disputations. They seem to have lost their appetite for things of the mind, although in truth none of the four were ever great scholars."

"Does one of the three have a mole upon his left temple, betwixt eye and ear?"

"Oh, aye. That would be John."

Goliards! I had heard of such wayward youths being not uncommon in the shire about Oxford. But such evil conduct was thought to be long past, scholars today being more tractable lads, less interested in looting the nearby villages and slaying those who would oppose their rapacious ways. Still, study can be tedious, and is not likely to produce much wealth, at least not in the near future. Those who want great reward for little effort could well be seduced into less noble occupations.

I now possessed names with which to confront Oswald and Edmund and was eager to do so. 'Twas past the ninth hour when my interview with Henry Whitfield ended. I would have pressed on that afternoon to Stanton Harcourt but such a decision would have been a cruel use of our beasts. So, as many times – too many times – in the past several weeks we halted before the gate to Eynsham Abbey requesting lodging and a meal.

We arrived as the monks were at their simple supper. We shared in the pottage and loaves brought to us in the guest chamber, and I was licking my chops when the hosteller returned with a request that I call upon Abbot Gerleys. I thought perhaps his sore had festered. Not so.

"Master Hugh," he greeted me when I entered his chamber. "I give you good day... or good evening, as the day is well gone. I shall be almost sorry when these felonies vexing us so are ended, for you will then have no reason to pass the abbey. I will miss our conversations. But look, there has been another house plundered. In Northmoor. The village is not an abbey demesne. Sir Ralph Wolford is lord of the manor. His cousin is here, Brother Andrew, and recently had news of the felony. The reeve's house was plundered of a Sunday, two weeks past."

"Whilst all Christian men were at mass," I said.

"Aye – well, a man who will break God's law to steal will defy His other commands also."

"Does Sir Ralph's bailiff have men he suspects?" I asked.

"That I cannot say. If the traveler who brought the news had such inklings, he did not share them with Brother Andrew."

"Then he's maybe as much in the dark as I am."

"Have you no suspects even now?"

"Suspects, aye. Proof of guilt? That I lack. But I am shaping a scheme to provide the evidence I need. God willing the demands I make on your hospitality will thin out soon."

"You are on the point of sending the villains to a scaffold?"

"Perhaps not," I said.

"No? If the felons are seized and their guilt is proven, why will they not hang?"

But the abbot answered his own question. "Ah, they have sometimes been seen wearing scholars' gowns. They are clerks."

"Mayhap. If my design succeeds I may know by this time on the morrow who is to be charged with the murders and villainies which have vexed us."

My design did not succeed. It did not fail of its own flaws, but because the schemes of others succeeded first.

Arthur, Uctred, and I mounted our palfreys early next morn and made for Stanton Harcourt, armed with the names of four young scholars who, I felt sure, were responsible for the mayhem in the shire. Should we present these names to Oswald and press him concerning the disappearance of the green woolen wisp, I thought we stood a reasonable chance of seeing the bailiff's resolve fail him. Putting the image of a noose before him would likely also loosen his tongue.

I dismounted before Sir Thomas's manor house, it being a courtesy when visiting a man's estate to greet him before attending to other matters. And Sir Thomas would surely have called my business that day his affair as much as my own.

He greeted me with a friendly "Good morrow," and when I told him 'twas Oswald I intended to visit he rolled his eyes and said, "'Tis barely the third hour. You will likely find the indolent fellow yet abed."

We did.

No amount of pounding on the bailiff's rattling door or shouting of his name brought the man to his threshold. It struck me that Oswald must be an uncommonly sound sleeper, with the sun filling his chamber through the oiled parchment of his window even before we started pounding on his door.

Arthur and Uctred looked as perplexed as I that the din had not brought the bailiff from his bed, if that was where he was. We three exchanged baffled glances. After several minutes of bruising my fist and abusing my voice proved ineffective at rousing Oswald I began to fear another reason for his failure to appear.

"You s'pose 'e's about manor business somewhere?" Uctred said.

"Not likely," Arthur replied, "if 'e's as lazy as Sir Thomas do say."

"Mayhap 'e's 'ad too much ale or wine last night," Uctred offered, "an' is sleepin' off an aching 'ead."

Possible. But though too much wine of an evening may cause deep sleep, it would have to render a man deaf to make him oblivious to the row we were making.

"Come," I said. "We will seek Sir Thomas and learn if Oswald may be about manor business of which Sir Thomas is unaware."

"Not likely," Sir Thomas said when I asked if the bailiff would be found at his duties. "Most of what's needful this time of year is reeve's business. Oswald will not find work for himself if it can be avoided. And since he knows that his days in my employ are numbered he does even less than before."

"No rapping upon his door or shouting of his name will bring him forth," I explained.

Sir Thomas frowned, thought upon my words for a moment, then said, "Come," and walked briskly across the village green, past the well, to the bailiff's house.

Perhaps he did not believe me. He beat upon the door, calling Oswald's name, with the same success as I had. None.

There was an iron latch to secure the door, but no lock. To further secure the door Oswald no doubt had a bar to drop when night came. I asked Sir Thomas if this was so.

"Aye. And another closes the door to the toft."

With that Sir Thomas quickly turned and walked around the house. We three followed. Sir Thomas lifted the latch of the rear door and when it failed to open put his shoulder to it. To no effect.

"Bah... both doors barred. Then he's not away. No man can bar both doors of his house and then leave it. He must be within." With that assertion Sir Thomas resumed pounding and shouting. A few folk of the village, curious about the racket, peered from their doorways to see what caused the tumult.

"He is dead," I said.

Sir Thomas regarded me with an open mouth, startled, as if I had announced that the king and Prince Edward would call this day at the ninth hour.

"Dead?" Sir Thomas said. "He was well enough yesterday. Why do you believe him dead?"

"He is either dead or so ill that he cannot raise himself from his bed. And if you saw him hale yesterday I believe it unlikely any malady would strike him down so quickly."

"Plague could do so," Arthur said.

"Aye," I answered, "it could, but the pestilence has vanished from the shire two years now. Plague does not take lone victims."

"'Less he be the first," Uctred muttered, and crossed himself.

"If he is ill he must be attended," Sir Thomas said. "Soon I will no longer employ him, but while they work for me I will not see my men suffer with no recourse to help. Wait here. I'll return shortly."

Sir Thomas hastened off toward his manor house and disappeared behind the dwelling. He soon reappeared, an axe in his hand.

"Stand aside," the knight said. Drawing back the axe he laid a vigorous blow on the plank just below the iron latch. The door burst open, banging loudly against the inner wall and springing back.

Sir Thomas pushed past the shattered door, propping the axe against it to fix it in place, and shouted the bailiff's name. There was no reply. I did not expect one.

The bailiff's house was modest. No glass windows here. It contained two rooms, with a loft above one end of the larger room, where children might sleep had Oswald a wife to bear him any. This larger room was also provided with a fireplace. The ruined door opened to this larger room and in it I saw a table, two benches, and a crude cupboard. But neither bed nor pallet, and no bailiff.

Sir Thomas glanced briefly about, then stalked through the room to an opening which led to another, smaller, chamber. Here we found Oswald.

He lay abed, a blanket bulging over his rotund form, his unseeing eyes staring at the rafters above him. I held my hand above his open mouth and felt no breath. About his mouth I saw traces of vomit which he had spewed up as he died. His body was cold and stiff with rigor mortis.

Sir Thomas crossed himself, then spoke. "Poor fellow. Died in his sleep."

"I think not," I replied.

"Oh? Why so?"

"A man asleep will have his eyes closed, and they will likely remain so if death overtakes him then."

"Hmmm. What if some pain awakens him before death comes?"

"His eyes would then open," I said. "But would his bedclothes not be put in disarray as he felt death approach?"

"I take your point," Sir Thomas said. "What man, even as indolent as Oswald, will lay abed and gaze calmly at the underside of his thatching as death comes?

"But if he did not die in his sleep," Sir Thomas continued, "what then? Did some man slay him? That seems unlikely. His doors were barred. How could a felon strike him down and then escape the place?"

I shook my head. "This death is odd. The man was not old and frail. He was vigorous yesterday, you said. It is possible some unforeseen malady came suddenly upon him, I suppose."

"But you think not," Sir Thomas said.

"Bailiffs are employed to think the worst," I replied. "Our work causes us to become skeptical of easy answers to perplexing situations."

"Are not the simple answers sometimes correct?"

"They are. And when 'tis so, I am pleased."

"You are a surgeon. If you examine the corpse closely might you discover the reason for this death?"

"I might."

"Then do so."

Some men sleep in kirtle and braes; others prefer to be unclothed under their blanket. Oswald was of the latter persuasion, which made examination of the corpse somewhat easier. Removing the blanket exposed his pallid rotundity to view. 'Twas not a pleasing sight.

I did not expect to find a wound. Wounds bleed, and no

blood stained either blanket or pallet. Nevertheless I inspected the corpse for a puncture, even the navel, ears, and anus. I had been tricked once in the past by a murderer who slew his victim by pushing a bodkin into the man's brain through an ear whilst he slept. I would not be deceived again in such manner.

I asked Arthur to help me roll Oswald onto his belly, and Sir Thomas watched intently as I concluded the examination and then turned the corpse again to its back.

"What have you found?" he asked.

"Nothing. He was not stabbed anywhere by any blade."

"There are other ways to slay a man."

"Aye. A hempen rope or strong hands about a man's neck will strangle him."

"Is there any way to know?" Sir Thomas said.

"There would be a bruise about the victim's neck," I replied.

Sir Thomas moved close to Oswald's head to examine the fleshy neck. The light in this chamber was not good, but good enough that if there had been red and purple impressions upon the neck they would be visible. There were none.

"A man being strangled will likely thrash about as he attempts to escape death," I said. "There is nothing amiss in this chamber. But murderers may, I suppose, return things to order which are awry."

"But you think not," Sir Thomas said.

"Aye. He was not strangled."

When Arthur and I had turned the corpse, Oswald's pillow had fallen from his bed to the rushes of the floor. Arthur had retrieved it, and held it before him as he watched me complete the inspection of the corpse.

"Ho," he exclaimed. "What is here?"

I turned and saw Arthur gazing intently at the pillow.

"What have you found?" I said.

"What it is I don't know. But there be a stain upon this pillow."

He held it out to me in such a wise as the light from the window could best illuminate it. I looked closely at the stain –

it had an unpleasant yellowish tint. Small dried particles clung there where the fluid had soaked in. I took the pillow and tentatively held it to my nose. The smell was repulsive. Oswald had indeed retched up part of his dinner as he died.

"What is there?" Sir Thomas asked.

"Oswald vomited as he died."

"Will a man commonly do that when death is near?"

"'Tis not uncommon, I think."

"I'll tell you what's uncommon," Arthur said. "When I picked the pillow from the rushes, that stain was upon the bottom. A man ain't gonna lose 'is dinner on the nether side of 'is pillow, I think."

I had been about to attribute Oswald's death to some natural affliction, of which there are many that will bring death. But Arthur's discovery dispelled that notion.

"There is another way to slay a man in his bed," I said. "If a pillow be held against his face he will soon perish."

"And there will be no bruise upon his neck, or anywhere else," Sir Thomas said, "if he is smothered, not strangled. Will such a death cause a man to spew up part of his last meal?"

"I doubt it not," I said.

"Murder, then. But who would slay Oswald? He was incompetent, 'tis true. But men are not murdered for their inadequacies. If they were, I should have done away with him long ago."

"He died, I think, because he knew too much."

"Too much about what?"

"He knew of the felons who have brought havoc to the shire."

"Oswald? How could he have exerted himself enough to have discovered them when you have not?"

"I think he did not need to exert himself, for he was one of them."

"My bailiff? A felon? But who then slew him, and why?"

"The brigands with whom he did the felonies slew him, I think."

"But why?"

"Somehow they discovered I was on my way here to demand information of him. And they guessed of my questions for him."

"You knew when you appeared at my door this day that Oswald was associated with a group of felons?"

"I did not know of a certainty, but I thought 'twas likely."

"And his companions did murder so he could not name them?" Sir Thomas concluded.

"I believe it so."

"Who are these men? Let me fetch the priest! We shall pursue them and send them to the scaffold." He departed the house and strode directly to the church. I thought it unlikely the knight would be so hot-blooded about this if he knew who I thought responsible for the deaths and thievery which had plagued the shire. I waited, with Arthur and Uctred and Oswald's staring corpse, for him to appear with the village priest. My reason for visiting Stanton Harcourt lay cold upon the bed, but gave me another reason for lingering in the village.

Men, or a man, had slain Oswald, this was sure. But how had they quit the house leaving both doors barred? For that matter, how had they gained entry? Invited, no doubt. If so, my suspicion that the bailiff was slain by men he knew and trusted would be confirmed.

Whilst the priest said the words of Extreme Unction over the corpse I prowled about the exterior of the house. I inspected the windows, looking for any sign of oiled parchments lifted and moved back into place. No such indication met my eye. It was clear that whoso did murder wished other men to believe that Oswald had died in his sleep, with no other involved in the death.

Grass flourished beneath two of the windows. No footprints would be found there, and the vegetation seemed vigorous, not flattened as if some man had recently stepped upon it. How long would grass crushed under a man's foot remain so before it became again upright? This was not taught in surgery classes at the University of Paris.

Soil, undisturbed, was under two other windows. The dirt was soft enough that, had men put foot upon it, an imprint would be made. None was there. No man had escaped the house through its windows.

I stood before the rear door, puzzled. It was as if felons had become angels and flown through the roof. The roof! I stepped back from the rear of the bailiff's house to examine the thatch. At first glance I saw nothing amiss, but closer examination showed a place near the chimney where the thatching reeds seemed to be turned. Elsewhere the thatch kept a uniformly gray tint, but a small section had a lighter shade, as if the place had usually been shaded from weather and sun.

Arthur and Uctred followed me about the house while I examined the windows and the sod and soil beneath them. When I stepped away from the dwelling to view the roof, so did they. And they saw what I saw.

"S'pose Oswald had a bundle of new thatch put up there aside 'is chimney?" Arthur said.

"Mayhap 'e 'ad a leak," Uctred added.

The off-color thatching was above the loft. "Come," I said, and led the way into the house.

A crude and apparently seldom-used ladder was propped against the daub. I moved it so that it rested at its top against the beam which supported the loft, then tested the first few rungs. They were tied to the uprights with hempen cords which were dry, brittle, and of great age. The loft was barely above my head when I stood under it. If a cord broke, my fall would not be great, and the rushes upon the floor would soften the impact. So I hoped.

I climbed to the loft and Arthur grasped the ladder to follow. I bid him remain below.

"Look to the cords which bind the rungs," I said. "They may support me, but you will tumble upon your head if you test them."

Arthur glanced at the cords, agreeing with my estimation of his near future if he began the climb, and stepped back.

The loft admitted little light, but enough for me to see

where two straps had been freshly snapped between a rafter and the wattles and daub of the end wall. These breaks had been cleverly fitted back together so the fracture would be hidden by the shadows to any but those who might search the place. The discolored thatching was directly above these broken crosspieces, if I judged correctly.

The man, or men, who had departed the house in this manner must have been young and agile to do so. The ladder had been replaced against a wall, so they had mounted to the loft by seizing the beam and pulling themselves up. The hole made in the thatch was large enough for a slender youth, and once outside the house, upon the roof, there would be a drop of no more than a foot or so greater than the height of a man to the ground – nothing to inconvenience a slender youth. I am past my youth and not so nimble now, but even I could manage the descent without injury.

I climbed down the ladder – carefully – and departed through the back door of the house. I stood close under the eaves below the discolored thatch and studied the soil there. I saw heel prints where men had dropped from roof to ground, striking the earth heavily. Some of these footprints had been brushed away, but a few remained. The men who dropped from the roof had done so in the dark and had not seen by moonlight all the prints they had made in the earth, so failed to obliterate all.

These indentations were unalike. The heels of two men had imbedded themselves into the soil. One of those who had made imprints wore a shoe, or mayhap a boot, which was missing a part of the heel. A semi-circle was absent from the heel print. I made a mental note of this, thinking the information might lead to a murderer. It did so, and sooner than I expected.

We three returned to the front of the bailiff's house to see the priest and his clerk removing Oswald's corpse. They struggled under the burden, and the coppiced poles of the litter flexed alarmingly.

Sir Thomas stood by the ruined front door and watched as priest and clerk labored to transport their load to the church. I wondered who could be found in the village to wash the corpse and keep vigil by candlelight through the night until Oswald could be properly planted in the churchyard. The death of a bailiff is rarely the occasion for weeping and mourning within his bailiwick. Mayhap Bampton will be different. I have tried to perform my duties to make it so.

As the blanket-covered corpse was carried to the church, Edmund Harcourt appeared from behind the manor house. He stopped to watch as the corpse passed, crossed himself, then strode rapidly to his father.

"Oswald has died in the night, so William said."

I wondered who William was and how he had discovered the information. Neither I nor Arthur nor Uctred had spoken to any man of Oswald's death. Perhaps when Sir Thomas hurried to fetch the axe he had spoken to a servant. But at that time no man knew that Oswald was dead. Did Sir Thomas surmise it was so? When he hastened to get the axe he had thought Oswald ill. I had suggested death, but Sir Thomas seemed to scoff at the thought.

"Murdered in the night," Sir Thomas replied.

"Murdered? Surely not! In his bed? How could such a thing be? Were his doors not barred?"

The lad was young and unskilled at guile. He was of an age and lineage which believes all will be well, no matter what mistakes are made along the way, until adulthood arrives to prove not every blunder can be brushed over.

How could Edmund know Oswald was found dead in his bed? He had a house in which to die, and could have done so anywhere. He might have been attacked before he had gone to his bed, before he had barred his doors. If Sir Thomas was puzzled by this he kept his peace.

"Oswald was a poor bailiff," Edmund pressed on. "We have not lost much with his death. You wished him away by Whitsuntide, anyway. And he had no success in discovering who slew my brother."

Sir Thomas listened to his son with a face that expressed no emotion. Seeing he would not be drawn, the lad finished lamely, "Well... dinner will be served soon... the cook asked me to tell you." After another moment's uncertainty, he turned back toward the manor house and the imminent meal. As he went, I – and Arthur, and Uctred – looked at his boots. They were of good quality, but not new; quite worn, in fact. As he walked away we saw the track of one boot left an ovoid breach in the dust where a part of the heel had been sliced or broken away.

So I explained to Sir Thomas how men had managed to slay Oswald and leave the house though the doors were barred from within. He listened with widening eyes, and asked to be shown the discolored thatching. I led him there, pointing out the depressions in the dirt where the murderers had descended from the roof and failed to obscure their footprints in the night. I wondered if he would notice the distinctive heel print. He did, but showed no knowledge of its source.

"You will not gain Bampton in time for your dinner," Sir Thomas said then. "Please dine at my table. There will be food enough, and places at the benches for your men."

I felt much conflicted over when and how much I should say to Sir Thomas of his son's complicity in the wickedness which had come to the shire. I decided to show him, and allow him to reach his own conclusions.

We departed the bailiff's house walking toward the manor house, then I stopped. Sir Thomas, Arthur, and Uctred continued for a few paces until they realized that I was no longer with them. They halted and turned to see what had caught my attention. When I knew I had Sir Thomas's attention I squatted and pointed a finger at his son's boot print in the dirt. I said nothing.

The knight bent to examine what I had pointed out. He said: "Why, 'tis the same as was behind Oswald's house. The same man has walked here."

And then he fell silent. His shoulders drooped. "It was my son walked here but a few moments past," he said. His words were a cry of pain from a wounded man. In truth, he had suffered a wound which would never heal.

There was no dinner served that day at Stanton Harcourt

manor house. Sir Thomas stood from examining the boot print, his back stiff as a poker, and stalked toward his house. We followed, aware of the thunderbolt about to strike, and unable to turn from it.

Sir Thomas threw open the door and called out for Edmund. The lad awaited his father in the hall; a valet was placing a dish of pork in egurdouce upon the high table as we watched.

"Take off your boots," Sir Thomas roared.

"My boots?" the lad said. "'Tis time for dinner. Why...?"

"Take off your boots," Sir Thomas shouted again. Edmund heeded the tone of his father's voice, sat upon a bench, and pulled off his footwear with no further delay.

Sir Thomas seized the boots, then grasped Edmund by the collar of his cotehardie and dragged him from the manor house. He said no more until he had hauled the lad to the rear of the bailiff's house. I watched as he held the misshapen heel close to Edmund's face, then pointed to the boot print in the soft earth and said, "Explain this."

The lad swallowed like a carp cast up on the bank.

"Uh... uh, I heard something in the night and came to see what had made the noise."

"Why then was your back to Oswald's house?" I said. "See how the footprint faces."

"Uh, I uh, heard another sound, so pressed myself against the house to – to hide from whoso might be about after curfew."

"Who was with you?" I said.

"With me?"

"Aye. Two men made footprints here. Who accompanied you?"

Edmund's reaction was telling. I might have swatted his skull with a barrel stave, so stunned was his expression.

"Who is this fellow Master Hugh speaks of?" Sir Thomas demanded.

"Uh... a friend... uh, from Queen's Hall."

"And he was here in the night? With you? Why did I not meet him?" Sir Thomas asked.

"Because," I said, "he did not arrive in Stanton Harcourt before dark. I inquired yesterday of the provost of Queen's Hall who Edmund's friends are. He gave me three names. One of the fellows somehow learned of it, and came here in the night to warn your son."

"Warn Edmund? But warn him of what?"

"That I was likely to press Oswald about his alliance with your son and his friends."

"What alliance could Edmund have with Oswald?"

"Will you tell him, or shall I?" I said to Edmund. The lad was silent.

"Your son and his friends are goliards. They found theft more appealing and profitable than study."

"What? My son and his companions have done the felonies in the shire these past months?"

"They have."

"But what of Oswald? How was he a part of the wickedness?"

"I'm not sure," I said. "'Tis my belief that he was not so stupid or inept as he seemed. Somehow he learned who the rogues were, and that Edmund was one of them, and demanded a price for his silence. This is why Oswald conveniently lost the green woolen fragment whereby we might have identified one of Edmund's felonious friends. 'Twas less troublesome to dispose of the wisp and feign ignorance of its disappearance than for the fellow to purchase a new cotehardie. They might have slain Oswald anyway, to relieve themselves of the cost of his silence, but when they learned I meant to visit here this day, and that from Queen's Hall I had learned their names, they conspired to slay Oswald. They feared I might question him so strictly he would fear the noose and give evidence against the miscreants."

Sir Thomas listened intently to this, and let it sink in. Then, "You slew your own *brother*?" he demanded in horror of his son.

"Nay, Father. Not so. I'd no wish to see him dead."

"If he knew you were among the villains who took him," I said, "he would have to die. If he lived he would name you as one who seized him."

"Aye. That's why only John and Ivo took him. And they were to be careful to speak no names. Henry did not know them, nor did he know I was in league with them." Edmund turned from me to his father, and his face changed. "Had you supplied me with funds so that I could live decently in Oxford I'd not have needed to extort shillings from you!"

Resigned to his situation, the lad accepted he had been caught out. I believe he considered further lies to be useless. He spoke more freely than I had thought he would.

"Why, then," I asked, "was he slain?"

"'Twas not our intent," Edmund said. I heard his throat tighten on the words and thought he was about to cry. "We would free him when Father paid ten pounds. We held him in the forest, in an old swineherd's hut abandoned there. But one night, when it was Ivo's turn to stay up and keep guard, he fell to sleep. Henry worked free of his bonds and ran, but crashing through the forest in the dark he made so much noise he awakened John. John roused Ivo and they gave chase. We didn't mean Henry to die. Ivo is fleet, and had armed himself with a cudgel. When he caught up with Henry he hit him – but only to halt his flight, not slay him. The blow caused Henry to stumble headlong into a stone wall, John said. They left Henry dead where he lay, beside the wall, unwilling to carry him away and perhaps be seen crossing the hayfield."

"And Hubert Shillside?"

"Who?"

"The man you robbed and struck down upon the Windrush Bridge."

"We slew no man upon the Windrush Bridge." Here was an unexpected claim.

"What of the man found slain near to Abingdon, his cart and oxen taken?"

"He knew Ivo. Had seen him about Oxford. Ivo would not allow him to live and bring a charge against us."

"And the man you slew and left in the forest near to Wytham? What of him?"

A puzzled frown came upon Edmund's countenance. "We slew no man there."

I believed him. Edmund had spoken freely enough of his other felonies when he understood that he was found out that I could find no reason for prevarication regarding one more murder.

"What of my surgical instruments and the book you stole from me?"

He mumbled, "We sold them in Oxford."

"To whom were my instruments sold?"

"I never saw. John sold them. Perhaps he'll remember."

"Which of your friends is left-handed?" I asked.

"Ivo."

"'Twas him, then, who slashed a traveler upon the road near to Abingdon," I said.

"Aye."

"You thought to overpower three men upon the road, but ran off when others of the party appeared. Is this not so?"

"Aye."

"Why then go to Eynsham Abbey? Why not return to Oxford?"

"We ran off and hid for a few days because we recognized the tanner when he appeared upon the road. We guessed him likely bound for Oxford, where he might recognize one of us on the streets."

"What of the lass of Church Hanborough? Was that your doing?"

Edmund did not reply, but hung his head.

"You and your friends are the scoundrels who raped that lass?" Sir Thomas said. Without another word he delivered a blow to the side of Edmund's head which left the lad sprawled in the dirt. The lad raised himself slowly to his feet, fearful of another stroke, which he surely deserved.

"Where is the one who helped you slay Oswald?" I said.

"He returned straightway to Oxford – last night."

"Where you will now go," Sir Thomas said, "to visit the sheriff... I have lost all of my sons."

Sir Thomas would not wait for his dinner. I watched as he permitted Edmund to draw on his boots, then hailed two grooms. He instructed his servants to prepare four horses and be quick about it. Within the hour we watched Sir Thomas and his grooms leave the village, taking Edmund to the sheriff. Many knights would not have done so, preferring a surviving heir to justice.

My empty stomach prompted me to seek our beasts and depart Stanton Harcourt in the opposite direction from Sir Thomas. I thought momentarily of begging a meal from the manor serving men, but judged it not fitting. There would be no dinner for us this day 'til we arrived home.

At the intersection of Bridge Street and Church View Street I sent Arthur and Uctred on to the castle with our palfreys. I proceeded afoot to Galen House where, between bites of capon in bruit and barley loaf, I told Kate and her father of the resolution of the felonies between Bampton and Oxford.

"No more journeys to Oxford," Kate smiled.

"One more. To find the monk who has purchased RHETORIC, and the surgeon who purchased my instruments. I want them returned."

When my meal was done I sought Will Shillside and told him of the conclusion to my investigation of his father's murder, unsatisfactory as it was. He was pleased to believe that, even though they did not admit their guilt, the felons had been apprehended. He told me later that the punishment inflicted upon the four scholars did not, to his mind, resemble justice. I had to agree.

As I suspected, the lads pleaded benefit of clergy before the King's Eyre and were sent to Bishop Bokyngham's court. There they were required to undertake pilgrimage to Jerusalem and wear hair shirts under their cotehardies which must not be removed until their return. By that time lice would infest the hair shirts and the degree of penance would be the greater.

Any pilgrimage is arduous, to Jerusalem especially so. A man will have many experiences upon such a journey, most of them bad. If he does not succumb to disease or thieves upon the road, or his ship does not sink beneath him, Musselmen may slay him for an infidel, or sell him into slavery. The penance was not so light as first appeared.

The monk who had purchased RHETORIC could not be found. Like Master Wycliffe he had departed Canterbury Hall. For Cambridge, another monk said. But John remembered the surgeon who had purchased my instruments – one of those who claimed ignorance of any such tools being offered, promising as if butter wouldn't melt in his mouth that he would surely let me know if they turned up.

When I confronted the man he claimed the scalpels and other oddments had been his these many years, and that a felon who said otherwise was not to be believed. But Lord Gilbert heard of my loss and sent word of the business to Sheriff de la Mare. He sent a constable to visit the surgeon. A few days later a youth arrived in Bampton with my lost instruments.

Somewhere, perhaps many years hence, some man will read Aristotle's RHETORIC and wonder how some pages became stained. The book will keep its secrets. Perhaps he will read this chronicle and understand.

Chapter 19

Edmund Harcourt's denial of responsibility for Hubert Shillside's murder vexed me. And the broken blade I had drawn from the man's ribs did also. I had set the crude weapon in my instruments chest, and each time I opened the box it reminded me of my uncertainty. Will Shillside seemed satisfied that, despite disavowing the murder of his father, Edmund Harcourt and his goliard friends were responsible for the crime. I was not. Edmund had been forthcoming about his other felonies. Why not admit the slaying of Hubert Shillside if he and his friends had done the deed? The doubt seldom left my mind.

So it was that I considered Shillside's murder one warm day in mid-May while I walked along the bank of Shill Brook seeking herbs for my depleted store. I knew of a place along the brook where feverfew and willow were to be found and went there to gather a sackful of the leaves of feverfew and bark of the willow. These are useful in reducing men's fevers, as well as lessening headaches and relieving the aching joints of older folk.

When my sack was full I sat upon the bank of the brook to enjoy the sun and fell to wool-gathering as I contemplated the flow. Once a few weeks past such a preoccupation had led to the discovery of Hubert Shillside's corpse. This day I made another find.

On the far side of the stream, where water deepened as it curved and undercut a bank, a small willow, its roots washed away, had fallen into the stream. Its branches waved gently in the current, and upon one of these boughs a brown object shaped like a pig's bladder was caught. I was puzzled as to what this could be, for it seemed foreign to the brook.

The thing could not be reached from my side of the stream, so there was nothing to be done, if I wished to retrieve it, but to remove my shoes and roll up my chauces and wade into the brook.

I found a leather pouch caught upon a willow sprig, bloated and rounded as it filled with water in the flow. I drew the pouch from its place and splashed back to the bank, where I dried my feet upon the grass, pulled on my shoes, then examined my find.

I had discovered a purse of excellent quality, made by a good cordwainer. Sturdy leather thongs were woven into its closure, but these had been cut cleanly. Why, I wondered, would a man discard such a valuable object?

I turned the purse over in my hands, and this question was answered. I had seen this purse before. Engraved on one side was the letter "H", painstakingly incised into the leather. Here was Hubert Shillside's purse, found, like the man, in a stream. But streams many miles apart.

I hastened back to the village and Broad Street, where is found Will Shillside's home and haberdashery. Alice answered my rapping upon the door, and recognizing me, bent to curtsey. This she need not do, for I am no nobleman, and she found the act difficult to do. Kate would, I thought, be called soon to serve as god's sib, for Alice must ere long become a mother.

Will heard my voice and appeared behind his wife. I did not wish to dismay Alice, considering her sensitive condition, so asked the young man to walk with me. I led him to the churchyard, and when he was seated in the porch I drew the purse from under my cotehardie and laid it in his hands.

His eyes opened wide, as did his mouth, when he saw the "H" engraved upon the damp leather.

"'Tis my father's purse," he exclaimed. "Where did you come by it? Where was it found? The lad from Stanton Harcourt is away on pilgrimage, is he not? Did his conscience trouble him so that he gave it up before he departed? 'Tis sodden. How so?"

"Edmund Harcourt and his felonious friends did not slay your father; nor did they have his purse. 'Tis as Edmund claimed. They were innocent of the crime, if not of many others. I found it not an hour past in Shill Brook, near to where the stream passes under the east bridge."

218

"How would it come to be there?" Will said, then answered his question. "The guilty man lives here, and thought to cast the purse into the brook and thereby discard evidence of his crime."

"Aye," I replied. "So I believe. I found the purse caught on a willow branch, else by now, after so many days, it would be in the Thames and carried to London. The man who slew your father thought to destroy evidence of his felony when he pitched him into the Windrush stream. As with the purse, he thought the flow would take evidence of his crime far away. The streams betrayed his sin."

Will sat silent for a moment, turning the purse in his hands, then spoke quietly, as if he feared some man might overhear.

"Who is the guilty man? Who do you believe has done this murder? 'Twill be some scoundrel of Bampton or the Weald."

"It will, and I believe I know who has done this evil. But I would not have his name bandied about so that he learns of my suspicion and takes flight."

"You will not name the man?"

"Nay. 'Tis for the best that I tell no man what I believe, not even you. If he learns of it he will do what he might to escape the scaffold, or if you have his name you may decide to take matters into your own hands, and not wait for the sheriff's justice. You would then be as guilty of felony as the murderer."

I may as well have named Walter Mapes, as matters befell. Will, I believe, told Alice of the purse. Indeed, he likely showed it to her, for he carried it with him when we left the church porch.

Alice, I think, then spoke of the discovery to friends, and one of these told Father Thomas, for early next morn he appeared at Galen House, curious as to whom I was about to charge with Hubert Shillside's death.

"'Tis said you found Hubert's purse in Shill Brook," he said.

"Aye. Yesterday, while seeking willow bark and feverfew."

"No doubt, then, that the felon is amongst us, eh, and not Sir Thomas Harcourt's lad."

"No doubt."

"And who is the culprit? Surely you must suspect some man."

"Aye, I do. 'Twill be the man who stabbed Shillside and left his broken blade in the haberdasher's ribs."

The priest's eyes widened. "The felon who slew Hubert broke his dagger in so doing?"

"He did."

"You did not say so when you discovered the corpse."

"You did not ask."

"We must speak more of this matter," the priest said. I invited him to seat himself upon a bench.

"What more is to be said?" I asked. "You seem troubled."

"I am. I have seen a dagger with its blade snapped off but a few weeks past."

"Where? Why did you not say so?"

"You did not ask. But I will tell you now. You watched as Father Ralph, Father Simon, and I sought Alain Gower's stolen goods and opened Walter Mapes' chest. There was little in it. Nothing of Alain's goods. But at the bottom, underneath an old, threadbare cotehardie, I remember a broken dagger."

"I wonder if it remains there," I said.

"We can discover if it is readily enough," the priest replied.

"Aye. And I have yet the broken blade I drew from Shillside's ribs. But we must seek other men before we confront Walter. He and his lads may object to our examining the chest, and we two are not enough to convince them otherwise.

"Walter Mapes attempted to enter this house and beat me because I had disparaged his name. So he said. But I think now he had another reason."

"He worried that you were near to identifying Hubert's murderer," Father Thomas agreed.

"And had no dagger to plunge into my heart while I slept, for it was broken in his attack on Shillside."

"Did he know that you had found a broken dagger embedded in Shillside's ribs?"

"I doubt it, but mayhap he did. I told no one of the find. No one needed to know. But Will and Arthur knew of it. If Will later told Alice and she eventually spoke of it, the discovery might have found Walter's ear."

"In which case he will have discarded the broken dagger I saw in his chest."

"Aye, likely. But we must seek it to be sure. I thought that by holding back the discovery of the broken dagger I might have information I could use against the felon, but I see now that was not the case."

"Ah, but it was," Father Thomas said. "Had you made this known Mapes would have rid himself of the dagger rather than placing it in the chest, and when I looked there I would have seen no broken dagger."

"Fetch Father Ralph and Father Simon and your clerks. I will seek grooms at the castle and meet you at the bridge over Shill Brook. I'll have the broken blade with me. We will learn if it matches the ruined dagger in Walter's chest, if the weapon is yet there."

At the castle I found Arthur and Uctred and we hastened to Bridge Street. With the priests and their clerks we were nine. The clerics were unarmed, but Arthur, Uctred, and I had daggers ready. We made a considerable show of force as we turned to the path to the Weald.

Our cohort was but fifty or so paces from Walter's hovel when from its open door we heard a shout, then another, followed by a feminine screech. The uproar startled us, and we halted in the lane. Another scream followed, then the sound of a blow against flesh, and then a masculine bellow. I looked to Father Thomas, and he nodded toward the house and set off at a rapid pace. I and the others trotted behind.

Before we reached the house Mapes' wife burst through the open door, Walter in pursuit. The woman was howling for aid, Walter crying out threats against her through his damaged lips, and waving over his head what appeared to be the broken shaft of some implement. Perhaps a pitchfork.

How this tool was broken I could not say, but as the woman saw us in the path she ran to us to escape Walter's wrath. I saw blood trickling down her face from under her dingy cap as she drew near.

Walter's wife staggered and fell to her knees before Father Simon, pleading for protection from her enraged husband. Walter, seeing that he was much outnumbered, skidded to a halt, lowered his weapon, and took stock of the situation. Without a word to us he turned, strode to his house, and disappeared through the open door.

Father Simon and his clerk kneeled in the path to comfort the battered woman while we others followed Walter to his house and pursued him through the door.

Walter yet held the broken shaft in his hand, and seemed for a moment ready to use it against us. But wisdom overcame valor and he backed away.

"What d'you want?" he growled.

"Why do you beat a defenseless woman so?" Father Thomas said.

"None o' your concern."

"Perhaps," the priest replied, "but your chest and what it contains is."

Father Thomas approached the crude chest and from the corner of my eye I saw Walter move as if to stop him. Arthur saw this also and stepped between them. Few men armed with only a thin staff will challenge Arthur. Walter stopped where he was. The man may be foolish, but not foolhardy.

The priest opened the chest and in the dim light inside the hovel rummaged about in its depths. He tossed out several items of apparel, then stood and spoke to Walter.

"Where is the broken dagger which I saw in this chest when I last examined it?"

"Broken dagger?" Mapes scoffed. "I've no broken dagger."

"Perhaps not now, but you had one not long past. Where is it now?"

"In the brook," Mapes' wife said. The woman had ceased her howls and, with Father Simon and his clerk, followed us to her home. She stood in the doorway when she spoke. I turned to her and she spoke again. "'E tossed it in t'brook a fortnight an' more past. Said 'twas good for naught. Wouldn't say 'ow 'e broke it."

Walter dropped his weapon and seemed ready to flee out of the rear door of the house. "Seize him," I said, but Arthur had anticipated my command and took hold of Mapes' arm as the words left my mouth.

"Show me where your husband discarded the broken dagger," I said.

A woman whose husband regularly beats her is not likely to feel much loyalty to him. Mapes' wife turned and without a word stumbled toward the brook about forty paces from her door. Father Simon and his clerk each took an arm to steady the woman. Walter's beating had left her wobbling upon her feet.

Arthur had a grip on one of Walter's arms and Uctred the other. Together they dragged the unwilling fellow along to the brook.

"Just there," the woman said, and pointed unsteadily into the stream. The brook at this place is perhaps six paces wide and knee deep, no more, but turgid. The stream bed and whatever might be on it were invisible to us.

Invisible to sight, but not to touch. For the second time in as many days I discarded shoes, rolled up my chauces, and waded into the brook. The current would not carry away a broken dagger, unlike Shillside's purse which, I suspected, had been disposed of in the same way, in the same place.

I thought it unlikely that a broken blade flat upon the stream bed would do harm to my bare feet; nevertheless, I stepped cautiously as I searched with my toes for Walter's discarded dagger. No man upon the stream bank asked what I was about. They knew.

Twice my feet found curiously shaped objects which, when I dipped an arm into the water, became but large pebbles. When I felt these with my toes I thought they could not be a dagger, but drew them out for a look anyway, as my toes are not familiar with the shape and feel of a dagger in cold water. But when my foot

223

found the dagger I knew what I had discovered before I lifted it from the brook.

I pushed my way to the bank through the current, where Father Thomas extended a hand to help me ascend its slope. From my purse I drew the broken blade which had been embedded in Hubert Shillside's ribs. It was a perfect match to the haft I had just lifted from the water.

A scaffold rises a few steps from the Northgate in Oxford, where felons meet their end and others who pass by are reminded to avoid evil deeds lest they find themselves upon the planks with no safe way to descend. Walter Mapes perished there for his crimes six days later.

I offered the pieces of broken dagger to Will Shillside but he would not have them. I can understand why. I keep them in my chest as a reminder of questions I should have asked Father Thomas but did not when he reported to me of his first inspection of Walter Mapes' chest. If ever again such a felony occurs in my bailiwick I trust I will be more astute.

Hubert Shillside's ten shillings were never found. Mapes' wife and her children denied knowledge of the coins, and although I watched for months for any sign that the woman had discovered some wealth I saw none. The family remained poor as ever. The sons were old enough to do a man's work, so the greatest change for Mapes' wife from this matter was that she was no longer beaten when she displeased her husband.

Likely Walter buried his loot some dark night, thinking to wait until Shillside's murder was all but forgotten before spending the coins. Mayhap, some years hence, some man with a spade will happen upon the trove and wonder at his find.

Four days after Walter Mapes did the sheriff's dance Alice Shillside gave birth to a tiny lass. The babe will have no grandfather to make for her a doll from a broken tree branch.

Afterword

Many readers of the chronicles of Master Hugh de Singleton have asked about medieval remains in the Bampton area. St. Mary's Church is little changed from the fourteenth century, when it was known as the Church of St. Beornwald. The May Bank Holiday is a good time to visit Bampton. The village is a Morris dancing center, and on that day hosts a day-long Morris dancing festival.

Village scenes in the popular television series *Downton Abbey* were filmed on Church View Street, and St. Mary's Church appeared in several episodes.

Bampton Castle was, in the fourteenth century, one of the largest castles in England in terms of the area enclosed within the curtain wall. Little remains of the castle but for the gatehouse and a small part of the curtain wall, which form a part of Ham Court, a farmhouse in private hands. The current owners are doing extensive restoration work. Gilbert Talbot was indeed the lord of the manor of Bampton in the late fourteenth century.

The Bampton town library building, now four hundred years old, was transformed into the Downton hospital for the television series. The building needs extensive repairs and the village would surely appreciate contributions to help maintain this historic facility.

Schoolcraft, Michigan
April 2017

Prince Edward's Warrant

An extract from the eleventh chronicle of
Hugh de Singleton, surgeon

Chapter 1

Our party reached Aldersgate after the curfew bell had rung. We could not enter the city, but rather sought refuge for the night at the Priory of St. Bartholomew. I traveled with Sir Giles Cheyne, his two grooms, Milo and Thomas, his squire, Randall Patchett, and Arthur, a groom to my employer, Lord Gilbert Talbot. That we were too late to pass the Aldersgate Sir Giles laid against me. I accept the blame.

I had attempted to avoid this journey, pointing out to Lord Gilbert my duties to him and his manor at Bampton. He replied that my duty to my future sovereign transcended obligations to him. Bampton's reeve, John Prudhomme, could assume my duties while I was away in London.

Sir Giles had arrived in Bampton with his grooms and squire on the fourteenth day of October on a mission for Edward of Woodstock, Duke of Cornwall and Prince of Wales. Edward, he said, wished for the services of Lord Gilbert's surgeon, who had eased his illness at Limoges. I am the only surgeon in Lord Gilbert Talbot's employ.

"When the prince commands me to send you to him," Lord Gilbert said, "your service to me as bailiff here must be dispensable."

Edward, Sir Giles said, was weak, in much discomfort, and perhaps near to death. With his father, the king, the prince had embarked in August from Sandwich with four hundred ships, ten thousand archers, and four thousand men at arms intending to retake Edward's possessions in France lost to the French king.

For six weeks foul weather prevented a landing in France, and the expedition was compelled to return to England. A failure. A costly failure. Six weeks at sea in storms of wind and rain will tax the healthiest of men, which Prince Edward was not. The experience worsened his illness, Sir Giles said, and he required my service as once before at Limoges.

I am no physician, but know enough of herbs that when I met Prince Edward at Limoges before he embarked on this disastrous mission, I told him that his symptoms might be relieved if he consumed tansy, thyme, cress, and bramble leaves crushed to an oily paste, then mixed with wine.

The prince suffered from numerous maladies: a bloody flux, fevers, then chills, and passing wind so foul that folk despaired to be in the same room with him. These ailments had begun whilst Edward was in Spain, winning honor at the Battle of Najera. At Limoges he was so weak he could not sit a horse. The herbs I suggested seemed to improve his health, enough that with his father he embarked upon the ill-fated attempt to reclaim his patrimony in France. But now, in the year of our Lord 1372, his affliction was returned. So Sir Giles said. The duke desired me to attend him at Limoges. He had lost faith in William Blackwater, his physician.

I was loathe to leave Kate and our children. The last time I did so, when Lord Gilbert required that I accompany him to the siege of Limoges, I returned home to loss and sorrow. Sybil, our second child, perished while I was in France and now with the Lord Christ awaits her mother and me and Bessie and John. The babe was not yet one year old when she died. Might I have saved her had I not been in France? Unlikely. I am a surgeon, not a physician. And if physicians could cure a babe's fever, few infants would perish.

But Bessie and John are thriving, and Kate's father promised to look after my family while I was away upon the prince's business. A year ago my father-in-law was skin and bones. I thought him ill and close to death. His business in Oxford was failing, and he was near to starvation. I convinced him to leave Oxford and live with us, at Galen House, in Bampton, and Kate's cookery soon had him hale. His locks are grey, but he is once again strong enough to see to the care of his own.

Lord Gilbert agreed that I could take with me to London Arthur Wagge, a groom of Bampton Castle who has proven useful to me in Lord Gilbert's service. Dealing with miscreants does not trouble Arthur. He outweighs most men by two stone, possesses arms as thick as most men's legs, and although no longer young, can with a scowl convince rogues to give up their felonies when I command them to do so.

The journey from Bampton to London may be completed in three days, but not if a cold rain pours down upon a traveler as he ascends the Chiltern Hills and a child requires a surgeon's care. So it was that darkness overtook us before we reached London and we spent Monday night at the Priory of St. Bartholomew.

The delay disappointed me. The sooner I gained Prince Edward's presence and prescribed some physics for his ailments, the sooner I could return to Bampton. And I had found Sir Giles an uncongenial travel companion. My rank was beneath him, and he felt it undignified that his prince would send him to bring me to London. A man of lesser station could have done so. This he remarked upon often. Sir Giles talked much on the journey but said little.

When passing through Stokenchurch a child of no more than three years stumbled in a muddy rut in the road before our party. Rather than drawing upon the reins Sir Giles, with a curse, spurred his beast – to leap over the boy, so he later said. The animal's iron-shod hoof struck the lad's arm. I wonder if Sir Giles would have behaved so had he known in how few hours he would greet St. Peter?

I halted my palfrey and dismounted to comfort the howling child. The lad's cries drew his parents and siblings from their house. Indeed, half of the homes in the village emptied, their occupants pressing about me, curious as to what harm I had done to the child. Had not Arthur's thick arms, neck, and chest been behind me I believe the boy's father would have thrashed me before I could explain what had occurred.

When the crowd quieted I told the babe's parents of the reason for his wails, and explained that I was a surgeon and could deal with the injured arm. Each time I touched the appendage the lad howled anew, but I was able to satisfy myself that there was no broken bone. There was, however, a laceration and red bruise, which would soon darken to purple.

The cut must be closed. My instruments sack was slung across my palfrey's rump, behind the saddle. I unfastened it and withdrew from a small box my finest needle and a spool of silken thread. Had I more time, and was I dealing with an adult, I would have asked for a cup of ale and into it poured a mix of crushed hemp seeds and powdered lettuce sap. In an hour or so after drinking this concoction a man would feel less pain as I closed his wound.

But Sir Giles sat scowling upon his horse, impatient to be away, and I was uncertain how a child might cope with crushed hemp seeds and powdered lettuce sap.

I instructed the lad's father to hold his child tightly, and told the mother to grasp the lad's arm and under no circumstances allow it to move. The parents seemed reluctant to do this until I spoke firmly to them about the calamity which might come to their child if his cut was not closed properly.

Tenants on a manor such as Stokenchurch will have no wine. I asked for a volunteer to seek the manor house, explain the need, and return with a cup of wine. A village matron bustled off and I set to work threading my needle.

I made six sutures and with each the babe wailed anew. When I was satisfied that the cut was closed well I took the cup of wine, which had appeared at my elbow while I attended the wound, and bathed the laceration. The lad bawled again as the wine stung his wound. I would have spared him this, but wounds bathed in wine heal more readily than those not so washed. No man knows why.

Generally I follow the practice of Henri de Mondeville, who taught that wounds left dry and uncovered heal best, but in the case of a child I thought it likely the lad would pluck at the wound and sutures if my work was left open. I asked the lad's mother for an old kirtle or chemise. She produced one which seemed clean, and I tore it to strips with which I bound the cut.

I told the child's father that he could sever the stitches with his dagger and pull the threads free on All Saints' Day. The fellow nodded and thanked me for my service to his child. I decided as I mounted my beast that when I returned to Bampton, in but two or three days, I hoped, I would travel this way to learn how the little lad fared. This episode is why we came to the Aldersgate too late to enter the city and waited the night at the priory.

Kennington Palace is south of the Thames, so to reach Prince Edward's home we had to cross London to approach the south bank across London Bridge. We had passed the Goldsmith's Hall and turned on to Cheapside when a gathering mob of London's inhabitants began to impede our progress.

"Hanging today," Sir Giles said.

He was correct. We spurred our beasts through the crowd, receiving black looks as we did so, and came to the Standard as a noose was being draped around the neck of a lad of perhaps sixteen years.

"Wonder what 'e done?" Arthur said above the clamor.

"Apprentice to a draper what stole a bolt of silk from 'is master," an obliging onlooker replied.

The lad stood in a cart as the noose was placed about his neck, and when the hangman was satisfied, he slapped the rump of the runcie which then drew the cart from under the apprentice.

He was a slight lad. The taut hempen rope did not break his neck, so he kicked as the tightening noose slowly strangled him. After a few moments the constables relented and allowed the boy's friends to rush to him and pull upon his ankles to end sooner his agony.

"Welcome to London," Arthur said grimly.

We were welcomed again after crossing London Bridge. Winchester geese accosted us as we entered Southwark, rightly identifying us as travelers upon the road. Sir Giles forgot his impatience and would have dallied with one of these strumpets but I told the knight that whatever he chose to do, I would journey on to Kennington Palace, the ramparts being now visible above the trees to the southwest.

Sir Giles scowled and apparently decided that if he was to escort a man to Prince Edward he should probably enter the prince's presence with the man he had been assigned to accompany.

Mel Starr